COUNTRY ROADS

A DAK HARPER THRILLER

ERNEST DEMPSEY

138 PUBLISHING

For my great friend Chris Anderson.
North!!!!

JOIN THE ADVENTURE

Visit ernestdempsey.net to get a free copy of the not-sold-in-stores short stories *Red Gold, The Lost Canvas,* and *The Moldova Job,* plus the full length novel *The Cairo Vendetta*, all from the critically acclaimed Sean Wyatt archaeological thriller series.

You'll also get access to exclusive content and stories not available anywhere else.

While you're at it, swing by the official Ernest Dempsey fan page on Facebook at https://facebook.com/ErnestDempsey to join the community of travelers, adventurers, historians, and dreamers. There are exclusive contests, giveaways, and more!

Lastly, if you enjoy pictures of exotic locations, food, and travel adventures, check out my feed @ernestdempsey on the Instagram app.

What are you waiting for? Join the adventure today!

1

DAWSONVILLE, NORTH CAROLINA

Merritt Wheeler didn't like the rendezvous point one bit. He'd done deals like this before, so it wasn't that he doubted his resources, or his connections. He simply doubted the location.

He'd scoped out the old quarry in the hills of western North Carolina before agreeing to the meeting. Initially, it seemed like a good idea. No one would see the deal go down out here in the middle of nowhere, and most of the time, he preferred the solitude, as opposed to how so many others in his trade sold their wares.

This one, however, felt different.

The buyer had requested to meet here, which was the first problem. Merritt always preferred to pick the spot, but the buyer had insisted, even suggesting he might back out of the deal if Merritt refused.

Merritt couldn't afford to miss the opportunity.

The items in question had been in his possession for too long, and until now, he'd been unable to find a way to sell them or a person willing to fork over this kind of money. The other goods he'd stolen were simpler to sell, at least for him, but they had all been paintings or sculptures. Never anything like this.

He sat in his gray four-door sedan, staring out over the shimmering water. The rippling surface sparkled, reflecting the moon and stars in the sky.

That was another thing Merritt didn't like about this whole shindig. Doing it at night would allow more room for trouble, and there were no guarantees the buyer wouldn't try to axe him out here, dump his body, and make off with both the money and the items.

His eyes wandered over to the passenger side, where the black case sat on the floor, secured with a couple of towels on either end so it wouldn't slide around while he drove.

Something stirred in the bushes to his right, startling Merritt. He snapped his head to the side and looked out into the darkness. The forest gave up no secrets, and he forced himself to calm down. He actually enjoyed being in nature and spent most of his time outdoors. It was one of the benefits his unusual line of work afforded him. He didn't have a boss to answer to, and very few people he trusted, other than his partner, Elliot Hankins.

Typically, Merritt worked alone, but for certain situations, he called in Elliott to run backup, as was the case in this scenario.

At the thought of his partner, Merritt leaned his neck over and spoke into the radio mic hidden under the seam of his shirt. "How's it lookin' out there?"

"Nothing yet, Merritt," Elliott answered. "You sure this is the right place?"

"Yeah, I'm sure." He peered through the windshield at the eerie beauty of the quarry and its liquid surface. "Only abandoned quarry with these coordinates."

"True. Although there are a lot of quarries in this part of the country."

"So I've heard. Just keep your eyes peeled. They should be here any minute."

He knew his partner would have his eyes on him. Elliott was reliable, and always happy to work for a quick payday. This occasion would net them both enough money to live on for years. Merritt had even considered retiring and moving down to Mexico. He could still steal a few pieces here or there south of the border if he needed. The lower cost of living that Mexico offered would make today's take last a long time. He even toyed with the idea of going into legitimate business—maybe open up a couple of restaurants, a cantina, or a small beach resort in some small, out-of-the-way place.

Merritt rolled his eyes at himself the second he'd thought of that last one. He certainly knew his way around a kitchen, not that he'd be the one cooking if he opened a restaurant in Mexico, but he knew absolutely nothing about the hospitality industry. He'd made his living stealing high-value items, not catering to the needs of a bunch of pampered tourists.

Still, the more he pondered the notion of moving south of the border and going into a real business, one that didn't involve hiding all the time, or breaking into high-security places...

He glanced over at the case again. "Those pistols have been more trouble than they're worth," he muttered, reinforcing his own judgment.

But not for much longer. Once he offloaded the guns to this buyer, his perspective on that would definitely change.

A two-million-dollar payday could have that effect on people.

Originally, the pistols had been valued at around $650,000. Such a rare and expensive treasure should have been kept in a much more secure location than the National Civil War Museum in Harrisburg, Pennsylvania.

He recalled the night as if it were just hours ago.

Staking out the museum had been a simple task, and the theft almost as easy. Most modern places would have alarm systems that locked down the entire building within seconds of a break-in. Merritt knew that wasn't the kind of system the museum had, so when he broke the glass, he simply stepped right into the building, hurried over to the exhibit where the pistols were on display, smashed the case, and took the guns.

The alarm didn't even go off the instant he smashed the glass. Even if it had, the police reaction time was far too slow, which he'd also calculated beforehand.

The cops had never come anywhere close to locating him, and Merritt had been sitting on the two pistols ever since, unable to find a buyer on the black market. Maybe he'd been too paranoid, keeping his searches infrequent so as not to draw attention from the cops. He'd tried to convince himself the cops were clueless, and no one was on his tail, but he always heard footsteps at night, movements in the shadows. Even when there were none.

Still, he knew it was far better to worry too much than not at all. That's how thieves got caught. That and thinking they were too good to fail.

Merritt knew his weaknesses and picked his targets accordingly— never anything too high profile but still valuable enough to bring in a solid payday. The pistols on his floorboard were the biggest ticket he'd gone for in his career, and he'd debated whether or not he should even try, knowing the sale on the back end would be trickier than usual.

Fortunately, he'd finally found someone after years of waiting, searching, and sitting on a couple of items that not only had extraordinary monetary value, but historical significance.

The pistols had once belonged to Simon Cameron, Abraham Lincoln's secretary of war. The two Colt pistols were still in remarkable condition after so many years, and more than a few times Merritt had wondered if the guns still worked. He wasn't about to find out, though. Discharging a 150-year-old firearm didn't sound like a good idea, not to mention if the thing fouled up, he wouldn't be able to sell it and would be left with only one. He dismissed the notion as childish and never touched the weapons with his skin for fear of ruining the wood or the metal.

Merritt wondered if the pistols had ever killed anyone, since weapons that had done so often fetched higher prices on the market. That part of his research had revealed nothing, though he did learn that the guns were given to Secretary Cameron by Samuel Colt himself, which was a huge deal. Merritt figured that little feature of their provenance probably added to the value.

Elliott interrupted his train of thought. "Headlights coming down the road, boss."

"Roger that," Merritt said. He felt the same tingle he'd always felt when he was about to move a valuable. The sensation felt like a combination of adrenaline and trepidation, as sales like this always came with an element of uncertainty, and danger.

He pulled the door open, got out of the car, and walked around to the passenger side. The sounds of late spring in the forest filled the air. Crickets chirped, and frogs sang their constant songs from a creek nearby.

Before opening the passenger door, Merritt took a second to absorb the beauty around him and the serenity of the moment. It relaxed him, more than he suspected it might, and he drew the clean mountain air in with a long, deep breath.

He exhaled, then opened the door and removed the case. He gently set it on the hood then looked back toward the forest, where the road disappeared into the darkness of the lush canopy.

Bright beams of light flicked in and out between the tree trunks. The lights turned and bounced, making their way closer to the quarry overlook. Merritt stretched his neck to both sides and looked back at the case to make sure it hadn't shifted. He would have hated to come all this way, to wait all this time, only to have the case with the pistols slide off his car's hood and crash to the ground, damaging what were two pristinely preserved weapons. So, he remained extra careful.

Merritt saw the lights stop moving for a couple of seconds and then continue forward. He stood by the car, waiting as his nerves tightened in his gut like a freshly wound baseball.

The seconds crawled by, and Merritt wished the buyer would hurry up so he could get his money...and get out of here. The sooner this was over, the better.

Finally, a black Cadillac Escalade appeared in the opening of the forest. Tires crunched on gravel, and the engine purred as the vehicle approached. The entire SUV was blacked out from wheels to windows, and Merritt couldn't see the occupants in the back, only the driver in the front.

The SUV pulled up and turned about thirty feet away from Merritt, parking at an angle that effectively blocked the way out. Merritt didn't think the buyer was trying to block him in, but he couldn't help but acknowledge the fleeting thought.

The vehicle's driver climbed out and opened the door, while two men climbed out of the other side of the SUV, one from the back and one from the front.

The buyer's bodyguards carried pistols; each man equipped with the same style weapon. Merritt had never been much of a gun guy. He used them out of necessity, and so far, he'd never needed to shoot his way out of a tight spot.

He kept his eyes on the men, immediately realizing he was severely outmanned, though he knew Elliott was watching from the shadows. If the SUV blocked his view, he could easily shift positions without drawing attention. Right now, Merritt knew that his partner had the buyer and his men dialed into his crosshairs, and if they tried anything stupid, Elliott would light them up.

Merritt couldn't see the buyer's face even through the open doors. The glow from the dome light seemed to flee from him as he turned away and walked around the back of the vehicle. Only then, in the light of the moon, did Merritt see his face. Even then, the man's black, beady eyes retreated from the light.

"Nice night for an antique sale," the buyer huffed in a slow, Southern drawl.

The buyer's rotund figure spoke of too many years of too many biscuits and gravy, and probably frequent trips to name-your-buffet. He wore an expensive black suit with a tie that looked like spring had puked all its pastel colors into one strip of fabric. It was the only thing colorful about the man—a glaring tribute to contrast.

The buyer sauntered toward Merritt, who fought the urge to retreat a few steps as the man approached. The buyer unsettled Merritt, in ways that no one else had before, and he'd only seen the guy for less than thirty seconds.

"So," the man said, "you're the one who pulled off that heist in Pennsylvania a few years ago."

It was more than a few, Merritt thought. *No need to correct him and risk pissing him off.* He briefly considered saying something clever, like "How do you know I didn't kill them?" But Merritt had a feeling the guy wouldn't appreciate it, or wouldn't believe it, so he went with the thief's truth.

"What heist?"

The buyer stared at him for a moment, as if assessing every breath and every twitch.

Then, he burst out laughing. The large man tilted back as he laughed then turned to face one of the guards standing a few feet away. "Did you hear this guy?" he asked. "What heist?" The guard barely flinched, only allowing his lips to crease slightly in acknowl-edgment.

The buyer calmed down and rubbed his nose when he was finally settled. "Oh, that's a good one. Smart man," he said, pointing at Merritt. "You never know if there are cops around."

He stole a glance to his left then right.

"Do you know who I am?" the buyer asked, elongating the "I" with his drawl.

"No," Merritt said truthfully. "I'm not from around here."

"No, you're not." He took a breath before speaking again. "My name is Mitchell Baldwin. Does that ring a bell?"

"Can't say that it does," Merritt said. "Normally, I don't introduce myself to clients. Keeps it simpler that way."

Baldwin nodded, seemingly in approval. "Yes, I can see how that would be a prudent practice in your line of work, Merritt."

Hearing his name stunned Merritt for a second, and he had to recover quickly to maintain at least a semblance of professionalism.

"You do your research," Merritt replied, doing his best to stay cool.

"I always do my due diligence in any of my business dealings."

"Is that what this is?"

Baldwin's lips barely creased. "Of course it is, son. You have a product I want very much. Two products," he corrected himself. "Do you not see it that way?"

"Of course. I just go about things differently." The truth was Merritt had exhausted all his resources in trying to figure out who the buyer might be. He'd obviously come across the name Mitchell Baldwin during several of his searches in the area, but he wasn't about to give the egotistical buyer the pleasure of admitting he'd read his bio.

He'd considered playing up to the man's narcissism. That, however, wasn't Merritt's style. He loathed men like Baldwin; small-town billionaires who thought they could buy and sell people, justice, and anything else they wanted. Then again, maybe Merritt was just jealous.

After the sale of the two troublesome pistols, he would finally have a leg up on becoming one of those types, though he had no plans of running a town. All he wanted to do was disappear.

"Where are the guns?" Baldwin asked.

"They're safe," Merritt replied coolly. "Where's the money?"

Baldwin cracked a wicked smile to the right side of his lips. "It's safe, too." He turned to one of the guards, who returned to the back door of the SUV and removed a black metal case from the floorboard.

The guard returned to his side, held it out in front of him, and flipped open the lid.

Merritt stared into the case. The stacks of green cash nearly glowed in the moonlight, or maybe he just imagined it did. This score was his ticket out.

"Now you show me yours," Baldwin said.

"Okay." Merritt walked cautiously over to his vehicle's passenger door.

He took his eyes off the buyer and his men, ducking in front the windshield to grab the case by the handle with one hand and the bottom edge with the other. He'd always been exceedingly careful with these items, knowing that if he did anything that marred them, their value would plummet.

Merritt stood up and turned, held the case out with both hands, walked around to the back of his car, and set the object on the trunk. After turning the combination lock, he pulled up the lid and stepped to the side so the buyer could inspect the goods.

"May I?" Baldwin asked, gesturing to the weapons now illuminated by the moon's glow.

"I wouldn't expect you to buy them without an inspection. Too many lowlifes out there trying to sell forgeries of pretty much everything, including antique pistols."

Baldwin eyed him curiously for three heartbeats then moved closer to the antique weapons.

He fished a pair of white gloves from his suit pocket and pulled them on tight.

At least he respects the goods, Merritt thought.

The buyer cautiously inched his gloved fingers to the first of the two pistols, as if afraid it might bite him, or more logically, shoot him.

Baldwin slipped his fingers under one of the weapons and carefully lifted it out of the case with the same gentle care he would a newborn from a pram. He pored over the priceless piece of history in his hands, admiring the craftsmanship produced by its maker—one of America's earliest innovators.

"I suppose I don't need to tell you the history of these pistols," Baldwin said as softly as his gruff voice would permit.

"I'm aware of it," Merritt answered. "Those guns were made by some of the most prominent craftsmen in American history. They're priceless."

Baldwin huffed, and his shoulders rose and fell with the sound. "Oh? And here I thought we had already agreed on a price."

The comment caught Merritt off guard, and he chuckled. "That's true. I trust they're to your satisfaction?"

"Yes," Baldwin said. "Very much so. You've done well. And you will be rewarded."

He placed the pistol back in its case and carefully closed the lid. "It's a shame," Baldwin said, "that you thought you could pull a fast one on me."

The brief moment of ease evaporated in an instant, and Merritt felt a rush of nerve-fueled adrenaline pump through his veins. "What?"

"Don't play dumb with me, boy," Baldwin sneered, rounding on him with a speed Merritt wouldn't have thought the stocky man capable of. Baldwin glowered at the thief through his black, beady eyes.

Merritt shifted his feet, suddenly uncertain of what was happening. The only thing that helped him feel a little secure was his partner watching him from the forest. If this deal went south, the sniper would make quick work of the buyer and his men before they realized what happened.

"You were planning on killing me, taking the money and the guns." Baldwin directed the accusation with a sharp tongue.

"What are you talking about?" Merritt shook his head. "We have a deal. Are you trying to back out or something? Because if you are, I'm out of here. We agreed on a price."

"And you thought you could get the drop on me and my men." Baldwin snapped a finger over his shoulder. "Show him what we found, Johnny."

One of the guards behind Baldwin moved abruptly. He returned to the back of the SUV and opened the rear door.

Merritt watched with rapt curiosity as the guard ducked into the back and pulled on something heavy. The second he saw what it was, Merritt's stomach turned.

Elliott rolled out of the back and hit the ground with a thud. He groaned. The sound didn't make Merritt feel much better, but at least his partner wasn't dead.

The guard retrieved Elliott's sniper rifle from the cargo area and rested the butt on the ground near his right foot. He stood several feet away from Elliott, who writhed on the ground, clearly in pain. What the men had done to him wasn't immediately evident to Merritt.

"A sniper, huh?" Baldwin groused. "I guess you really didn't have an idea about who you were dealing with, kid."

"You got it all wrong, man," Merritt pleaded. "I—

"Oh, I suppose you're going to tell me you ain't never seen him before," he jerked his thumb at Elliott, who only moved slightly on the ground, lying on his side.

"No. I mean—"

"Johnny," Baldwin cut Merritt off again.

The blond-haired guard took a pistol from his jacket and aimed it down at the injured man. The muzzle popped.

Merritt watched in horror as the guard executed his partner with a bullet through the skull. The weapon's report echoed across the quarry and into the forest, diffused by the trees and their dense canopy.

Baldwin turned and faced Merritt, who stood there staring in disbelief at his dead partner, trembling as he gazed at the wound on the side of Elliott's head.

Words failed Merritt. They stuck in his throat like a piece of unchewed meat he could neither swallow nor spit out. All he could manage was a few stammered, unintelligible sounds. He'd never seen someone killed before. He was a thief. Murdering people wasn't his thing. In truth, most thieves tried to avoid violence at all costs. It was one of the reasons they spent so much time sneaking around. If they could dodge confrontation of any kind, they would.

"We knew you would try something like this," Baldwin explained. "At least, I had a feeling you might. It's a shame. We could have done more deals together in the future. But you had to be greedy."

Merritt shook his head in protest, but there would be no reprieve. He knew that without tearing his eyes away from his dead partner to look Baldwin in those obsidian orbs planted in his face.

"I wasn't planning on robbing you," Merritt said, somehow finally able to speak. "He was backup. That's all. In case you and your goons tried to pull a fast one on us." Merritt made no effort to conceal the vitriol in his voice. He lingered somewhere between throwing up and bum-rushing Baldwin in a wild display of fury.

Baldwin squared toward the man. He clicked his tongue in a mocking sound, looked back over his shoulder at the body, then shook his head, letting his hands flail out wide. "Maybe you're telling the truth. But how was I to know that?" He snorted, casting a derisive glare at the thief. "Who are we kidding? I was going to kill him anyway."

Resignation settled in Merritt's eyes. Memories flooded him, and a pile of regrets mounted in his mind, not the least of which was showing up to this sale unprepared, and unarmed. The least he could have done was brought a pistol, maybe taken out Baldwin, even one of the guards before the others shot him dead.

One of the other guards grabbed Elliott's body by the ankles and dragged it over to the precipice. A second guard stepped in and helped lift the corpse, a man on either end. They swung it two times then tossed the body over the edge.

A sick part of Merritt counted the seconds until he heard the distant splash echo through the man-made canyon. Bile climbed up his throat. And the way Baldwin stared at him as he would a porterhouse didn't settle that nauseated feeling.

"You see, son," Baldwin said, cocking his head to the side, "there ain't much in this world I hate more than a thief."

"Ironic, since you're stealing from me now."

Baldwin huffed at the barb. "I don't consider it stealing if you're taking something from a thief, boy."

Merritt shook his head. "You don't have to do this," he groveled. "You can take the guns. Take your money. Just let me go. I won't tell anyone what happened here. I didn't see anything."

"Oh now, Merritt. You don't want to go out like that, do you? Begging for your life like some kind of pathetic weakling? Have some dignity, man. In the end, that's all we have."

"No. Please. I can disappear. You'll never hear from me again. I swear. If you just—"

The loud pop from a pistol cut Merritt off. Focus vacated his eyes, and after a second, gravity pulled him to the ground. One of the other guards stood by the body, his arm still extended. A thin stream of smoke trickled from the muzzle, twirling in the cool moonlit air.

"You're right, Merritt. I won't hear from you again," Baldwin mused. He waited a few breaths, staring curiously at the body, then picked up the case from the car's trunk and nodded to the executioner.

The guard dropped his gun into Merritt's car, then helped Johnny stuff the body into the driver's seat of the sedan. Johnny started the car and aimed the front wheels toward the cliff's edge. After he shifted the transmission into gear, he slammed the door shut and let the vehicle idle forward.

The bodyguards stepped back and watched with their employer as the car rolled slowly to the precipice. It paused for a second as the front tires dropped over the edge. Then momentum and a little push from the rear wheels sent it over.

Baldwin heard the loud splash as he turned and walked back to the SUV, cradling his prize in his arms.

2

TOKYO

Dak risked a look back over his shoulder as he ran. The wind in his ears muted the sounds of the men following him, but he knew they were there, and the glance behind him confirmed it.

A quick twist of his shoulders kept Dak from colliding with a young woman with a small child holding her hand. He would have offered an apology, but there was no time. The men chasing him weren't going to slow down anytime soon.

The smell of fresh fish filled his nostrils with every hard breath, and it was all Dak could do to force away the odor and focus on escaping. He'd never cared much for fish, or seafood in general, and even less for the scent.

The Tsukiji Fish Market was packed, literally to the gills, with people of all ages shopping for fresh fare. Which made running nearly impossible. The only solace Dak took was that the men following him likewise had to deal with the dense mobs of market-place patrons.

He squeezed the package tucked under his arm like a football as he danced, spun, and twisted through the gauntlet of vendor stalls and seething masses of shoppers. Two things weighed on

Dak's mind: getting caught by Hobu's men, and dropping the package.

Finding the thing had been hard enough.

Dak's employer, the eccentric video game millionaire (and twelve-year-old) Boston McClaren, had heard about the vase through one of his connections—something that still boggled Dak's mind. How a twelve-year-old had any kind of connections to anything other than school or hanging out with friends was beyond Dak.

Then again, Boston was no ordinary kid. After amassing a fortune as an internet personality for his video game dominance, he became a global sensation. Now, Dak worked for him, locating and recovering stolen or lost artifacts—usually after they'd been moved around on the antiquities black market. Such was the case with the vase tucked under his arm.

This particular item had been stolen two years before from one of the imperial collections, a personal possession of Emperor Kammu, who reigned in the eighth century. Until recently, no one had been able to confirm its whereabouts. Somehow, Boston had gotten wind of the vase's location and current owner. As with other artifacts Dak reclaimed, this one would be returned to the museum instead of to Boston. While he had a small collection of legally claimed or purchased artifacts and relics, Boston's real passion—aside from video games—was, apparently, philanthropy.

Dak wondered if the kid understood—at any level—what he had to do to recover those artifacts. He preferred to think the kid had no clue, considering some of the things Dak had done. At the moment, he couldn't worry about that.

He weaved around an old woman with a brown bag hanging at her side, then split between a couple of men in their twenties as he sprinted ahead.

The mobsters chasing him worked for a local kingpin by the name of Takibi, who was near the top of the food chain with a Yakuza gang.

Dak knew the risks before he took the gig, but he'd dealt with people just as bad as, and sometimes worse than, the Yakuza—

though they were certainly down there among the most savage criminals. He'd heard horror stories about how they executed their enemies that made the concrete boots and car bombs of the American Mafia seem quaint, like a primitive violence from a simpler tribe.

Somewhere behind him, a woman screamed, and Dak knew he'd barely increased his lead on the pursuers, if at all.

Up ahead, he could see daylight at the end of the marketplace, where the alley gave way to another street where cars packed the asphalt.

A raindrop splashed on Dak's face, and he briefly looked up at the churning dark gray clouds overhead. The deluge was coming soon, and he figured he might be the only person in the marketplace who would welcome it.

Dak neared the next street, and as he panted for breath, he felt a rush of relief flood him with the realization that he could lose the men at the corner, melt into the sidewalk traffic, and disappear.

He continued his dance, moving closer and closer to the opening, navigating through and around the shoppers until he was only thirty feet from the sidewalk. Then, his relief evaporated.

At the end of the promenade, three gangsters blocked the way. They stood out amid the ordinary market patrons with their matching black suits and neck tattoos that barely peeked out from under white collars.

Dak skidded to a stop several feet from the men.

All three stared back at him with devilishly dark eyes devoid of emotion or empathy. Like well-trained dogs, they only knew one way —obedience.

"Man," Dak said, panting for air, "there sure are a lot of y'all."

"You're coming with us," the man in the middle said.

Dak noticed the people all around them seem to bend their path like water over stones. Dak figured the ordinary folks must have recognized this for what it was and were either too scared to stand up against the gang or they simply figured it was none of their business.

"You know, I would love to," Dak said, still catching his breath, "but I have a train to catch. Places to go. People to see. A museum where this thing belongs. You know. The usual."

One of the men stepped forward and extended his hand.

"Don't you touch me!" Dak shrieked in a high-pitch falsetto.

The bald man froze, his hand still extended toward the American. Several passersby turned and looked at them, with Dak cowering like a child cradling his favorite toy. He heard the other men rushing up behind him. His warning to the gangster had only slowed the man for a second, and with the others about to cut off any retreat, Dak was completely surrounded.

A split-second thought clicked in his brain and he acted in an instant, shoving his hands skyward with the package. The men running up behind him abruptly stopped. Dak saw the sudden fear in the goon's eyes as the man realized what the American was threatening.

In case he didn't catch the drift, Dak told him. "Come any closer, and I break this."

"You do that, and you're dead," the gangster sneered.

"Yeah, but I'm dead anyway, right? Can't let the guy live who stole from Daddy."

The man's right eye twitched, and Dak know he'd hit a nerve.

"Yeah, that's right. So, here's what's going to happen. You're going to back up. And I'm going to walk away."

The guy peered at Dak, a strange look of satisfaction in his eyes. Dak had seen that look before, and it almost never bode well for him. It was an expression that said "checkmate."

"You don't understand," the goon said. "This is no longer about a piece of property or money; it is about honor."

"Oh," Dak nodded emphatically. "I get it now. So, this isn't about the vase." He continued bobbing his head. "That's a relief. I guess if that's the case, then you boys won't care if I do this."

Dak bent down, swinging the brown paper package between his legs like a kettlebell, then back up again. At the apex, he released the object. It sailed high in the air, and the gangsters immediately converged to rescue the valuable artifact.

The second the package left Dak's fingertips, he broke to the left and ran. Behind him, the Yakuza enforcers scrambled. He didn't see the leader reach up and touch the object, inadvertently tipping it away. He also didn't see the thing bounce off two other guys' hands before it crashed to the ground with a crack.

Dak blended into the crowd as he pushed forward, running as fast as he could toward the subway station.

He didn't look back to see the gangsters bend down to inspect the damage to the rare artifact, or their surprise when they peeled back the brown paper packaging to discover an ordinary jar, broken into huge chunks of clear glass.

By the time the men realized they'd been duped, Dak was descending into the bowels of the city. He scanned his metro card, careful not to rush and screw it up. With the green light, he hurried through the turnstiles and across the platform to the escalators leading deeper into the tunnels.

He worked his way by the people standing on the escalators, being as polite as possible while trying to put as much distance as possible between him and the Yakuza crew. Rounding the corner at the bottom, Dak hurried down the platform.

A light from within the tunnel, accompanied by the sounds of wheels on tracks, announced the arrival of the next train. *Right on time,* Dak thought.

He looked back at the escalator, the seconds ticking by in his head like a hammer on nails. Dak was certain that at any moment the Yakuza would appear at the bottom of the escalator. But as the train ground to a halt, the men never appeared.

The subway doors opened and dozens of people exited. When the flood of passengers dissipated, Dak stepped onto the train and grabbed ahold of the metal bar overhead, watching through one of the windows.

"Come on," he muttered, bouncing up and down on his toes. His gut tightened as the train continued to sit.

Then his fears materialized as two of the Yakuza appeared halfway down the escalator.

"Come on," Dak repeated. "Why are we not moving?"

The two men barged past people on the escalator, knocking one poor woman into the wall in the process. They reached the platform and scrambled around the corner, sprinting toward the train.

The leader was one of the men in pursuit, and while the other guy went right, he went left, charging down the landing toward the rear of the train where Dak stood watching. A voice came over the speakers, and the train shook for a second. The leader spotted Dak in the last car.

The two men locked eyes as the doors started to close. With a last dive, the Yakuza goon lunged toward the narrowing doorway. Dak watched with pleasure as the man's hand and face smacked painfully against the closed doors. The guy slumped to the ground for a second, then popped up as the train started to move. He walked alongside it, then started to jog, then run, unwilling to give up.

Dak smiled childishly at the man and waved as he mouthed, "Bye-bye."

The gangster slowed down as the train sped away into the tunnel. All he could do was watch as the thief disappeared down the tracks.

Dak stayed on the subway through three stops, then changed directions, went another two, then changed one more time until he reached his destination.

He climbed back up to streetside and looked around until he spotted the sushi place he'd chosen as the rendezvous.

The foot traffic was much thinner in this part of the city, and while many cars still filled the streets, fewer pedestrians passed by. Dak looked around, surveying the area where people sat at bars, cafés, and shops. No sign of any trouble.

He relaxed slightly and strolled down the sidewalk to the sushi bar, where a young man sat at the outdoor counter on a red stool, a plate of sushi in front of him, and a glass of Coke to his left. He wore a blue windbreaker and blue jeans with black sneakers. The St. Louis Cardinals hat on his head was turned around backward so the bill nearly hid his neck.

Dak sidled up next to the guy and rested his elbows on the

counter, noting with a flashing glance to his right, the gray backpack at the foot of the stool.

"Were you followed?" the young man asked. He couldn't have been more than twenty-one or twenty-two, but his boyish looks caused Dak to wonder if he were even that old.

"Of course I was," Dak said.

His contact nearly choked on a piece of salmon at the matter-of-fact way Dak made the confession.

"What?" The guy stared back at him with wide, fearful eyes.

"Relax, Ryu," Dak eased, holding up a hand. "I lost them at the fish market."

Ryu looked around over both shoulders, uncertain if he could trust the American.

"See?" Dak continued. "No one followed me here. I doubled back twice, took too many stops and trains for them to be able to keep up." He stole a look up at the top of a traffic pole at the next corner. *Unless they have access to the camera system,* he thought.

"Good," Ryu said with relief. "How did you know they would catch you?"

"Know what you can do, kid. And more importantly, know what you can't do."

The chef stepped up to the glass display and smiled. He asked for Dak's order, and while Dak had no intention of eating, he knew he couldn't just sit there. So he ordered a salmon roll and a spicy tuna roll then went back to the conversation.

"I knew I could get the vase," Dak said. "But I knew they would be on me before I could get away. So I let them chase me to the market, where I made the switch."

When Dak arrived at the fish market with the package, he'd placed Ryu near one of the entrances, just behind a corner stall in the shadows. The plan had been timed to perfection. Ryu left the decoy package on a wooden table. When Dak ran by, he left the real vase on the table, swapping it out for the decoy. The second Dak took the fake package, Ryu grabbed the real one and ducked into the corner. The Yakuza never saw him as they sprinted by in pursuit. And when they were gone, Ryu simply slipped out the exit and made his way to the subway station.

"It was a good plan," Ryu said. He lifted a piece of sushi with a pair of chopsticks and stuffed it into his mouth.

"I appreciate the compliment," Dak said. "Now I need to get this thing to the museum."

"You know they'll arrest you on sight, right?" Ryu said between chews.

"Yeah," Dak admitted. "I considered that. Which is why I'm not going to walk in there holding the thing out in the open. I'll take it to the curator, get the reward, and be on my way."

"And pay me."

Dak huffed. "Already done, kid. Check your account."

For a second, Ryu looked as though he might take his phone off the counter and look, but he shook his head. "I trust you, Dak."

"Careful doing that, Ryu. Maybe I'm someone you can trust, but there are others out there you can't."

"I know, but you're a friend of Will. So, I know you're good people."

Dak nodded his agreement. Will Collins had been instrumental in helping Dak locate the vase, especially through his introduction of Ryu, whose connections in the criminal underworld proved vital to the success of this recovery operation.

"What will you do next?" Ryu asked. "On to the next treasure?"

"Something like that," Dak grumbled. He refused to turn his back to the street, instead continuing to sit sideways on the stool, his head on a swivel, turning back and forth as he continued watching for trouble.

"You sure are wound tight," Ryu commented as he placed a sliver of ginger on a piece of sushi, then topped it with a dab of wasabi.

Dak didn't immediately respond, instead letting memories from the last few years play out on the screen of his mind. As quickly as the visions appeared, they were gone, and he returned to the moment at the counter. "You'd be wound tight too if you had a crazy person who thinks you ruined their life sending assassins to kill you."

Ryu was in the process of delivering another piece of sushi to his mouth, but he stopped with the food in midair. He stared over at the American with curiosity and a dose of disbelief. "Yeah," he finally agreed. "I guess you're right. I wouldn't be as relaxed." He shoved the sushi into his mouth and chewed.

"Probably not."

"Although," Ryu protested by holding one chopstick up, "I do deal with people who, if provoked, would kill me in a second. So, different but same. That's the price we pay for living such extravagant lives."

Dak chuckled at the last part.

"Who is this mysterious benefactor of yours?" Ryu changed gears. "Some crazy millionaire who pays you to recover artifacts he doesn't want to keep for himself?"

Dak curled his lips to one side. "Something like that."

"Where'd you find someone like that?"

Dak bent down and picked up the backpack. He slung it over his shoulder and smirked at Ryu. The chef placed the two rolls Dak ordered down on the counter.

"If I told you, it wouldn't be a secret, would it?" Dak popped a slice of salmon roll into his mouth.

"Mystery," Ryu corrected. "I said they were a mystery, not a secret."

Dak shrugged. "Okay. Anyway, I don't give their information out. In any way, shape, or form. Gotta keep them safe, you know?"

"I suppose someone like that would be a high-profile target," Ryu conceded.

Dak hummed agreement as he stuffed another piece of sushi into his mouth. The two said nothing for several minutes until Dak was done eating. Then he drew some bills out of his pocket, placed them on the counter, and patted Ryu on the back.

"You did good, kid. You did great, actually."

"Thanks. Happy to help. I'll see you around, Dak."

"See you around, Ryu."

As Dak strode down the sidewalk with the backpack over his

shoulder, he felt the phone in his pocket vibrate. He pulled the device out, checked the number, and answered.

"Were your ears burning?" Dak asked.

"What?" Boston replied, confused.

"Never mind. What's up?"

"I assume you're still in Tokyo."

"Yes, sir. I was just about to drop off this lovely piece of pottery to the director of the museum."

Dak stopped at the corner and waited for the signal to change. While he stood there, he continued surveying the area for potential trouble. Fortunately, none appeared.

"Wow. That's amazing. Was it difficult?"

Dak sighed. "Don't ask questions you don't want the answers to, kid."

"Yeah. You're right. I don't want to know. I mean, I do, but I don't. You know what I mean. Anyway, if you've done that, then maybe you're ready for another assignment?" He sounded hopeful.

"Another one, huh?" Dak asked. "That's not normally how this has worked."

"I know, but this is a really interesting one."

The light changed and Dak crossed the street, then turned left to cross the next, again forced to wait for the signal to change.

"They're all interesting, B."

"Okay, that's true," the boy allowed. "But this one comes with a murder mystery."

Dak wasn't sure he felt comfortable talking about something as heavy as a murder. "Um, what?" he managed.

"A world famous thief was found in a quarry today by some kids who happened to be trespassing on the land. They saw something down in the water, and it turned out to be a car with a body inside."

"That's macabre. What does this have to do with anything? I'm not in the business of solving murders."

"Yeah. Pretty messed up. The dead man in the car was a thief by the name of Merritt Wheeler. They said he died a few days ago. How this ties into you is, I think, Wheeler was the one who stole a pair of pistols from a Pennsylvania museum several years ago."

Dak walked across the street when the signal changed and he continued down the sidewalk, keeping a brisk pace.

"What's with the pistols?" Dak asked, keeping his tone low enough that people around him didn't wonder why he was talking about guns.

"They belonged to Abraham Lincoln's secretary of war," Boston explained. "A gift from Samuel Colt."

Dak's eyebrows raised. "Impressive," he said. "And you think this Wheeler was the one behind it?"

"No one got a good view of the thief. The cameras didn't produce any images that made identifying the culprit possible. But the few images the cops were able to gather definitely fit Wheeler's body type."

"That's a big stretch," Dak warned.

"I know. I'm reaching a little, but it's worth looking into."

"What is?"

"The body was found on property that belongs to the Baldwin Corporation, a billion-dollar construction materials company. They mostly do gravel and concrete."

"Strange they ended up with a body on their land. Let me guess, you think the company had something to do with it?"

"No clue," Boston admitted. "That's what I pay you for."

Dak snorted a laugh, caught off guard by the kid's wit. "Fair enough. I'll look into it. I'm getting tired of eating sushi anyway. Where is this place?"

"Kyoto."

"Wait. What?" Dak stopped in midstride.

"I'm kidding. It's in North Carolina."

Dak laughed. "Hilarious. I'll check in with you when I have something."

He ended the call and continued down the sidewalk, clutching the priceless vase under his arm, a James Taylor song about going to Carolina playing in his head.

3

DAWSONVILLE, NORTH CAROLINA

Hattie Markham saw the black Escalade the second it appeared over the ridge to the east. She stared up the hill at the SUV, dust churning into the air behind it as the vehicle rumbled down the gravel road toward her farm.

Hattie sighed, lowering the sweater she'd been knitting. She knew who it was. This wasn't the first time Mitchell Baldwin had visited her family's land.

The farm had belonged to the Markhams for more than five generations, going all the way back to the days prior to the Civil War. The family had been simple folk, working the land as their ancestors had done. The property produced three primary crops: sweet potatoes, corn, and hops.

The latter had become a boon over the last decade with the rise of craft brewing all over the United States. People were starting breweries everywhere, as well as all the home-brewing hobbyists that enjoyed an afternoon on their back porches or in their garages simmering mashes for IPAs—which were, apparently, one of the easier beers to make.

Hattie didn't care much for beer. She'd always been a bourbon girl. But if hops continued to fill the family coffers, she didn't judge.

She wasn't rich. Being wealthy had never been one of her goals in life. Hattie didn't care about money, fancy cars, big houses, any of that. Her needs were met and she lived a simple life.

The only bump in the road had been just over a year ago when her husband George died from a heart attack while out in one of the fields. She'd known him since the two were in high school. They started dating their senior year—one of those high school sweetheart stories that seemed to be a rarity in modern times.

George had worked hard his entire life. He never complained, always happy to have completed an honest day's work with his hands. He loved the farm, and loved his wife and their daughter, Heather. The people in town respected him, too, as evidenced by the incredible turnout at the funeral.

Hattie couldn't believe it had been a year already. The days had dragged on without him, but the year passed in the blink of an eye; a small part of her felt guilty about that. With all the responsibilities falling to her, she took over the family business and ran the farm as well as George ever did. She brought on help to manage the day-to-day operations, particularly the parts that involved harder manual labor. Hattie knew how to drive a tractor, and the combine, but she didn't do those things much anymore. For all intents and purposes, she'd retired from active, physical roles on the farm and had resigned herself to more of a management role.

The SUV continued down the long, winding road, picking up speed as it bounced along.

Hattie knew why Baldwin was coming to pay her a visit. It was the same reason he'd always come, even before George died. When he was still alive, it was George that Baldwin pestered.

He wanted the Markham land.

Baldwin was in the stone business. His quarries dotted the landscape all across the Southeast, with a huge cluster located in the hills of North Carolina. She knew the company was worth billions, which she thought would be enough.

Not for Mitchell Baldwin.

The man and the figure he cut across the economic and political life of the modern South hearkened back to the days of the old American empire builders: the J.P. Morgans, the Rockefellers, the Carnegies, the Vanderbilts. Like those magnates of old, Baldwin wasn't just about making money. He'd done that a long time ago. Now he sought power, and his enormous ego wouldn't do without it.

She watched the SUV make the last turn at the bottom of the hill, where the road swung around past an old oak tree that had been on the property since the first Markham arrived here more than 170 years before.

Hattie sighed, foreseeing the conversation that she knew was forthcoming. She wished her daughter were there, but Heather was off trying to make a living as a journalist in Charlotte. The only heir to the Markham farm, Hattie had hoped her daughter would follow in the family footsteps and take over someday, but she'd never had it in her. Heather detested the work and hated the weather just as much. The summers were too hot, and the winters too cold, though there wasn't nearly as much to do during those down months.

The disconcerting truth was Hattie didn't know what was going to happen to their land when she died. If Heather was not inclined to keep up the family tradition, Hattie wasn't going to force it on her. Not the way George had.

He'd insisted that Heather would someday take over the farm, but she'd steered away from it her entire life, to the point that she relocated to the city when she finished college at the University of North Carolina.

George claimed she was trying to run away from who she really was, which Hattie believed only pushed her further.

Her husband meant well, but George was a direct man, blunt and to the point, often lacking the subtle way of communicating that worked better with their daughter.

Heather came back to visit every weekend, and had always done so, but she made it clear: no matter how much George badgered her, she had no plans on returning to the farm for more than short visits.

The SUV's tires crunched to a stop in front of the white farmhouse's front porch. Hattie didn't acknowledge it, instead reaching over to the little white table to her right for the glass of sweet tea she'd been sipping for the last twenty minutes. She took a drink and set the glass back down, letting the cool liquid soothe her.

The sun was already high in the morning sky when the SUV's driver climbed out and opened the back door for his boss. Hattie wasn't surprised to see Baldwin wearing a suit that probably cost as much as one of her good tractors, though she had no point of reference for things of that nature. She'd never cared much for fashion, instead preferring to make clothes, or wear the ones she bought at the department store for several years until they nearly fell apart.

Baldwin smiled at her and walked toward the steps. The driver shut the door and stood by the vehicle.

"Mornin', Hattie," Baldwin said as he approached the first step. He stopped at the bottom, not willing to risk venturing up to the porch without being invited.

Hattie knew the man practiced proper Southern etiquette, at least in some regards. But underneath the smooth veneer lurked a wolf in a $2,000 suit.

"The answer's still no, Mitch," Hattie said, like she was reprimanding him.

"I didn't ask a question."

The woman rolled her eyes. "Don't play coy with me, Mitchell. We both know why you're here, and it's not to see how I'm doing, or make friendly chatter." She stood up and walked three steps to the door. "But come on up and have a seat. I'll get you a glass of tea."

He lowered his head like a young boy who'd just been caught in a lie by his mother. The woman disappeared into the house through the screen door, and he climbed the steps to the porch and helped himself to a rocking chair on the opposite side of the little table where Hattie's glass sat.

He eased into the seat and the chair's white-painted wood creaked under his weight. He looked out over the land, nestled in a valley between densely forested hills on every side. Birds chirped in an apple tree to his left in the center of a lush green lawn. A few other trees dotted the area around the house. Oaks, maples, a tulip poplar, and some tall pines stood nearly equidistant apart in various spots in the grass.

Baldwin admired the land as he sat there waiting for his host to return. The human side of him could understand why Hattie Markham didn't want to let the place go. It was a little slice of paradise. *Well, it wasn't little,* he thought.

The Markham farm occupied hundreds of acres, stretching all the way up and over the mountains on every side. Part of him considered it a shame that this piece of Eden would end up a quarry—the land stripped of its beautiful resources, the valley littered by heavy machines lumbering rock and industrial materials, big processing facilities, and offices.

That was progress, though.

There were still plenty of other beautiful places around the world, including the properties where he had homes.

Progress was only the tagline he attached to every move he made. The truth was Baldwin was a businessman, plain and simple. The only thing he cared about, in the end, was growing the business.

With no heirs, it was all he had, and the way he saw it, the best path to keeping his beloved company was growth. On top of that, he certainly enjoyed the power and influence it gave him. Not that he needed favors from anyone, but it was nice to have a politician or a judge in his back pocket if the necessity arose.

He heard Hattie padding across the floor inside and straightened his posture before she pushed the screen door open and reappeared with a fresh pitcher of tea and an empty glass.

She set the glass down on the table and poured the tea, placed the pitcher next to it, and sat back down in her rocking chair. Hattie picked up her glass and took a sip, sighed in satisfaction, then began rocking slowly back and forth.

"This farm sure is pretty, Hattie," Baldwin said, lifting the glass and taking a swig. He let out a refreshed "ah" and raised the drink toward her. "And this tea is perfect. Not too sweet, not too unsweet."

"I mix it half and half," she chirped with a touch of venom in her voice. "But you didn't come here to talk about my tea. And I would appreciate it if you didn't try to smooth me over with compliments about the land you want to rip apart."

Baldwin forced an awkward chuckle. "Oh, Hattie. You sound just like your late husband. George was always straight to the point. I liked that about him. No beating around the bush."

"He hated you."

"I know." Baldwin made the concession as he bobbed his head. "He was a firebrand. Shame about his heart. Gone too soon."

George hadn't been a spring chicken, but he hadn't been old either, with still many good years ahead of him—or so Hattie would have hoped.

The timing of his death had bothered their daughter, Heather, and she'd insinuated on more than one occasion that foul play couldn't be ruled out—despite the conclusions reached by the autopsy.

Hattie was too submerged in her grief to hear of it, claiming that years of too many steaks and potatoes had gotten the better of George. There'd been no warning signs, but that was often how widow-maker heart attacks worked. Fine one minute. Gone the next.

It stung Hattie to hear Baldwin talk about George in such a patronizing way, but she kept her emotions in check and simply said, "Yes. It was too soon." She drowned the fire in her heart with another gulp of tea.

"We all end up there one way or another," Baldwin continued.

"Yes. We do," she agreed. "Now, if you'll excuse me, Mitchell, I have some knitting to do before the boys come in from the fields. Finish your tea if you like, but my answer is still the same as it's always been. I'm not selling the farm, so there's no point in discussing it."

"I knew you would say that."

Hattie snorted, casting a derisive glare at her uninvited guest. "And yet you still drove all the way out here."

He took another drink, then set the glass down on the table and faced her. "Hattie, I know you don't like me."

"Is it that obvious?"

Baldwin ignored the quip and kept going. "And I understand why. This farm has been in your family for generations. I get it."

"Then why do you want to destroy it? Just leave us alone, Mitchell."

"When you're gone, what's going to happen? Your daughter doesn't have any interest in the farming business, from what I've heard. And you don't have anyone else to leave the property to. Unless there are some nieces or nephews I don't know about somewhere."

Hattie's eyelids narrowed to slits. The angry scowl on her face could have melted ice. "What I do with our farm when I'm gone is none of your concern, Mitchell. Unless that was some kind of threat."

"It wasn't." The denial came with a single turn of his head. "I would never consider such a thing. I'm simply making a point."

The fire in her eyes flared. "And what is your point? That the land that's been in our family for hundreds of years should be sold to you so you can destroy it?"

"No. But there's no stopping life from going on, even when the two of us are gone." He turned his head and picked up the glass again. This time, he held it several inches from his lips as he stared out at some random, distant point.

Hattie didn't know what to make of the sudden melancholy from the usually brash businessman, or of the way he'd made mention of when they were both gone. It caught her slightly off guard and she found herself curious as to what he was thinking, but figured he would share whether she asked or not.

She wasn't disappointed.

"As you know," he said, "I have no heirs of my own. When I'm gone, I don't care what happens to my company."

"I'm sure your employees would be glad to hear that."

"That's not what I meant, Hattie." He took a sip and held on to the glass with both hands. "I mean I don't care if the new leader makes a pivot, changes the way Baldwin Corporation does business. I'll be dead, after all. I won't know what's going on."

Hattie's suspicion never lowered. She was, after all, still talking to a wolf.

"You going to get to the point sometime this year, Mitchell, or are you going to let this conversation keep circling the drain?"

He snorted a laugh and bobbed his head. "Hattie, you know I want to buy this property. That's no secret. And we both know you're not interested in selling. But I want to make one last offer."

"The answer is still no. There's no amount of money you could offer."

"You haven't heard the offer."

"Don't need to," she snapped. The bun in her dark gray hair jiggled with her retort. "I don't care about money, Mitchell. I understand that's something you can't get through your thick skull, but there are some folks in this world who hold other things in higher regard than money: honor, tradition, family. You wouldn't know about any of that, though."

To her surprise, he nodded. "You're right," Mitchell agreed.

Hattie wasn't sure she'd ever been more shocked in her life.

"That's why I'm giving you a different kind of offer, Hattie. I can run this company forever, and while my leadership team, the board, all of them are full of brilliant strategists, I need someone who sees things differently." He paused for only a second, then said, "Along with the price of ten million dollars, which is way above market value per acre, I am willing to hand over the entire company to your daughter when I die. She can do with it as she pleases."

Just when Hattie thought she couldn't be more surprised by the man, he upped the ante. "What did you say?"

"Ten million," he repeated. "And when I die, your daughter can take over. The board will be at her disposal. If she wants to tear down everything I've built, that's up to her."

"You're kidding."

"Nope. The company will need new blood when I'm out of the picture, a fresh perspective."

"Heather is a writer, a journalist. She doesn't know the first thing about running a big corporation." Hattie knew merely calling it "big" was almost an insult. Baldwin was an international behemoth.

"Neither did I when I started, and that's why I think she could be the perfect person for it."

Hattie raised an eyebrow, still suspicious of the man and his offer. "I don't like you."

"I know."

"And my daughter isn't too fond of you, either."

"Apples and trees and gravity, Hattie." He could see she didn't get the reference, so he went on. "Just think it over. I know you don't care about money, but you care about your daughter. And the combination of the money I'm offering for your land, along with the majority ownership of the company, will take care of her and generations after her. It would be a disservice to her to not even consider it."

He tipped the glass to his lips and knocked back the rest of the tea in two big gulps. "Ah," he sighed again, placing the glass back on the table with a grin. "You do make good tea, Hattie." He stood, straightened his suit jacket, and looked out over the railing to the land beyond his driver and the SUV in the driveway. "Just think about it, Hattie. That's all I can ask."

He left her with that and ambled down the steps.

Mitchell could feel her watching him as he made his way to the SUV. The driver stepped to the back door and opened it for him, allowed him to climb in, then closed it before getting in and starting the engine. Mitchell didn't risk a look back at the woman until he was safely behind the tinted windows. Even then, he only twisted his head slightly to get a view of her. She still wore the same shocked expression, and he knew he'd thrown her for a loop with his offer.

"Did she take it?" Johnny asked from behind the wheel as he turned the vehicle around on the circular driveway.

"No," Mitchell said, watching the landscape pass by outside. "I don't think she ever will. And even if she did, there's no way I'm going to ever hand my company over to that hippie daughter of hers. But I had to do it, Johnny. If she doesn't accept, we will be forced to use other measures."

"Say the word, sir."

"I will, Johnny. I will. When the time is right."

4

DAWSONVILLE

Heather Markham held the phone to her ear, contemplating the question. Her friend on the other end of the call waited for an answer, breathing audibly through the speaker.

Until a few minutes ago, Heather was certain she could go through with it. She'd talked herself into it, pumping courage into her veins with a shot of whiskey. The drink calmed her nerves a little but not enough; she still felt the cold edge of fear cutting against her abdomen.

Now, she sat in her car outside the Baldwin Corporation's main quarry, a massive complex that spanned more than two hundred acres. The corporation's headquarters sat atop a hill overlooking the property, and the surrounding area, for miles.

Heather ran a finger through her tangled, curly blonde hair and stretched it out until it was taut. She took a deep breath in through her nose and exhaled.

"Did you hear me, Heather?" her friend asked, making sure the line hadn't gone dead.

"Yeah, I heard you."

"Well? Are you sure you want to go through with this? I don't want to put you in any danger. If you feel at all unsafe about this, don't do it. Just walk away. We'll find something else on them."

"No," Heather insisted. "I'm fine. I can do this."

She said the words, but they didn't come with a side of conviction. Instead, doubt tickled her tone.

Heather had been working on this piece for months, and she knew if she walked away, all the work she'd put in—the long hours and short nights—would all be for nothing. Even more importantly, the people she was there to help would be left dangling without a lifeline.

They would have only two choices: leave, or let things continue as they always had, and most likely die an early death. *A miserable, painful death.*

She'd been working as a reporter for the *Charlotte Times* since graduating from the University of North Carolina two years before. Heather mostly covered feel-good stories, little pieces in the local community that typically ended up on the back of the lifestyles page.

That was before she found out about what was going on here in Dawsonville.

Nestled in the hills of North Carolina between Asheville and Charlotte, the town of Dawsonville embodied every possible meaning of the word *quaint*. Its town square hearkened back to a simpler time, when neighbors met at the local barber shop or salon to talk about the latest news, or sipped iced tea on the porch with friends as the sun crawled across the sky.

Behind that Mayberry veneer, however, lurked a sinister secret.

The Baldwin Corporation, steered by its chairman, Mitchell Baldwin, had gone from a fledging gravel company in the 1960s to a multinational behemoth. Mitchell's grandfather, Martin, founded the organization, ran it for twenty-five years, and then Mitchell's father, Marion, took the reins and operated as the chairman for twenty-three years. Now in his mid-sixties, Mitchell ran the show.

The Baldwins had a reputation for being cutthroat businessmen. They did things purely by the numbers, maximizing profits wherever they could, which often meant cutting corners. Sometimes, that

meant laying off workers, though the Baldwins made an excellent
show of caring for their neighbors. Or pretending to. They'd pay big
severance checks to keep people from raising too much of a stink, but
in the end, the Baldwin Corporation always profited.

The company had become adept at covering their tracks at every
turn, but they'd slipped up, and now Heather was primed to expose
their dirty deeds to the world. Maybe then, after she went public with
the unethical practices of Baldwin, her mother could relax.

Mitchell Baldwin had been pressuring Heather's parents and,
most recently, her mother, to sell the family farm. Based on the man's
track record, Heather considered it fortunate that her mother was
still alive. When her father died, Heather teased the idea that
somehow Baldwin had been behind his death, but there was no way
to prove it, and the autopsy report revealed natural causes.

Still, Heather wondered now and then.

Now, she had a chance to end Baldwin's pestering and manipula-
tion once and for all.

She learned that the company had been illegally dumping chemicals into the soil, which had recently started leaking into the local
water supply. People in one area of town began getting sick several
months prior, all showing the same symptoms. Two older victims
passed from complications due to the illness, but no one raised the
alarm as to what could have been the source.

Until Heather got the call last week.

She began putting pieces together and investigated the practices
of Baldwin Corporation in greater detail, all of which led her to this
quarry where she believed she'd find the facility responsible for the
illegal dumping.

The investigation had taken more hours than she could have
imagined at the onset, but now she was here, trespassing on Baldwin
property to see if she could get hard evidence that would bring the
company to its knees. An odd twist of fate had brought renewed scrutiny to Mitchell Baldwin's materials business when a body, still inside
their car, was found in one of the company's quarries.

The police officially ruled it an accident, saying that the victim was drunk when they drove over the edge and down into their watery grave below.

Heather didn't buy a word of it. Why would someone drive all the way out there to an abandoned quarry just to drive into it? Seemed like a lot of work for a suicide. And then the manner of it didn't make sense either. She'd heard of people driving over cliffs or into walls, but this was a first.

Based on everything she'd learned about Baldwin and his company, Heather felt confident foul play couldn't be ruled out, despite what the local authorities claimed.

"Just be careful," her friend said. "If you're right about how they do things, they could come after you."

"I know," Heather said, the voice through the speaker snapping her back to the present. "I'll be fine. Besides, if anything happens to me, you can tell the cops. Either way, Baldwin loses."

"Yeah, but I don't want anything to happen to you."

"Trust me, Julie. I'll be fine. I'll talk to you when I have what I need."

"Okay. Be careful," Julie reminded her again.

"Always."

Heather ended the call and stuffed the phone into the pocket of her slim black pants. She wore a matching black long-sleeve shirt and a dark gray baseball cap. Down by the quarry, she saw the security guards roaming around the perimeter on their patrols.

There would be more in and around the main facility, but she wasn't going there. She knew they would have that place locked down, and she wasn't there to break into it. All Heather had to do was get some footage of the pollution Baldwin was allowing to spill onto the ground, and she could go straight to the paper and television outlets with the story.

She took a deep breath, climbed out of her car, and made her way down from the hilltop toward a forest that surrounded the processing facility. Once she was out of the moonlight, Heather switched on her phone light and turned it to the dimmest setting so as not to catch the attention of any guards going astray on their patrols. She cupped the front of the phone to keep the light directed at the ground as she marched through the underbrush.

Heather had used some drone footage to get the layout of the property, though she'd been forced to fly the device at its highest altitude to keep from arousing suspicion from the workers and security detail at the quarry.

As far as she knew, no one had noticed, and she'd been able to get a clear picture of where the runoff was occurring. Those images, combined with some closeups from the ground would be more than enough to cause a full-on investigation, both from local authorities and from the feds. *The EPA*, she knew, *will have a field day*.

Every twig that snapped underfoot caused her to freeze, and she thought more than once she heard the security guards talking nearby. Other random noises injected fresh paranoia into her mind—the rustling of leaves, a squirrel on a branch, a bird chirping from somewhere in the dark canopy above.

Finally, after ten minutes of trudging through the forest, the sound of trickling water touched her ears and she felt a surge of hope rush through her as she stepped out into the clearing.

Thick green grass rolled for thirty feet down a gentle slope to a creek. Another grassy hillside mirrored the one where she stood, climbing back up to the forest on the other side.

Heather checked to her right, in the direction of the facility, then left, where the creek wound through the woods on its journey toward the town of Dawsonville. She pivoted in the grass and walked to the right, following the water upstream toward the manufacturing plant. Lights twinkled in the plant and on the tall antennas that towered over it.

She didn't have to journey far to find what she was looking for.

At a bend in the creek, the dancing stream met a thick drainage pipe with a grate over it. The pipe was around a foot in diameter and spilled a murky liquid into the creek at a slow, steady rate.

Heather watched the pollutants churn into the once-clear creek. The mixture flowed downstream toward the town, probably seeping into a few farms along the way, on top of the wells and city water supply. The chemicals carried a foul stench with them and the odor burned into Heather's nostrils. She shook her head and waved a hand around in front of her face to dispel the scent. The effort proved in vain.

She wrinkled her nose and activated the camera on her phone, careful to dim the light before pointing the device in the direction of the facility. Heather snapped dozens of pictures, getting various angles, of the clear water before it was soiled by the pollutants and the aftereffects. She also made sure to get shots of the building behind it, complete with a big white Baldwin Corporation sign hanging in full view.

Heather looked around to make sure no one saw her, and then took off back toward the forest.

She felt a wave of relief wash over her the second she left the clearing for the cover of the woods. Her feet moved involuntarily faster and she felt her pace quickening. The sooner she got out of here, the better.

The second she got back to her car, she'd send the images to Charlotte and things would be set in motion. She stopped next to a tree, considering the idea. *I should send them now,* she thought.

Heather looked at her phone, ready to text the pictures to Julie. She sighed with expected disappointment. "No bars out here in the sticks," she said. "I really need to switch carriers."

She hoped there might be a better signal up on the hilltop where she'd left her car, but suspected nothing would change, which meant she'd have to wait until she got back on the main road or closer to town.

Clutching her precious evidence in her hand, Heather marched up the hill through the woods and back out into the open where a grassy knoll led to her car and the gravel road out of here.

Her head twisted back and forth, her eyes scanning every piece of the land around her for signs of trouble. She felt a growing sense of confidence as she arrived at the car. She quickly climbed in and started the engine, checking twice to make sure her headlights were still off.

She rolled her eyes at her own action, knowing it to be ridiculous. *You drove here with them off, idiot.*

Heather shifted the car into drive and steered it around the gravel overlook, careful not to tap the brakes and caused the taillights to blink bright red. She watched in the rearview mirror as the clearing disappeared around the first curve in the road, and along with it the Baldwin production facility.

She kept her lights off, driving by the light of the moon for another few hundred feet until she was certain she'd put enough distance between herself and the facility that no one would see the headlamps.

With the lights finally on, she sped up a little, guiding the car down the winding gravel road toward the main county road back into town.

Heather rounded one of the last curves and abruptly slammed on her brakes when she nearly drove straight into two black SUVs parked across the gravel. Two men stood by the vehicles, guns in their hands hung close to their hips, but Heather got the distinct impression they could be trained on her with deadly accuracy within seconds.

She gripped the steering wheel so hard her knuckles turned the shade of pearls. Heather swallowed, watching as the back door to the second SUV opened and a familiar face emerged.

Mitchell Baldwin stepped in front of his guards and walked around to the driver's side, where he waited with arms crossed. He stared down at her for a few seconds, as if waiting for her to roll down the window.

For a second, Heather considered slipping her foot off the brake and stomping on the gas. She'd damage the car, probably totaling it, but she'd take out Baldwin's gunmen, and maybe have a chance at getting away.

How did he know? That question racked her mind in recurring waves, crashing against her brain like the sea against a rocky shore. *There's no way he could have known. I was careful.*

He tapped on the window, jerking her from her thoughts.

She hesitated, then rolled down the window.

"Nice night for a drive through the woods, isn't it?" Baldwin asked. His patronizing tone scratched at her nerves.

She didn't immediately reply. Baldwin furrowed his brow, then put on a confused face. "Heather? Heather Markham? Is that you?"

"Yes...yes, sir, Mr. Baldwin. It's me."

He bent over to get a better look, then pulled his head back to emphasize his shock. "What in the world are you doing out here at this time of night?" He turned to the guards and waved at them. "Put those guns away, boys. It's just Hattie's daughter." The guards appeared to be uncertain. "Seriously, y'all put those away. You're scaring this poor girl."

He shook his head and returned his focus to Heather. "What are you doing out here at this time of night? We thought there were some trespassers down this way. Your car triggered a sensor. I just happened to still be on the grounds when the boys here called it in. I was immediately concerned, especially considering what happened here a few days ago."

"Yes," she managed, barely able to speak despite his soothing tone. "I can imagine things have been a little crazy around here, what with someone killing themselves on your property and all."

He nodded. "Yeah, terrible thing. Some folks just can't deal with the stresses of life, I suppose. Of course, a group of kids found the car, which could have been a much worse issue. I'm just glad none of them were hurt or saw the body. That kind of thing can haunt a child for life."

"I would think so," she agreed. She couldn't hide the nervous tremor in her voice and hoped Baldwin hadn't noticed.

He stood up straight again and looked around. "So, what are you doing out here? Just trying to get some fresh country air on a gorgeous night?"

"Yep," she said. "It gets so stuffy in the big city. I miss nights like this out here in the mountains. Clear skies full of stars. The smell of pine in the air."

"Sounds like you miss it," Baldwin offered.

"I do. Don't get back here often enough."

"Well, we sure would love to see more of you around these parts." He put his hands behind his back and leaned forward, tipping on his toes for a second before straightening again.

The man's voice made Heather sick to her stomach, and the fake show of politeness he was putting on only worsened the nausea.

"Thank you," she managed. "I'm sorry I was trespassing on your property. It's just so peaceful out here. And the stars were so beautiful, I figured no one would mind."

"Not at all," he agreed far too easily.

"I guess I'll just be on my way. Nice to see you again, Mr. Baldwin."

"Good to see you, too, Heather." He stepped back from the door as if about to let her leave, but within a second his face tightened into a frown. "Did your mother tell you about my offer?"

"Which one?" she forced through a laugh.

He chuckled for a second. "The one I gave her earlier this week."

"Oh. I guess it slipped her mind because she hasn't told me about it, but I'll be sure to ask her when I see her tomorrow."

"Yes," Baldwin hissed. "Actually, I have a better idea."

She puzzled at the sudden change in his demeanor.

"I think I have a better offer for Hattie now. And it's far more valuable to her than money."

Heather had been so focused on Baldwin and her fears that she didn't see the guard sneak around the other side of the vehicle.

"Get out of the car, Heather," Baldwin ordered, any cordiality gone from his voice.

"What?" She turned her head, a terrible fear creeping up through her gut and into her throat. She saw the armed guard through her window, pointing the pistol at her head.

"What is this?" Heather asked, panic pulsing in her tone. "Tell your guy to put his gun down."

Baldwin merely shook his head. "No, I don't think so. See, you were trespassing, Heather. The land is clearly marked 'No trespassing.' The whole prosecution warning is on there too. And yet you appear to believe those rules don't apply to you."

"I'm sorry," she blurted. "I won't do it again. Okay."

"Oh, I know you won't, sugar." He leaned forward, menace dripping from his eyes. "I know you won't."

5

Dak arrived in Dawsonville late in the afternoon, three days after leaving Tokyo. Tired from the jet lag of traveling all the way across the world, he checked into a small hotel near the interstate a few miles outside of town, and after a light dinner crashed in the welcoming embrace of the hotel bed.

The next morning, he woke to a thin beam of sunlight streaming through the narrow gap between the curtains. Dak looked over at the clock and was shocked to see he'd slept till nearly nine o'clock in the morning.

He rubbed his eyes and scooted up a little to rest his head on the headboard. "I don't remember the last time I slept till nine," he muttered.

Dak took a quick shower and then got dressed, putting on a T-shirt and jeans before heading out to the car. The morning air felt cool against his skin, but Dak knew it was merely a tease. The summer heat would rapidly melt away the cooler air, and before long, the hills would be plunged into a sauna.

After spending some time in Chapel Hill and Asheville, Dak was well aware of how hot and humid North Carolina could be, just like the rest of the South.

The hotel sat just a half mile from the main square of Dawsonville, and it being a lovely morning, he decided to walk rather than drive. All the hours of sitting on planes and in cars for the last several days had worn on him, and he needed to get the blood flowing again.

The journey into the little town only required a short walk at a brisk pace, but Dak took an extra few minutes along the way to take in the sights. Late nineteenth-century homes lined the street leading to town, most of them with wraparound porches with big columns supporting the roof. Every one of the homes appeared to be in pristine condition. The landscaping around the houses displayed an impressive array of flowering shrubs and lush green trees. Pines dominated the forest behind the homes, but oaks, poplars, and maples also occupied much of the woods.

As Dak reached the edge of the town square, he noted the throwback feel of a long-forgotten era that reminded him of the hometown of Marty McFly in the Back to the Future movies. Dak had been in several hamlets like that before, including a few near his home in Tennessee.

He'd wondered, as he visited those other towns, how the people were able to keep up a livelihood, especially the small businesses that operated there. As he suspected, several of the local shops he passed had gone out of business. Three had for lease signs hanging in them. A couple were listed for sale. Others didn't even bother.

All told, Dak noticed eight shops that were no longer open for business.

Some people might have blamed the bad fortune on the pandemic that had rocked the world and shuttered hundreds of thousands of businesses in the United States and around the world.

But Dak knew it was more than that. He'd been in towns like this years prior, and the story was always the same: Some businesses made it and were able to stick around through the good times and the thin. Villages like this one, though, didn't provide enough foot traffic to keep most in the black, and often they went under without the necessary cashflow to keep things going.

Deep down, Dak felt for the business owners as he walked by toward the center of town, where a tall statue stood in the center of a square, grass-covered park. Four oak trees guarded the corners and a black wrought-iron fence enclosed the park. The metal barrier opened in four spots, one on each side of the street that encircled the park.

Few pedestrians walked the sidewalks in the square, though parked cars lined both sides of the busy town streets.

Dak walked by a hair salon and noted the women inside chatting about something he was certain he didn't care about. As he walked by a coffee shop, he saw several older men inside talking, again about something he probably didn't want or need to know.

One thing Dak noticed right away about Dawsonville, as was the case with most small towns he visited, was the slower pace of life. People here weren't in a hurry to get anywhere, or to get much done. That wasn't to say they were lazy or didn't work. Everyone he'd seen so far was retirement age or close to it.

He passed a little hardware store, a clothing retailer, an outdoors shop that sold kayaks, paddle boards, camping equipment, and a plethora of other gear in that vein.

At the next corner, he spotted a quaint diner that looked like a relic from the fifties, complete with the silvery chrome sign out front that declared the place to be Gene's Diner.

Dak crossed the road and walked into the restaurant that time could never forget. Elvis played on a jukebox in the corner. Everything in the joint seemed like a tribute to the bygone era of doing the twist and swinging by the diner after school for a milkshake.

The only thing that differed from the ambiance were the customers in their current clothes, some looking at their smartphones.

Dak noted the contrast and made his way to a spot at the counter at the rear of the diner. An older man, maybe in his sixties, sat alone in the back corner booth eating a stack of pancakes with bacon and scrambled eggs. Dak gave the man a single nod as he approached. The man returned the gesture, albeit with a look of curiosity on his face, as if seeing one of those smartphones in the era when only rotary existed.

Dak didn't give it much thought, other than the guy looked rich, and he wondered for half a breath if that might be the Mitchell Baldwin he was looking for. After saddling up on the stool, Dak slid the laminated white menu closer to have a look at the offerings. Along with the fare the man behind him was consuming, Dak noted the usual items he would expect to find in any diner in the Southeast: fried chicken and waffles, biscuits and gravy, grits, hash browns, and an assortment of fruit and egg combinations—some with toast— filled out the breakfast options. The second half of the menu featured the lunch and dinner items. Dak smiled when he saw the macaroni and cheese offered in the vegetable section. The right side of his mouth curled up at the thought. *Only in the South.*

A pleasant middle-aged woman with blonde hair pulled back into pigtails walked up to the counter from the other end of the room. She wore a red-and-white-striped button-up shirt, a white paper hat pinned to her hair, and a white apron over a cherry-red skirt. Dak's initial thought was that if someone in a time machine picked her up and took her back to the fifties, she'd fit right in.

Her name tag declared her to be Susan.

"What can I get for you, hun?" she asked in a pleasant Southern accent. She flipped out a white note pad and hovered a pen over the page as she waited for Dak to give her his order.

"Hello," Dak greeted. He felt, even when he was trying to sound nice, he still sounded like someone who was about to rob the place. "I'll have a coffee to start, if that's okay."

"Of course, hun. You want sugar and cream with that?"

"No, thanks. Black is fine."

"One black coffee, coming right up." She winked at him and walked over to a pot sitting on the back counter between the griddle and a refrigerator full of milk, chocolate milk, apple juice, and an assortment of plastic tea jugs.

Dak looked over the menu for a few more seconds before he

made his decision and then slid the thin plastic back across the counter.

Susan returned with a brimming cup of steaming, dark brown coffee. She set the white ceramic mug down on the counter and nudged it toward him.

Dak nodded appreciatively. "Thank you."

"You're welcome, sugar. Know what you want?"

"Yes, ma'am. I'll have the grits, two eggs over medium, and a side of hash browns."

"You want cheese on those?" Susan never looked up from her pen as she asked.

"Yes, ma'am. And onions, if you can do it that way."

She smirked at the request. "Scattered, smothered, and covered, huh?"

"What can I say?" Dak shrugged as he picked up the mug, "I like the way Waffle House makes their hash browns."

Susan finished jotting down the order and winked at him. "I do, too." She turned and barked Dak's order to the young man running the griddle.

The boy set into motion, quickly retrieving two eggs from a nearby bowl. He cracked them and they instantly started sizzling on the hot, oily surface. The cook then threw on a batch of hash browns and pressed them hard into the griddle before tossing in some diced onions.

Dak sipped his coffee, mesmerized by the young man's simple work. He glanced over at the door as it opened when one of the patrons exited.

Then, as he set the mug down and returned his gaze to the cook, a voice interrupted Dak's thoughts.

"You really should try the biscuits and gravy here." The voice came from behind Dak, and he didn't have to turn around to realize it was the man sitting alone in the booth.

Still, Dak twisted and looked back at the guy. He didn't want to be rude, after all, and he knew how these small-town types could be.

They often took offense if an outsider was spoken to and didn't return their cordiality.

"Yeah, I looked at those," Dak replied. "If I had time to go take a nap after I leave here, I would have chosen them instead."

The husky man chuckled as he shoveled the last scraps of food from his plate into his mouth. He chewed for a few seconds, then set down the fork, leaned back, and swallowed. "They sure do make a fine breakfast here," the man said. "But you're right about the biscuits and gravy. They make you tired somethin' awful."

"Sounds like the ones my grandma used to make."

"Yes, sir." The man looked down at the empty plate one more time, perhaps hoping he could manifest one more slab of bacon from the universe's kitchen. "It's a wonder all these Southern recipes we have down here haven't spread across the world like kudzu."

"Could be," Dak said. "If it ain't broke..." He raised his mug to the man.

"Don't try to fix it. You got that right."

Dak turned back to the counter to find Susan walking toward him with a plate in one hand and a ceramic bowl in the other. She set the food down in front of Dak and asked if he needed anything else.

"No, ma'am," he said. "This is great."

"Let me know if you need anything else, sweetie." She spun around on her heels and walked back over to the other end of the counter to refill an older man's coffee mug.

Dak dug into the food like an animal that hadn't been fed in days. He'd stopped to eat on his journey, but that journey had taken a few unexpected detours and hadn't always afforded him the best dining options. That made meals like this one all the better.

"You have a good one, son," the stranger said from behind Dak's right shoulder. He was standing now and had collected his things to leave. Dak noticed the fresh hundred-dollar bill on the table.

"Thanks. You too," Dak replied, bobbing his head. He watched the man walk toward the door and stop to thank Susan on his way out.

Dak added a dash of pepper to the eggs and grits, then continued devouring the food until it was gone in short order. He sighed in satisfaction at the empty plate before sliding it forward. He washed down the meal with some more coffee and watched as the generous man walked out through the front door and onto the sidewalk. He'd no sooner turned to the right and walked into view through the center window when a woman stormed up to him. The woman looked like she was probably a few years older than the man, though Dak had never really been good at gauging those kinds of things.

The woman looked angry and wagged a threatening finger in the man's face. Dak saw the tears streaming down her face and wondered what the man could have done to draw such ire.

The man replied to the woman. It was easy to see he was trying to appease her or make her feel better about something, but his efforts only seemed to make things worse. She slapped him on the shoulder as hard as she could, then turned and marched away, still crying but holding her head high in defiance.

Dak watched the spectacle with casual disinterest, at least outwardly.

Susan finished chatting up the customer at the other end of the counter and happened a glance Dak's way. She noticed his empty plate, excused herself from the other patron, then walked over to Dak.

"All finished, hun?" Susan asked, reaching for the plate.

"Yes, ma'am. Thank you."

"Looks like you didn't hate it."

"No, ma'am. Haven't had a good meal like that in a while."

She eyed him curiously, then picked up the plate and set it in a metal sink to her right. "What brings you to Dawsonville?" Susan asked, rinsing off the plate quickly before drying her hands on a nearby towel.

Dak lifted his mug and shrugged. "Just passing through."

"Where you headed?" she pressed, turning to walk back to the coffee pot. She picked it up and brought it over to him, waited until he'd taken a sip from his mug, then topped it off.

"Thank you. If I drink much more, I'll be on the moon by this afternoon. Not everyone makes coffee this good."

"Well, aren't you sweet? It don't take much. Just clean water and enough coffee beans to kill a horse," she laughed.

"I like my coffee strong. Nothing wrong with that."

"Hey, if it doesn't kick you in the back of the throat, then it's too weak."

Dak chuckled at the comment.

"Where you from?" She picked up a rag and started wiping down the counter.

The woman was friendly, but she was asking too many questions, and Dak started feeling the pressure to either lie or evade the question altogether.

"I'm from Tennessee," he said, keeping it vague but also specific enough that she might accept the answer. He pointed at the window to where the rich man had been standing outside when he was accosted by the woman. "What was that about out there? Who is that guy?"

Susan looked toward the window and her face immediately darkened. Her eyes took on a nervous tightness, and she leaned forward as if what she was about to say was illegal. "You really aren't from around here. That's Mitchell Baldwin."

"He runs the Baldwin Corporation, right?"

"Mm-hmm," she hummed. "And everything else in this town. That man has more money than the entire population of Dawsonville, and probably all the surrounding counties combined."

"It's a big company."

"You got that right."

"What was with the altercation with the woman?" Dak asked, returning his gaze to Susan.

"Can't say I know for sure, but the woman is Hattie Markham. She owns a big farm not far from here. Baldwin's been pressuring her for a while now to sell the property to him. I heard it's because there's a big rock deposit there on her land, but you know how rumors are."

"Yeah," he agreed.

"But I don't know if that's why Hattie looked so upset just now,"

Susan continued. "Baldwin has been after that farm since before her husband passed. Back then, Baldwin was making offers to him. From what I hear, George said he'd never sell the place. I don't blame him. It's a pretty piece of land, and it's been in the Markham family a long time."

Dak considered the information. He took swig of coffee then asked, "If you don't mind me asking, how did he die?"

"Heart attack," Susan said, a hint of sadness tracing her words. "Before it happened, George was as healthy as a horse. From what I hear, his last doctor visit was a good one. Doc Parker said his cholesterol was good, blood pressure where it needed to be." She rolled her shoulders a cocked her head to the side. "I guess if it's your time, it's your time."

Dak wanted to ask about an autopsy, but he decided he'd pushed the issue far enough. Asking too many questions on a specific subject tended to cause people to remember you, and he wanted to remain as unmemorable as possible.

"Never can tell, I guess." Dak offered the bland statement without meeting her eyes.

"No, I suppose you can't," she agreed.

Dak decided to push his questioning a little further. "Why doesn't he just leave them alone?"

"Baldwin?" She raised an eyebrow. "You don't know Mitchell. That man would own the entire town if he could. I'm talking every square inch of dirt he could get his hands on. Already owns most of it. Most of the retail places around here are owned by him."

"I noticed some of the businesses here in town were closed. Does he own those shops?"

"He rents out a lot of the buildings here to local entrepreneurs, but if they fall on hard times and can't pay the rent, well..." She ended her sentence prematurely, her voice fading away rapidly.

Dak didn't ask why. He could tell from the look in her eyes that the woman was afraid. She wore an expression that told him she'd said too much, even if she wasn't trying to let him see that.

"Times are tough," Dak said, using a cliché he doubted she would remember him quoting.

"You got that right." She slid him the bill, as if that last comment were the perfect segue. "Let me know if you need anything else, sugar. No rush. Feel free to hang around as long as you want.

"Thank you. I think I'm good. Although I am curious as to why Mrs. Markham would accost Baldwin here on the sidewalk. I get that he's been trying to buy her farm, and she's not having it, but why now? Why would she walk up to him out of the blue, in broad daylight, and cause a scene?"

Susan shrugged. "She's had a tough year or so. Her daughter moved to Charlotte to take a job with the paper there. I heard she's doing investigative reporting. I can't say for sure, but I heard that Heather went missing. No one's heard from her for several days. Maybe Hattie blames Mitchell for it."

Dak nodded and went back to drinking his coffee, allowing Susan to go about her tasks behind the counter. He waited a few minutes, relaxing as he finished his drink, then placed a twenty on the check, which would cover his bill and add another eight dollars to the tip. His meager offering wouldn't compare to the one Baldwin just left after his lunch, but it was generous enough.

He stood and walked out of the bar, thanked Susan once more for the service, and stepped outside into the warming morning air.

He looked in the direction Hattie Markham had stormed off and noticed her sitting in a gray pickup truck down the block. The woman wiped her eyes and revved the engine to life.

Dak wasn't about to jump to conclusions regarding Baldwin and the disappearance of Markham's daughter. Maybe Baldwin abducted her; maybe he didn't. Either way, if Hattie Markham had a bone to pick with Baldwin, she might just be the perfect person to help Dak with his objective and, along the way, maybe find answers about Heather, too.

6

Dak collected a little intel from Susan about Hattie Markham, including the general area where her farm sat in the countryside just outside of town. After paying his tab, he hurried—albeit with great restraint—back to his vehicle, and sped out of town until he managed to catch up to Hattie in her pickup truck. Dak remained at a safe distance until he saw her turn into the Markham farm's entrance off the old county road. Tailing the woman proved to be a challenge, but Dak figured she'd have just as hard a time losing him once they were out of town and in the country. There weren't many driveways, and much of the surrounding landscape was either farmland or forest, and there was far more of the latter.

He hung back farther than he normally would, simply because there were no other cars on the road, and the last thing Dak wanted to do was spook the poor woman. She was already missing a daughter. The last thing he wanted was to make her think someone was coming after her.

The result was a lot of near stop-and-go driving. Dak would slow down when he pulled the gray pickup into view, and when he lost sight of the truck, Dak sped up to near-dangerous speeds to make sure he didn't lose her.

Thankfully, the drive was short, and when Hattie turned into her long gravel driveway, Dak appeared over a ridge up the road in time to see her taillights disappear through the gate.

Trees lined the Markham property, providing a natural barrier to the outside world, but at the top of the hill, Dak could see over the treetops and into the little piece of paradise beyond.

Green pastures rolled up the slopes of the next hill to the ridge. Trees dotted the landscape at the hill's peak, providing shade to several cows lazily standing around chewing grass.

Dak let his car roll down the long hill until he reached the bottom of the valley, then he slowed down and turned into the driveway. He left the county road and looked out the windshield and through the opening in the trees. The mechanical gate was slowly swinging shut again, and Dak nearly missed his chance to get through. He barely managed to squeeze the front of the sedan through enough to trigger the sensors that triggered the gate's reopening.

Up ahead, Hattie Markham's truck was already near the hilltop, her back tires sending a trail of dust pluming into the air in its wake.

Once through the gate, Dak paused and waited until the pickup disappeared over the ridge. When it was gone, he stepped on the gas and accelerated around a short turn, then up the long hill.

Just as his car reached the peak, the woman's pickup truck came into view parked off to the right of the gravel road. Dak felt the air sucked out of his lungs, and a tight knot wrenched his stomach.

Hattie stood outside of her pickup truck with a rifle in her hand, and it was pointed straight at Dak.

He slowed down, pulling the car off on the side of the road and brought it to a stop. He put up his right hand and rolled down the window with his left.

The woman fired a shot just past the driver's side of the car. Dak shrank back from the window with a start. He peered out through the windshield and made a show of putting both hands up. Then he turned off the engine and waited for the woman to speak.

He didn't have to wait long.

"Keep your hands up where I can see 'em, and don't make any

sudden movements." Hattie barked the orders in such a way Dak couldn't help but wonder if she'd done this before.

Dak nodded and cautiously opened the door, then stepped out with his hands up high over his head.

"Why were you following me?" Hattie asked. "You work for Baldwin? You tell him he already knows my answer. I gave it to him in person last week. And I gave it to him again today."

"No, ma'am," Dak replied, hands still high. The sun burned brightly even through his aviator sunglasses. "I don't work for Baldwin. In fact, today was the first time I've ever laid eyes on him."

She studied him for a couple of breaths. He'd seen that look before, when people were trying to determine if someone were lying or telling the truth.

"Then what do you want?" she asked. "Who are you?"

Dak winced against the bright sunshine, but he never faltered. He'd stared down the barrel of a gun before. Although he had a feeling this woman was far more dangerous with a firearm than many of the men he'd faced.

"Name's Dak," he said. "I just wanted to talk."

She scowled, and he saw her grip on the rifle tighten. The weapon had only slumped a few inches, but she corrected that, lining up the sights on Dak's chest.

"You ever heard of a phone?"

"Yes, ma'am. But I don't have your number. And would you have answered me if I called? I don't know about you, but I don't answer calls from strangers."

"And stalking someone back to their home is a better idea?" she scoffed. "I'm calling the police."

He shook his head. "No you're not." Dak took a risk, and it was a big one considering how little he knew about this woman, and the town. "You don't trust the cops here any more than you trust Mitchell Baldwin."

Dak hoped his brazen assertion wasn't taken the wrong way, though he wasn't sure the right way was any better.

He noticed the woman's grip loosen, ever so slightly. The barrel sagged a few inches. "Who are you?" she pressed the question again. "What do you know about me and Baldwin?"

A disarming grin spread across Dak's face. "I know he's been bothering you about selling your land to him for a while now. I know that you've had this property"—he waved around at their surroundings—"for generations. And I also heard your daughter went missing a few days ago."

The gun lifted again. "What do you know about Heather?"

Dak shook his head. "Nothing, ma'am. Other than I heard she's been missing for a few days. But you think Baldwin had something to do with it. Don't you?"

The woman breathed hard for several seconds, and Dak couldn't tell if she was about to break down in tears or send a round through his ribcage.

Dak didn't dare take another step forward, but he gauged both the woman's curiosity regarding his statement as well as what she intended to do with the rifle, and came up uncertain. If there was one thing Dak didn't appreciate—aside from people who don't return grocery carts to the cart corral—it was not knowing what a person with a gun was going to do with it.

He could see the indecision written on her face, the conflict in her eyes. This woman didn't want to shoot him. That much he knew, but he also knew if she pegged him for a Baldwin guy, she'd be more than happy to drill a bullet through him.

"You say you heard my girl is missing," Hattie stated, her voice punching through the valley breeze with all the power of a dry twig. Pain cracked the words, and Dak knew he'd touched something not even the strongest of wills could resist. Hope.

"Yes, ma'am. I promise, I wasn't trying to spook you. And I didn't know if anyone in town would give me your number, or if you'd even answer, like I said." He weighed her intentions carefully and then risked asking, "Is it okay if I put my hands down? My gun is in the car. Other than that, I'm unarmed."

"Why do you have a gun in the car?" she barked, flicking her head in the direction of the vehicle.

Dak smirked with a chuckle. "I suppose I could ask you the same thing, ma'am."

For a second, the woman seemed as if lost for words. She looked like she wasn't sure if she should kill him for being a smart aleck or slap him on the back and offer him lunch.

"Where did you say you're from?" The question fell somewhere in the middle. And Dak was fine with that.

"East Tennessee. Few hours from here."

"More than a few," she huffed. "Who told you about Heather?"

"Susan, at the diner," Dak said. He hoped he hadn't thrown poor Susan under the bus, but he was hedging his bets that Hattie had reached a point of desperation.

"She should keep her mouth shut," Hattie grumbled. The gun in her hands lowered. "What is it you do, Dak? You some kind of private investigator or something?"

Dak's head bobbed gently, almost as if moved by the wind. "Something like that."

Hattie's head inclined and she peered at him, giving Dak one last assessment. "Follow me," she ordered, jerking a thumb back toward the farmhouse in the valley below. "You try anything, though, and I'll kill you."

Dak nodded, lowering his hands slowly. "Yes, ma'am."

7

D ak sat on the front porch in one of the rocking chairs, absently moving it back and forth with the slightest effort from his feet. Taking in the late morning view, Dak understood why Mrs. Markham didn't want to let go of the farm, all the history and tradition aside. Sure, it had been in their family for a long time, but places like this weren't the kind you simply let go for a hefty sum, unless the sum was big enough to buy you similar property, or better if that was possible. Dak had seen some incredible places in his travels. Some ugly ones too. This one, though, he knew was hard to beat.

Farms with rolling hills, a few mountains, and lush valleys such as this one had always been a favorite of Dak's. His land in the Sequatchie Valley was similar in some ways, though more dramatic than this particular parcel. His cabin in the forest on the Cumberland Plateau sat only a few minutes' walk from a rocky brow that overlooked one of his favorite vistas. The second Dak laid eyes on that property, he knew he had to buy it.

This one would do nicely as well. He knew, though, if Baldwin got his hands on the Markham land, he'd strip it bare, devastating the local wildlife and the environment. On top of that, the farm that had been in the Markham family for so long would be erased, as if it never existed. The only thing that would remain would be the memories held by the last living Markhams, and when they died, so would those.

John Prine's song "Paradise" came to mind as Dak waited for Hattie to return to the porch. The sweet melody of a song he'd heard hundreds of times fluttered on the morning breeze.

Footsteps from inside cut off the lyrics, and Dak instinctively sat up a little straighter, despite his posture already being rigid.

The screen door creaked open, and Hattie appeared in the doorway holding a clear pitcher of iced tea and two empty glasses. Dak almost laughed at the sight of the last item she carried. Tucked under her armpit, Hattie squeezed a bottle of Jack Daniel's.

He stood up and extended his hands. "Here, let me help you with that."

He reached for the whiskey, but she turned her torso away, blocking him from the bottle. In the same fluid movement, she shoved an empty glass toward him. "I'll hold the whiskey, if you don't mind."

Dak grinned. "Of course." He took the proffered glass and set it on the little table between the two rocking chairs.

"I like a little whiskey with my sweet tea," she said, setting down the pitcher and second glass next to the first.

"Only the finest ladies do."

She whipped her head around to steal a quick look at him, trying to determine whether he was joking, sincere, or being rude. The disarming grin on his face, and the accompanying wink, told her there was only the best of intentions.

"Yes, well, the women at the church may not agree with me, but what they don't know won't hurt them."

"No, I suppose not."

She eased into her rocking chair and motioned to the one Dak had been in, silently inviting him to have a seat. Then she twisted the cap off the liquor bottle and poured two fingers into each of the glasses. The ice inside cracked at the touch of the warm whiskey.

After replacing the lid, she filled the glasses with tea and handed one to Dak. He took it with an appreciative nod and raised it high. "Thank you. Cheers."

"*Salud* to you as well."

They each sipped their drink. Dak licked his lips. "Glad to see I'm not the only one who likes to put whiskey in their tea."

"Best way to drink it."

"It is good," Dak agreed and drank again.

Hattie gave a nod. "Yeah, it's definitely better than the one I gave Baldwin the other day."

"He paid you a visit?"

"You don't sound surprised."

Dak shrugged. "He's a rich businessman set on global domination. It's what they do. They're persistent, sometimes arrogantly so, to the point that they will pay a visit to your personal residence to try to get their deal done."

"It's more than persistence," Hattie countered. "Men like Baldwin don't take no for an answer; at least, they don't like to. He bugged my husband constantly about this land, but George wouldn't give in. Some things are more important than money."

"Like family. Tradition. Legacy."

Hattie huffed a laugh for the first time since Dak met the woman. "You don't sound like a Baldwin man."

Dak twisted his head and clicked his tongue, took another sip, and said, "No, ma'am. I guess I don't." He looked down at the tea in his hand, the condensation dribbling down the clear sides of the glass. The ice inside floated and jiggled, clinking against the interior walls whenever he moved his hand. "So, Baldwin's been bugging you, too, huh?"

She offered a "pfft" in reply then added, "Once George passed, the body was still warm when he started coming around. The man has no sense of propriety. I would expect more from a well-to-do Southerner."

"Sometimes people lose sight of what's important, and etiquette.

Seems pretty tacky that he came over here bugging you about your land, and so soon after your husband passed."

Dak immediately felt bad for bringing up the death of George, but she didn't seem to take offense to it. In fact, this woman didn't seem like she was offended by much except for a lack of common courtesy from others.

"Baldwin never cared much for being proper. The man has spent his life stepping on those beneath him. Or those he considers beneath him," she corrected.

"I've met the type," Dak said, though he didn't think of anyone specific. In his life, he'd run into an assortment of scumbags. He glanced at the tea in his hand again and said, "This tea is really good, by the way. Not just because of the whiskey, either."

"Thank you." She cast him a wry, sidelong look.

He returned the expression along with a question. "Did you offer Baldwin tea when he last paid you a visit?"

She chuckled under her breath. "Of course I did, son. I can be polite, even to the people who are looking to screw me out of everything I've ever worked for." She paused and looked at her glass fondly, as if recalling some distant memory. "Although I didn't pour whiskey in his tea."

"Smart move."

"Yeah," she said, turning to face the fields and hills beyond the porch railing. "I did put a little something extra in his drink, though."

"Oh?" He arched an eyebrow. "What was that? Obviously not poison."

"No, I'm not a murderer. If I'm going to kill someone, I would have done it the way I was about to with you earlier."

"I have no doubts."

"Mr. Baldwin did get a healthy dose of Visine in his tea, though." She started laughing. Dak had just taken a sip and did a full spit take, spewing the tea into the air in a fine mist.

"Wow," he said, his lips creased in a beaming smile.

"Yeah, from what I heard, he basically crapped himself as he was getting back into town. Stopped at the diner you were at before.

Susan said he blew through the door and beelined it to the bathroom. But the door was locked, so he had to go into the women's. Probably the best story I've ever heard."

Dak burst out in laughter while rocking back and forth. "That. Is. Awesome." He shook his head in disbelief. "Please tell me that really happened."

Hattie leaned forward and peered at him. "Apparently, it was quite the spectacle. Those bathroom walls in the diner are pretty thin."

Dak kept laughing for another minute, imagining the entire scene playing out: the sheer terror on Baldwin's face, the panic in his eyes, the stocky man lumbering through the diner, moving as fast as he could to save himself—and his drawers—from catastrophe.

The laughter waned, and Dak found himself nearly in tears. The peaceful calm of the farm overtook the conversation, and Dak embraced the silence. This place felt like a real home, and that thought struck him hard.

"All those things I mentioned are important. Family, above all," he shared. "But there was one I forgot."

"And what's that?" She looked to him with genuine curiosity brimming in her eyes.

"Home," he said. "This place is your home. Not some apartment building or the suburbs. This land is a part of you. No amount of money can change that. I've met people from all over the world in my previous line of work."

"Military?"

"Yes, ma'am."

"I thought so." She sounded pleased, not at herself but at his selflessness. It was a kind of admiration, and Dak didn't miss that unspoken thanks.

"Many of the men and women I served with didn't have a home. They bounced around as kids, several of them the children of servicemen and women. None of them felt the attachment to a place like this."

"What about you?"

A cardinal chirped in one of the nearby tree branches, calling to its mate or issuing a warning to other birds that a predator was nearby. Dak wasn't sure which it was, but if it was the latter, he doubted the creature was trilling a warning about him.

"I had a home. Still do. My parents live nearby in Tennessee." He grew thoughtful again and didn't say anything for several seconds. Hattie didn't interrupt, sensing his pensiveness from his absent stare. "I miss it," he said finally. "I look forward to the day when..." he faltered. "When I can settle down."

Hattie offered a consoling smile. She reached across the table and put her hand on his forearm. "No offense, Dak, but you don't seem like the settling-down type."

He snorted then replied with a nod. "Yeah, I suppose you're right."

She took another drink then licked her lips. "I almost shot you," she said. "Now I'm finding myself sipping sweet tea and whiskey with you. Some people might say I'm crazy."

"Definitely sketchy letting a stranger into your home."

"You're a safer bet than Baldwin and his goons. So," she said, "you're former military. You served abroad. What brings you to Dawsonville, and Mitchell Baldwin's doorstep? You said he has something you want?"

Dak took a deep breath and sighed. "My job is unusual. I'll spare you the details, but I travel the world looking for missing artifacts, usually stolen. I track them down and get them back to their governments, or to the rightful owners."

"So, you work as a freelancer doing that? Sounds dangerous." Her expression didn't change with the concerned statement.

"It is. And no, I suppose I'm not a freelancer. I work for a guy in Tennessee. Those artifacts usually have decent rewards attached. Sometimes not. My employer is a bit of a philanthropist that way."

"He doesn't want the artifacts you recover?"

"Not usually," Dak said. "When he does, they're usually things that don't belong to any government or person."

"How many of those have you gotten for him?" She truly seemed drawn into this conversation.

He huffed. "None yet."

She hmmed at the response. "Interesting. So, you're some kind of relic runner then. Have to say, I've never heard of that kind of job. I'm sure the answer to how you came by that gig is even more complicated, so I'll leave that one alone. But I do want to know what it is Baldwin has that you're looking for. More importantly, why did you come here to see me?"

"I guess that would make sense," he admitted. "Several years ago, someone stole a pair of pistols from the National Civil War Museum in Harrisburg, Pennsylvania. The guns are extremely valuable. They were given to Abraham Lincoln's first secretary of war, Simon Cameron, by the inventor of the Colt Revolver, Samuel Colt himself."

He stopped for a second, noting the impressed look on her face. Dak wasn't surprised. The woman clearly knew her way around a firearm, as he'd almost experienced firsthand. "No one's been able to catch the thief yet. And there were no leads left at the scene."

Hattie processed the information, blinking slowly. "And you think Mitchell Baldwin stole those guns?" She scoffed at the notion. "That man would be a bull in a china shop. Not a snowball's chance in Hades he'd be able to pull that off. One of his men, maybe."

Dak shook his head. "I don't think Baldwin stole the pistols. I do believe he bought them, though, directly from the thief."

"And what makes you think that?" She stared at him with an intensely curious gaze.

"Because the thief was found dead on Baldwin's property a few days ago."

8

Heather twisted the makeshift lockpick she'd forged from a hair clip, trying to get something to click or move inside the door lock. She had no idea how to pick a lock, but she wasn't about to be held prisoner by anyone, especially Mitchell Baldwin.

She'd seen people picking locks this way in movies and television shows but had never actually witnessed the act in person. It didn't take long for her to realize that the stuff she'd seen in films wasn't nearly as easy as it looked. Of course, they were only movies, but she knew that often experts were brought in to provide consultations for such things. There had to be some element of realism to it, or all the moviegoing locksmiths in the world would raise the alarm.

It had been a twenty-minute ordeal that felt more like two hours of fidgeting with the lock. She didn't even have a plan for the unlikely event that she succeeded in picking the stupid thing. *What am I going to do, run through the halls of Baldwin's mansion, sticking to the shadows until I could somehow escape through a back door?* She'd be picked off before she even made it to the main floor above.

For a basement room, which essentially functioned as a dungeon, it could have been much worse. The place was decked out with a cream-colored leather sofa, matching chairs on either side, a gas fire-place, a flatscreen television that took up space on a mountain-stone mantel, and a spare bedroom in the basement's interior corner. It was small but accommodated her privacy, along with a bathroom connected to the bedroom. If she wasn't being held against her will, Heather would have been comfortable here.

Then again, it creeped her out that there were no windows to the basement. She didn't know if it was sunny outside or if it was raining. She'd been allowed outside in the courtyard behind the mansion for fresh air and exercise, and Baldwin had been kind enough to allow those little outings three times a day.

I wouldn't describe his actions as "kind enough," she thought.

Heather knew why she was being held captive. Baldwin wanted her mother's land, and now she was being used as a pawn to get it.

She had no idea what he planned in regard to cashing in his valuable chip. It's not like he could force Heather's mother to sell the place and simply return her daughter with no questions asked.

Or could he?

The police didn't dare meddle with Baldwin's affairs. Most of the people in Dawsonville seemed to understand, and accept, that nuance of their town's culture. Heather had been baptized in that corrupt dynamic since birth. It was one of the things she loathed most about her hometown.

The people were friendly, and it was far less busy than the hustle and bustle of Charlotte, with its sprawling suburbs and growing downtown. She enjoyed the quiet way of life here, the slower pace, but she'd longed to move to the city, like so many other young people who grew up in predominantly rural areas. It was the old cliché: Kid grows up in small town, dreams big about making something of herself in the big town. While Charlotte wasn't her final goal, it would work for now, and she didn't mind using a few stepping-stones on her way up.

Now, Heather wished she'd stayed in Charlotte. She'd walked right into the spider's web. And for what? A story?

She shook off the regret tempting her to abandon hope. It wasn't helpful. Coming to Dawsonville had been more than just writing a story to inform and entertain the paper's readers. Someone needed to knock Baldwin down a peg, but the man was made of Teflon. Nothing stuck. People had considered suing him before, but he simply paid them off quietly, away from the prying eyes of the public and the court system. Sometimes, Heather figured, the payments weren't always in cash.

Rumors abounded regarding mysterious deaths in Dawsonville, and every single one of them revolved around a person either associated with Baldwin or with property he desired.

Property like her mother's.

It was usually death by natural causes, though there were a few "accidents" now and then. One person, for example, someone high up in the food chain of Baldwin, was killed in a boating accident on a nearby lake. But the most interesting fatality revolving around Baldwin was the death of local farmer Clarence Weatherby.

The Weatherby farm wasn't as vast as the Markham property, but it contained many of the same materials Baldwin needed for his business. Old Clarence had turned Baldwin down, and reportedly threatened Baldwin. Heather didn't know what threat Clarence could have possibly posed, but when his body was discovered at the base of a sixty-foot cliff on the edge of his farm, no one bothered to raise an eyebrow. The cops called it an unfortunate accident and urged the locals to exercise more caution when out hiking or surveying their property.

There were others, Heather was certain, but no one would ever know what really happened. Men like Baldwin would never feel the icy hands of justice. They could buy their way out of anything.

Unless someone broke a story that would cast the Baldwin Corporation under a spotlight, one that would expose all their shady practices to public scrutiny. She'd hoped that as investigations started rolling, more and more layers of Baldwin's operations would be exposed to the world, and there would be no rock he could hide under, no island for him to escape to that would offer him sanctuary.

Heather felt something click inside the door, and for a second, she thought she had the lock picked, but when she stood up to twist the knob, she found it was still locked.

She sighed, frustrated, and then knelt at the threshold again. After a calming breath, she inserted the lockpick into the hole again. This time, Heather focused with even greater intensity, her ears listening for any sound that might signal success. For several minutes, all she heard was the same quiet scraping sound of her tool's tip rubbing against the lock's interior.

Sweat coated her fingers as the anxiety of the moment overtook her body. The perspiration made the tool slippery in her hands, and she fought to keep pressure on it when she believed she'd found a mechanism inside the lock that might trigger it to be freed.

It took effort to fight away her irritation at the lock. *Who puts these kinds of locks on interior doors, anyway?* she wondered. She'd never seen one like this in a room. It was always one of those things that had the little screwdriver slit. Heather wished that was the only thing keeping her in this room. This one locked from the outside, and with a more complex mechanism.

As she applied pressure against something inside the doorknob, Heather heard a click. Her heart raced, and her breath caught for a second. She'd done it. She couldn't believe her luck.

But the problem of escaping past the guards and finding transportation out of Baldwin's property still loomed large. And she needed a weapon; that much she knew. Without one, she'd stand little chance of getting out of here alive.

The second she got this lock figured out, she'd find something she could use. There had to be a random object in the room that would pass as a weapon, a blunt object at the very least. Maybe she could take one of the legs off the couch, smash a guard over the back of the head, take his gun, and then she'd be in business.

Being raised a Markham, Heather had grown up around firearms. She'd spent countless hours on the shooting range her father had constructed on the farm. It was nothing fancy, but it had honed her skills with small arms as well as long guns.

The thoughts of her farm, and her father, led her to wondering what her mother was thinking now. By now, her mother would know she'd disappeared. Hattie wasn't stupid. On their last visit, Heather had done her best to be coy about what she was doing in town, but she'd also wanted to give her mother a little hope.

"I have a lead that I think will help us take down Baldwin," she'd said. "And when I'm done with him, he'll be ruined."

Hattie just wanted to be left alone, but she knew how dirty Baldwin was and that the man surely had blood on his hands. Heather knew her mother didn't approve, but she didn't tell her daughter not to do it, either. Deep down, Hattie knew the only way to get a man like Baldwin off their backs was to take him down in a way he couldn't see coming, a way he couldn't avoid or defend.

So, her mother had remained quiet on the issue, only voicing concern about Heather's safety once.

Now, Heather wished she'd listened. But what could she do? Simply stand by on the sidelines and watch as this man wrecked thousands of lives, running over anyone in his way without so much as a second thought?

She couldn't abide that. And Heather knew her father would have felt the same way. Her mother, too, if she didn't have to be so protective.

They'd taught her to stick to her intuition, and her moral code. And that's exactly what she intended to do.

Except she'd been caught on Baldwin's property. Initially, she'd expected to be taken to the police, which wouldn't be a much better fate. The savvy citizens in the town figured Sheriff Tom Meachum was on the Baldwin payroll—unofficially, of course.

Heather snapped her focus back to the lock in front of her. Using her makeshift tool, she pressed against something inside the knob, and heard it click once more. Elation flooded her body, but as quickly as it hit her, the feeling evaporated at the sight of shadows beneath the bottom edge of the door.

Someone was right outside.

Had they heard me? She had no way of knowing but assumed the worst. Heather staggered backward until she reached a chair, and deftly slid her lockpicking tool between the cushions a split second before the door opened and one of the guards stepped in. The man merely moved to the side, making way for his employer.

Baldwin stood in the doorway wearing a red polo and khakis. The sight of him sickened her, but she wouldn't give him the pleasure of knowing he made her uncomfortable. And uncomfortable was putting it mildly.

He took a step into the room and stopped, blocking the only way out. "Like the room?" he asked.

She didn't answer.

"I hope it's suitable," he continued, seeing she was unwilling to respond, instead only glowering at him like a feral beast. "Of course, if I get what I want, you won't have to stay here long. That's what all of us are hoping, right? To make this go away as quickly as possible?"

"If you think my mother is going to sell her land to you in exchange for me, you got another thing coming. People know where I went. They know what I was investigating. And you don't have any of them in your pockets like so many of the locals. These are out of your reach, and if I don't report in, they're going to come looking for me. And they won't be alone. You'll have every federal investigator in the region breathing down your neck. And then what will you do?"

Baldwin stared back at her as if her comments were of no consequence. "You must be thinking of your friend at the *Charlotte Times*. Miss Julie Carlisle?" He gauged her response and could easily see she was doing her best to remain stoic and not let on that the mention of Julie's name dismantled her.

The thought caused a sickening grin to crease his face, twisting the skin around the corners of his eyes. "Oh, you thought I didn't know about that?" Baldwin shook his head as if disappointed in her. "You really should be more careful about who you send messages to with your phone, Miss Markham."

Her face drained of any color it had left, and the breath left her lungs in a single, lengthy exhale.

"You're too late," Heather ventured, praying he couldn't see the bluff in her eyes. "She already has the pictures. It's only a matter of time until—"

"Desperation isn't a good look on anyone," Baldwin cut her off. He held up the phone so she could see the picture from the processing facility. His face darkened to match the stormy tone of his voice. "I know those messages didn't go through, Heather. No cell service out there. The facility relies on Wi-Fi, and as luck would have it, you were just out of range of our signals."

Her nostrils flared, and her face reddened.

"Unfortunate, I have to say, for Julie, though. You dragging her into this and all. Real shame. Beautiful woman, worked hard to get where she is."

Terror filled Heather's eyes, and the gravity of what she'd done collapsed on her like an avalanche. She'd brought Julie into this, and by doing so had put her friend's life in jeopardy.

"If you lay a finger on her—"

"Whoa, now. Take it easy, sugar. I'm not going to do anything to her." He allowed a temporary, fleeting relief to pass over her like the gentlest Southern breeze before he added, "Accidents, however, happen all the time, don't they?"

She trembled with fury, and if Heather could have consumed him with lightning bolts from her eyes, she would have.

"Or home invasions. Those are becoming more frequent lately, what with times being so tough for so many folks. People just don't know what to do. So they end up breaking into homes, stealing things that don't belong to them. Now and then, those incidents end badly. Someone gets shot or stabbed. It's sad."

"You monster!" She surged forward to strike him with her balled fists, but one of the guards stepped in front of Baldwin at the last second and blocked her charge. Heather swung her arms in vain, pathetic attempts to hit the guard and free herself from his grip, but his fingers locked around her wrists with unbreakable strength.

"No need to use names like that, Miss Markham," Baldwin

drawled. "After all, if you'd just left things well enough alone, I would have never even heard of Julie Carlisle. Shame. In a way, you did this to her."

He moved by the struggling woman and stopped by the chair where she'd been sitting when he came in. He looked over the edge of the armchair and spotted something shiny sticking out from between the armrest and the cushion. Baldwin picked up the hair clip and shook his head, studying it with a bemused gaze. He held it up to her, looking at her with disappointment. "Did you really think you were going to pick the lock with this?"

She said nothing, clenching her jaw tight.

He laughed. It was a hollow, mocking sound. "What was your plan if you succeeded? Were you going to take out my men? Somehow slip past all the cameras, and then steal one of my cars?"

Heather's chest swelled and shrank with every breath.

"I guess you didn't really think that one through, did you?" He shrugged and stuffed the clip into his pocket. "Oh well. I just came by to make sure you were comfortable. I could, of course, give you less pleasant accommodations, but I was trying to be civil."

She shook her head, the fight in her waning with fatigue. "Men like you know nothing about being civil."

"Now, Miss Markham. That's not very nice. You were trespassing on my land. Technically, that makes you a criminal. What does a criminal know about being civil?"

"If you do anything to Julie, I'll kill you. Do you hear me?" she roared and found herself surprised at the sound of her voice.

Baldwin blinked slowly then made his way back to the door. The guard shoved her back, and she stumbled to the floor next to the chair. The billionaire stopped and looked back at her. The expression in his eyes was a disturbing blend of pity and menace. "I wouldn't worry too much about your friend, Miss Markham. Once your mother signs over your land to me, you'll both be joining her."

He walked out of the room, followed closely by the guard, who closed the door shut and locked it once more.

Heather sat there trembling for a minute before the tears started to flow. There was nothing she could do—except hope that Julie would somehow be okay.

9

For a second, Hattie looked as if she didn't believe what Dak said. "Hold on a second. You're telling me that the man you believe stole those pistols from the museum is the same guy they dredged out of the Baldwin quarry?"

"The dead man's name was Merritt Wheeler. On the outside, he looked like an ordinary citizen. Held a job as a freelancer, which is pretty common these days. Built websites for people, ran a small business-to-business operation. Everything he did, based on what I've learned, was remote. Doesn't appear to have ever really met up with his clients for a face-to-face, which either makes him a recluse or a man who was hiding something."

"Nothing wrong with being a little reclusive," Hattie countered.

"No, ma'am. There isn't. My intel suggests, though, that wasn't the reason for Wheeler's disappearance from society."

She searched him for an answer before she asked the question. "Where did you get that information?"

"Do enough digging through tax records, you eventually find all kinds of information. It also helps I have a friend who used to work for the IRS."

Hattie blurted out a laugh. "I wasn't aware people who work for the IRS have friends."

Dak chuckled. "Guess I walked into that one, but yes, actual people work there. Not evil monsters."

"Yeah, I know. Just folks doing a job. Doesn't mean I have to like it when I send them a check or get a letter in the mail."

"It sure doesn't. Anyway," he detoured, "I have more information on Wheeler that tells me he was the guy. It's not a coincidence he's the one who turned up dead in Baldwin's quarry."

Hattie thought for a few heartbeats. She peered out at nothing in particular, but her voice was direct. "What do you want from me, Dak?"

"I need your help finding Baldwin's place."

"So you can do what?" she asked, looking over at him like his hair was on fire. "Waltz in there and take those guns from him? I think maybe you've underestimated who you're up against."

Dak nodded his agreement. "That's true. Baldwin has armed guards, unlimited resources, and I assume his home is like a fortress."

"You can say that again."

"And what about you?" Dak asked, venturing onto ground he knew was dangerous. "You think Baldwin kidnapped your girl. What are you going to do about it? Will you go to the feds? Maybe the papers? Perhaps the media outside of Dawsonville?"

The woman shook her head in dejection, her eyes falling to the tea in her hands. "I have no proof. But I know he's the one responsible for her disappearance." Her tone darkened to a point of deep, utter sadness. "I just hope she's still alive."

"Me too," Dak said. He wanted to help the woman, comfort her by telling her that he was sure Heather was still alive, but there was no way he could know that, and he wasn't going to pander to Hattie's sentiments. Partly because Dak figured she would see right through his empty words.

Instead, he took a different tack. "When was the last time you spoke to Heather?"

"The day before she disappeared," Hattie answered. "She came over here. Told me she was working on something big for the paper in Charlotte but wouldn't tell me what it was. I didn't pry, but I got a feeling I knew what she was working on."

Dak raised both eyebrows. "Oh? What's that?"

Hattie sighed. "Lot of people have been getting sick in Dawsonville lately. No one's saying anything, and maybe they don't know, but I think Baldwin's been polluting the water, along with the land. Healthy people, getting sick and dying out of the blue. Doctors say they don't know the cause, but I don't believe it. I think Baldwin pays them off."

Now things were starting to add up. Heather was here doing an exposé on Baldwin's pollution problem, and he or one of his goons must have caught her in the act, perhaps on his property. If she'd been snooping around to find proof of wrongdoing, it didn't take much effort for Dak to see how it all played out.

He wondered if Heather had figured out a way to take the tycoon down. Men like Baldwin were untouchable, by nearly everyone and everything.

There was one exception: Exposing Baldwin's utter disregard for the well-being of the people and the environment of Dawsonville would bring him down. The public outcry would be enormous, and there wouldn't be anything the local cops could do to keep Baldwin from being dismantled around the world. The fallout would be epic. Dak doubted the company would shut down, but Baldwin would face trouble on several fronts, and probably fines and jail time. Of course, billionaires didn't go to jail. And Dak wondered if Heather had really planned out what the end game might look like. Men like Baldwin didn't lose wars. Battles, sure, but they always found a way to get things to work out in their favor in the end.

Dak meant what he had said, though, about hoping Heather was still alive. In the back of his mind, he believed the young woman wasn't dead. That didn't mean her status couldn't change in the next couple of days, depending on how Baldwin tried to play things. Dak feared the man might start using grotesque tactics such as cutting off digits and mailing them to Hattie to persuade her to sell. It was a little surprising the man hadn't done that yet, or something along those lines.

"Has Baldwin contacted you since Hattie disappeared?" Dak asked.

"No."

"He will. He'll come to you with a treaty, offering some kind of deal that if you sell the land, he'll give you your daughter back."

"Sounds pretty bold to me," Hattie chuffed. "What could he do to keep us from telling the world?"

It was a good point, but one Dak had considered. "Like you said before, without proof, who's to say you two didn't just make up the whole story?"

"True."

"But he will come to you. Soon, I'm guessing. I think he wants to make you sweat, worry about your daughter's well-being. After your encounter on the street, though, I'm guessing he'll be making an appearance here again soon."

She grumbled something, and Dak thought he heard her mention shooting Baldwin if he showed up again, but Dak figured that would never play out, not with the armed entourage Baldwin always had around. Unless Hattie was willing to die to make sure he was gone. Looking at her, he wasn't sure he could scratch that off the list.

Also, there was a bigger issue at play concerning shooting Baldwin, and Dak knew the woman had considered it. If she killed Baldwin, she'd never see Heather again. She would likely die wherever she was being kept prisoner. Dak didn't say it, but there was still another problem with all of this.

Once Hattie officially sold the land to Baldwin, the tycoon would have her and Heather killed. That ending was all but certain in Dak's mind, and it was one he couldn't abide.

Hattie had, apparently, reached the same conclusion. "I don't reckon it matters much," she said. Her forlorn words barely reached Dak's ears, so he leaned closer to hear clearly. "Baldwin is going to kill us either way. He can't leave a couple of loose ends lying around.

The option to sell and move on with our lives is no longer on the table. We might be all right for a while. I'm sure that's how he'll play it. He'll pay me the money, make it look official, and then Heather and I will die in some unfortunate accident. Or maybe he simply does it before. It's possible, but getting his hands on the land legally will be more difficult that way."

"Well, I guess we can't let that happen, now can we?"

She looked at him like he was wearing the pink bunny suit from the movie *A Christmas Story*. As an adult. "What are you saying?"

"I'm saying I want to help you. Baldwin has something I need. Something that doesn't belong to him. It's a stolen piece of history and it needs to be returned to the museum in Harrisburg. He killed the man who stole it. And now he's taken your daughter hostage to leverage you into selling your family's heritage. Like you said, we can't take him down through the legal system. Your daughter had the right idea about finding proof of wrongdoing. Getting the dirt on Baldwin, exposing him to a massive audience, was a good plan, but she put herself in harm's way to do it. Your kid's got guts, I'll say that. And I can see where she gets it from."

The woman blushed slightly at the compliment. "I'd say she gets it from George, too. He didn't take crap from anyone."

"Sounds like he and I would have gotten along just fine."

"Yeah. I guess you probably would have." She paused for a moment, as if hesitating to ask the question teetering on her lips. "What will you do?" she asked, but Dak could tell she already had an idea of what the answer would be.

He took a long breath before speaking and rubbed his chin with his left thumb. "Men like Baldwin only understand one way of doing business. They play dirty. Fortunately, I know how to play dirty, too. But there's another concern here."

"What's that?"

"Heather's contact at the paper in Charlotte. She could be in danger. If Baldwin finds out who she is—"

"He could kill her," Hattie finished.

"Yes. Do you know who she is?"

"Her name is Julie Carlisle. She's the editor of the paper. Heather's mentioned her a couple of times. I'm not sure how close the two are, outside of their work relationship, I mean. She's the one who gave Heather the chance to do some work for the paper. Investigative journalism is what she called it. I told her to be careful, like every parent always tells their child from the day they're born."

"And the kids never listen," Dak hedged.

"Not usually," she agreed.

"I'll start with Julie and see what I can find out. Maybe I can retrace your daughter's steps and figure out where she might have gone to get the dirt on Baldwin's operation."

Hattie looked at him with pleading, tear-filled eyes. The sight of this hardened woman on the verge of tears punched Dak in the face like Mike Tyson in his prime.

"Why would you help me?" she asked, her eyes searching him for the truth. "You don't even know me. And I nearly shot you."

Dak took a sip of tea before he answered. "Well, first of all, I had a feeling you wouldn't. Second, you made me one of my favorite drinks. But most importantly, you need my help. At least it feels that way. In my journeys, at least lately, I've been running into people who are in difficult situations where they can't help themselves. I don't know why I find good folks like you, and others, who aren't able to fight their most difficult battles. Maybe it's some kind of weird fate thing. I don't know. But I know that as long as I'm breathing, and able to do something, I have to help."

His words cracked the dam holding back Hattie's tears. One dribbled down her right cheek and soaked into the shoulder of her shirt. "Maybe that's the Good Lord putting you in a position to help where you can." She wiped away the tear stain on her cheek before she went on. "I once heard someone say that destiny is the path we are meant to be on, but along the way, we are met by fates—places where we must make decisions that will determine the rest of our journey to our destiny."

Dak nodded. He'd heard that once too. For some reason, he

thought it was in a fantasy book he'd once read in the barracks in Iraq. A Kel Kade story, if he remembered correctly.

"Maybe you're right," Dak admitted. "I've wondered the same thing a few times, but it always makes me feel a little narcissistic. I don't think I'm that important in the grand scheme of things."

"Great people never do, Dak," she said and took a sip of tea. After she swallowed, Hattie continued. "I can't ask you to do what you're suggesting. You could get killed."

"Story of my life the last few years, Mrs. Markham."

"Please, call me Hattie."

"Wish I could, Mrs. Markham. But that's not how I was raised."

She smiled at him in approval. "Well, you were raised right. That's pretty rare these days."

"I'll be sure to let my parents know." Dak emptied the contents of the glass, sucking down every last drop. He sighed in satisfaction then set the glass down on the little table. "Don't worry about me getting killed. I've seen worse than Baldwin and his goons. Not richer, I don't think, but definitely my share of nasty characters. I'll figure something out."

Hattie drifted away for a minute, her eyes scanning the horizon like the father in the story of the prodigal son, watching for his lost child to return. "I wish you the best of luck, Dak. And between you and me, I hope you kill Mitchell Baldwin. If you do, let me know. I've got plenty of places to bury the body here on my land."

Dak looked at the woman, expecting to see a joking glint in her eyes, but there was none. He pressed his lips together and nodded. "If it comes to that," he said, "I'll let you know."

10

CHARLOTTE, NORTH CAROLINA

Dak parked his rental car outside a white house in the suburbs of Charlotte and looked beyond the black aluminum fence to the front door. The black roofing, windows, and front door were a popular trend, and he could tell the home had been built in the last few years during the explosion of construction all over the nation.

The home was beautiful, like all the others in this neighborhood, but Dak wasn't here to admire the architecture. He needed answers, and Julie Carlisle might be able to help.

He wanted to get out immediately and stretch his legs after the two-hour drive, but Dak waited, watching the front door of the home as the sun cast its dying rays over the mountains to the west.

A total stranger showing up unannounced would probably not be well received. Thinking back to his childhood, traipsing around neighborhoods like this one with his cardboard fundraising suitcase full of candles and knickknacks for homes, Dak was struck by the realization at just how different times were now.

Back then, door-to-door salesmen were common, including schoolkids who walked around subdivisions without much supervision as they tried to raise money for school projects and competitions. The world wasn't like that anymore. On the rare occasion he saw children playing outside in the yard, or in the street, there was always a parent watching from the front porch or from the shade of a tree. Evil people seemed to be everywhere, and preying on children had become shockingly commonplace.

His thoughts drifted again to his childhood and walking with neighborhood friends to the park up the street, about a half mile away. They never thought anything of it. He was always careful, of course. He and his friends had always been taught not to talk to strangers, and that was pretty much all they needed to know.

Dak looked around at the homes, taking note of a man in green shorts and a white T-shirt mowing his lawn while puffing on a thick cigar. Another neighbor down the street pulled weeds out of her landscaping. She wore a round straw hat and blue gardening gloves to go with her loose-fitting green T-shirt and beige shorts.

Suburbia. This place looked like every suburban neighborhood Dak had ever seen. Sure, the houses were newer, but everything was just like it was back in the eighties when he was a kid. The architecture was different, as were the vehicles, but the vibe was still the same for the most part. Dak imagined neighbors chatting as they washed their cars, sharing tricks of the grilling trade during cookouts, and laughing on the back porch while their children played together in the yard.

The nostalgia faded, and Dak brought his focus back to the white house to his right. The address on the mailbox matched the one Will gave him.

Dak wondered if Julie Carlisle knew about Heather's disappearance. He guessed she might have heard something about it, perhaps from Heather's mom, though Dak got the impression the two women weren't in regular contact with each other. If Julie hadn't spoken to Hattie, then odds were, she didn't know about the kidnapping.

There was no way to be certain that Heather had been taken, but that was the angle Dak was following. He doubted Heather Markham went for a walk in the woods and got lost, when she just happened to be working on an investigation that could take down a multibillion-dollar company.

If she did know, Julie would probably be worried about her friend.

Dak got out of the car and swept the street with his gaze one more time, then closed the door and started walking slowly toward the house. He tried to look as nonthreatening as possible, in case the woman happened to be looking out the big front window to the left of the entrance.

As he neared the front porch, Dak wondered if he shouldn't have gone to her workplace earlier in the day where more people would be around. He'd discovered that often, when dealing with questioning, those being interrogated were usually more comfortable when there were others around. They felt less threatened than if they were being singled out for answers.

Which was fine, unless it was one of those instances where Dak wanted the other person to be intimidated.

This, however, wasn't one of those times.

He climbed up the steps, took another look over his shoulder, and quietly moved to the door.

He could see through a side window built into the doorframe and noticed the foyer just inside. The room was dark, but a light was on in the kitchen. He checked his watch, noting it was just after 6:30 p.m. Julie would be home from work by now. There was no car in the driveway, but she probably parked it in the garage.

Dak stopped close to the door and pressed on the doorbell. He heard it ring inside the home and waited for the subsequent footsteps as Julie made her way to the entrance. Dak continued waiting for thirty seconds but heard no one moving in the home. He craned his neck to the right and risked a peek through the window again. He detected no movement in the kitchen, no sounds of the television coming from the living room. It was dinnertime, and people were busy making supper. Maybe Julie had stopped to get something to eat on the way home. It was possible she was sitting at a restaurant or bar with coworkers after a long day at the office.

He rang the doorbell again after waiting two minutes. Dak detested when people incessantly rang doorbells over and over again in hopes of getting a homeowner's attention. Then Dak wondered if the woman would even answer a cold call like this. He'd known some friends who simply ignored the doorbell and waited until the person left to see who it was, if they weren't expecting someone. Solicitors, or door-to-door sales people, were one of the few kinds of people who had never gone away, dating back to the time when Dak was a kid. It seemed one of the few old ways that some sellers were unwilling to release, despite the advent of the internet and social media to reach new customers.

Dak stepped back once more and waited. This time, he listened even more intently, expecting to hear the sounds of someone coming to the door. Again, not a peep.

He checked the street again, then gave it another thirty seconds before deciding to look around back.

He descended the steps and walked around the house to his right, past the closed garage door and around the corner, careful to make sure no one was watching him. The lawn-mowing guy didn't seem to have noticed him, and he didn't spot anyone lurking in the windows of the house next door, though it was possible a curious Lookie-Lou was watching him from across the street.

That was a chance he was willing to take. He needed answers, and Julie Carlisle was the first resource on his list. A woman's life hung in the balance.

Once around the corner, Dak skirted the edge, staying close to a hedgerow until he found a side door into the garage. He stopped and looked through the door's window. Though the glass was mostly blocked by a white flap hanging down from the top, he still managed to see through enough to locate Julie's car inside.

She's home, Dak thought. Worry fluttered in his gut and he picked up his pace, heading toward the backyard. He stopped at the fence gate, pulled up the lever, and continued around the corner. The back-yard was much larger than he'd first thought, with bright green fescue stretching a hundred feet to a forest. A screened-in back porch overlooked the lawn, and the second Dak looked at the door at the top of the steps, his suspicions spiked.

The white screen door hung open, the edge resting against the doorframe. Dak searched the woods behind the house, scanning the areas behind the neighbors' yards as well. He didn't see any signs of trouble, but with so many trees, if someone were out there it would be impossible to find them if they didn't want to be found.

He hurried up the steps to the open door and peered into the enclosed area. The back door was similarly cracked open. Dak considered drawing the concealed subcompact pistol he carried, but that was the last thing he wanted Julie to see if she abruptly stepped out onto the back porch for a snack or a cold drink.

To be safe, he kept his hand close to the weapon in case he had to draw it quickly. Something wasn't right here. It was a feeling Dak knew never to ignore. Trepidation filled his mind as he eased the door open and stepped onto the back porch. He maneuvered around the furniture and walked over to the back door, where he could see through the glass into the kitchen. As he'd suspected, it was empty. The lack of any activity in the house only fertilized Dak's blooming concerns.

He entered the house and carefully nudged the back door closed just a little tighter than he'd found it, but still not completely shut.

"Julie?" he said loudly, doing his best to be heard by the home's owner but not any neighbors who might be outside. "Are you home?"

No response.

"Miss Carlisle?" Dak risked saying a little louder than the first time. "I'm a friend of Heather Markham." He didn't figure the lie was that much of a stretch; after all, he was trying to find Heather.

He received silence again.

Dak's concern pushed him to cross the living room to the stairwell in the far corner. He looked up the stairs but saw nothing of interest. Pictures of a young brunette woman on vacations in different parts of the world lined the walls. Julie was pretty, and from the look of the pictures, stayed active with hiking through forests or trekking across

Europe. Dak wondered how long ago those photos were taken, but they looked fairly recent.

He continued up the stairs, fearful that he might catch the woman in a bathrobe stepping out of the shower, and for a second, Dak hesitated. He froze halfway up the steps, thinking better of his intrusion. *What if she's armed?* She might well shoot him right there without so much as a second thought. After all he'd been through—the gun battles, the wars, the small armies of trained professionals who'd tried to kill him—it would be Dak's luck to get killed by the editor of a newspaper.

He focused his energy on his hearing and listened closely for any signs of movement at the top of the stairs, or perhaps the sound of running water from one of the bathrooms.

Again, nothing.

Dak sighed and continued up the stairs until he reached the landing at the top. A door to his right led into an office, where a modern contemporary writing desk sat against the wall. A television hung from the adjacent wall, and more pictures of Julie and her travels filled the rest of the wall space. The laptop on the desk sat closed, indicating it hadn't been used in the last few minutes, though she could have finished moments before Dak walked in.

He turned to the open door to the left and looked into the master bedroom. No sign of anyone. He looked straight ahead into the guest bathroom at the end of the hall where it split at a T, branching off to a bedroom to the right and the left.

Those would be spare rooms, maybe Julie was doing some kind of work in there, perhaps cleaning, or a hobby.

"Julie? My name is Dak Harper. I'm a friend of Heather and Hattie Markham. I just came into town to see if you could help me." He spoke to the empty house as if it might answer him, or produce the hiding, frightened woman. "I'm trying to find Heather. I don't know if you heard, but she's missing."

Nothing.

Dak drew the pistol from his concealed holster and held it low by his waist. He didn't want to scare Julie, but now Dak's worries had shifted. The back door had been left open. Her car was in the garage. And she wasn't answering.

Moving into the bedroom, Dak surveyed the space in a single second then moved to the closet in the back-left corner. When he reached the doorway, he pressed his back against the wall and peeked in. The long walk-in closet was as empty as the rest of the house.

Just as he was starting to accept that no one was home, and that Julie must have gone to one of the neighbors or out for a walk, he noticed something through the open bathroom door on the other side of the room.

A foot jutted out from behind the wall, the heel resting on the floor.

"Julie?" Dak's voice carried concern now, and he rushed across the room.

He reached the doorway and pushed it the rest of the way open. Julie lay on her back, her head twisted to the side slightly as if sleeping. But her chest didn't rise and fall with breath. A red line across her neck told Dak everything he needed to know. She'd been strangled.

He caught movement in the closet just past the sink a few feet away. Dak raised his pistol, but something shiny flew at him and he narrowly ducked out of the way before the metal box struck him in the face. He snapped the pistol up again, but this time it was met by the tip of a black boot. The weapon flew out of Dak's hand and clattered on the floor in the corner under the sink.

The killer lunged at Dak; a piano cord clenched in his fingers— the murder weapon he'd used to take Julie's life. Menace filled the attacker's cold, dark eyes. His full, dark brown hair jiggled with his movement. The man was probably in his late twenties.

Dak dodged the man's surging attack as he tried to loop the piano cord around Dak's neck. After the quick sidestep, the man's momentum carried him to the door. Dak countered with a high knee to the midsection, and the killer's wind left his lungs.

The man doubled over, incapable of returning the favor. Dak spun around and grabbed the man's lush hair at the back of his skull and rammed his head into the doorsill. The man's forehead thudded against the trim, and Dak felt him relax with every blow. The murderer dropped the piano cord on the floor and clawed behind him, trying to scratch Dak's hand, or grab his wrists.

The grip was too strong, and Dak continued issuing the punishment until the man collapsed to the floor.

The assailant tried to escape into the bedroom, crawling on all fours. Dak bent down and grabbed the piano cord. He twirled it around his hands like a giant piece of dental floss and straddled the killer's back, letting the cord dangle around his neck for a second. Then Dak yanked hard, squeezing the thin metal wire against the killer's throat.

The assassin reared back, and for a second, the cord went slack. But only for a second. Dak tightened it once more, and this time the man had nowhere to go as Dak pulled him close.

The killer wiggled and fought, scratching at Dak's face with his fingernails in a desperate attempt to free himself from the strip of irony choking the life from him. Dak kept his face far enough from the killer's reach and put his knee into the man's back, forcing him down with his weight.

With a slap, the man's palms hit the floor, and with Dak on top of him, he couldn't summon the energy to push back up.

As every second passed, the killer's struggle weakened. He gasped for breath, tugged at the piano cord around his neck, probably much the same way Julie had before she died. The thought only fueled Dak's rage and he twisted the cord tighter in his hands, ignoring the lack of circulation and the pain of the wire digging into his own skin.

A last gasp, then a gurgle, escaped the man's lips before Dak felt the body beneath him slump to the floor. Dak didn't let off for another minute, instead continuing to choke the man until he was sure the guy was dead.

After a minute, Dak let go of the cord and caught his breath. The fight had been a short one, but he'd been lucky. The killer had got the drop on him, and if the man had been armed with a gun, too, the outcome might have been different.

Dak wouldn't make that mistake again.

He stood up and looked around the room, which was now a murder scene. He hadn't touched anything except the cord he'd used to kill the assassin, and there was no way anyone could connect that to Dak. Still, he didn't like the idea of being there. Even though the neighbors appeared to pay him no mind, it's likely one of them saw him, or his car, or both.

The car would be easy enough to ditch and replace with another rental. He'd used one of his false identities to get the vehicle, so no one could track who the real renter was.

Dak looked around the room one last time, making doubly sure he didn't leave any evidence that could somehow link him to the crime. Satisfied the room was clean, Dak picked up his gun, then walked to the door and paused. He stared back at the body of Julie Carlisle, and a lump caught in his throat. A knot in his gut matched the icky feeling, and Dak felt a wave of regret smash into him.

He didn't want to leave her body there, on the floor like that, but he had no choice. The cops would put together an explanation about what happened, probably linking the dead man on the floor near her to Julie's demise. How they explained the assassin's death, Dak didn't know, nor did he care. What he did care about was that Baldwin had crossed a line.

The tycoon had taken an innocent life, and nearly took out Dak in the process. Dak knew that it was only a matter of time until Baldwin eliminated Hattie and her daughter—if Heather was still alive.

Dak made his way back down the stairs, careful not to touch the railing or walls. He already felt a surge of paranoia pulsing through his mind, and lingering here at the crime scene only made it worse.

He stopped at the bottom of the stairs, surveyed the empty house, and made for the back door. A second before Dak reached the exit, he noticed the workstation in the corner of the living room. Notepads sat on the surface in a neat stack to the right of the keyboard. Dak looked out through the back door's window and then reluctantly hurried over to the desk.

Dak carefully peeled back the pages to the top notebook until he found a name he recognized on the third page.

Heather Markham was written in black ink at the top of the paper. Mitchell Baldwin's name was a few lines down, with notes about the pollution and the corruption going on in Dawsonville. A few more names occupied lines farther down. One was the name of the sheriff Dak had heard about, Tom Meachum. Dak didn't recognize the other name, and he was certain he'd have remembered it if he had seen it before—Joe Notekabortsky. The only detail next to Notekabortsky's name was the word *mechanic*.

"Must be a mechanic in town," Dak mumbled. "I wonder how a mechanic connects to all this."

Dak heard a door slam somewhere across the street, and he jumped at the noise that may as well have been a firecracker going off in a bathroom. He closed the notebook with his fingernail and rushed back to the rear door. Dak left quietly as the sun set behind the mountains to the west, and skimmed the side yard around to the front. At the corner, he looked around, surveying the street for any witnesses, but everyone had gone in for the evening. The man mowing his lawn was no longer there, and no children played in the street or in their yards.

Dak walked calmly, but briskly, back to his rental sedan, climbed in, and started the engine.

As he pulled out of the subdivision, heading back toward Dawsonville, questions rang in his mind: *Who is this mechanic? What does he know about the Baldwin Corporation? How does he connect to Heather Markham? And most importantly, who is Baldwin going after next?*

11

Baldwin stepped out of his SUV and looked up at the older woman sitting in her rocking chair on the porch, a black hunting rifle across her lap.

"Little early for target practice, ain't it, Hattie?" Baldwin asked cheerfully.

"The target just got here," she countered.

He didn't miss the threat. "Now, Hattie, I came here to tell you I'm sorry for whatever it was I said that upset you on the street yesterday."

"You didn't come here to apologize, Mitchell. I know you better than that. You came here to take my land away."

His head bobbed stupidly. "I understand why you say that, Hattie. And it's true, I'm here to make you another offer, even more generous than the last."

"The answer is still no, Mitchell. And if you don't bring my daughter back safe, I will kill you. I don't care what your boys do to me."

She indicated Baldwin's driver with a flick of the head. The man stood by the open back door to the SUV, remaining stoic.

"I have no doubt you would keep your word on that, Hattie. No doubt at all. Which is why I'm making you my final offer." He walked toward the steps.

"That's far enough, Mitchell," she spat. The rifle across her lap twisted in his general direction. She didn't aim it right at him but enough so he would get the gist.

Baldwin halted in his tracks and didn't dare venture another inch forward. "If you shoot me, you'll never get to see your daughter again, Hattie. We both know that."

"Decided to come forward with the truth, eh, Mitchell?" She hissed the words at him like a serpent.

"We both know what will happen if you go to the authorities with this, Hattie. Your daughter will die, quite painfully, I might add. She's comfortable right now. I'd prefer to keep it that way."

She didn't like the way he said "comfortable." That's how people described loved ones just before they died. The term usually meant heavily medicated, hopped up on so many drugs that the soon-to-be dearly departed never felt a thing. Or very little.

"I could just kill you, call the feds, tell them to get a warrant to search your place, and then everything would be peachy. Well, except for you." She let the threat flutter in the breeze.

Baldwin didn't seem affected by it, which didn't surprise Hattie. He'd been the target of many of her barbs in recent times, and until he either gave up, or died, that wasn't going to change.

"You're not going to kill me, Hattie," Baldwin drawled. "I've ordered my men to execute—if you'll pardon the phrase—plan B if anything happens to me."

Hattie knew what he meant. He was going to kill Heather, and there was nothing Hattie could do about it. She silently prayed that Dak had somehow managed to find a way into Baldwin's home. The present moment would have been an opportune time to make his move, what with Baldwin standing at her front door. He'd never suspect the former Delta Force operator to show up and tear through his property, and his guards.

It was wishful thinking. Hattie knew that. But that fact didn't stop her from doing it. She also wished, in part, that he was here with her right now. She could kill Baldwin, Dak could eliminate the driver, and the two of them could dispose of the bodies together before heading out to take on Baldwin's fortress.

Hattie knew it wasn't going to happen. She didn't know where Dak was at the moment, but she would have seen him approaching the second he cleared the top of the ridge, just as she'd seen Baldwin on his approach. Hattie doubted Dak had been successful in his search, but she had to keep up hope. Her daughter's life depended on the stranger, and she wasn't going to give up yet.

"Now then," Baldwin continued, "what do you say we put all of this behind us and sit down for some business."

"I'd prefer you stand, since you won't be staying long. My answer is the same as it's always been, Mitchell. You will never own Markham land as long as blood flows through my veins."

He'd expected that answer. Baldwin wasn't foolish enough to think anything had changed since his last visit. He knew the woman's frosty stubbornness would never be melted by the passage of time, though he was surprised that she seemed unwilling to even consider his offer since her daughter's safety hinged upon it.

"Hattie," he said, his voice full of resignation, "I don't want anything to happen to Heather."

"Says the guy who kidnapped her," Hattie snapped, cutting him off. "The only reason I haven't killed you and your little crony over there"—she motioned to the driver with a flick of her head—"is because as long as you're alive, so is Heather." She choked on a tear, swallowed it, and kept going. "So, I'm going to make you an offer, Mitchell."

He stared at her through eyelids so narrow you could have blindfolded him with dental floss. He remained unmoving, a monument to apathy.

"Bring back my daughter, and never come here again, and I'll let you live. But if you harm a single hair on her head, if you do anything to Heather against her will, I will spend the rest of my days making sure you suffer every second for the rest of yours. Do you understand, Mitchell?"

The man tilted his head back. The morning sun gleamed on his tanned forehead just below his hairline. "I've tried to be civil, Hattie. I've been cordial to the point it hurts my teeth for being so sweet. But you just won't listen to reason, will you?" He looked down at the ground while making a dramatic show of shaking his head. "I have offered you an extremely fair price. And even now, as your daughter's life hangs in the balance, you still won't do a deal with me. So, I'm changing my offer."

Hattie chuffed. "You gonna drop your trousers, bend over, and kiss your own behind right here? Because that's an offer I don't think I could refuse."

"As funny as I'm sure you think that would be, Hattie, no. That isn't my offer. My offer is along a different line. You threatened me."

"You threatened me, too, Mitchell. And my daughter."

"And now she is going to pay for your insolence and your short-sighted point of view. You said not to harm a hair on her head. I won't touch her hair. But I'm thinking of something a little more old-school. Like maybe I send you pieces of her, one at a time. A finger here, a toe there. I'm sure you remember the first time you counted those digits on her birthday." He watched the storm brewing in her eyes with every word. "Isn't that what all mothers do when their child is born? They count the fingers and toes, make sure the numbers are right? It will be like reliving that day, except this time all those cute little digits will be grown up, and they will no longer be attached to your daughter."

The rifle in Hattie's hands erupted with a loud pop. The ground at Baldwin's feet exploded, sending gravel and debris all over his shiny shoes and the lower part of his pants.

The man jumped, throwing his hands up close to his face as if that would save him from any of the driveway shrapnel. The driver at the SUV started at the sound, then instantly drew his weapon and stalked forward as he'd probably done many times in training.

Hattie didn't doubt the man's accuracy. She knew all the men

Baldwin employed were lethal with firearms, and probably a few other forms of weapons. Everyone had heard the stories, and while some of them were simply urban legends used to keep the citizens of Dawsonville in line, she could tell that this man knew how to handle a pistol. From where he stood, though, he'd be lucky to hit the exterior wall of her house. With every step toward her, however, his accuracy increased.

The dust blew away, and Baldwin lowered his hands from his face. The driver joined him by his side, keeping the weapon trained on the woman in the rocking chair. Neither of them had even seen the subtle twist of her hands, or the quick pull of the trigger.

Hattie hadn't even aimed. She'd fired from the hip and put a shot right at Baldwin's feet.

Baldwin sucked in a deep breath through his nostrils and blew it through his lips in an impressed whistle.

"That was a dandy of a shot, Hattie," he said, holding up one hand to signal the driver to stop his advance. "I bet you could take the beak off a buzzard without even looking down the sights."

"I'll take something off you if you don't leave my land, Mitchell."

The smug grin on his face evaporated, replaced with an irritated scowl. "You have until Friday at noon to let me know your final answer, Hattie," Baldwin said. "That's two days. I do hope you'll change your mind. For poor Heather's sake. Would be awfully tough to write for *The Times* with a few fingers missing."

She didn't respond, instead matching his searing scowl with one of her own. Hattie wanted to tell him where to go, where he could shove his deal, but for all her resolve, she felt a crack in her heart. There was no way she could resign Heather to that fate, to any of the threats Baldwin made.

Mitchell said nothing else as he turned around and ambled back to his SUV. Hattie watched, wondering if he might turn around for fear of catching a bullet in the back. But he never did. Instead, the man climbed into the backseat through the open door and waited until the driver closed it.

Hattie sat there on the porch for ten minutes after the vehicle disappeared over the ridge. A trail of dust drifted into the sky, spreading by the second until it created a dirty haze.

Two days. The thought sucked the air out of her lungs, and for the second time in her life, Hattie Markham felt completely helpless. She couldn't even bring herself to hope that the stranger named Dak would be able to pull off a miracle.

12

D ak woke up earlier than usual the next morning. He always had trouble sleeping when there was something pressing on his mind, and lately that seemed to be the rule rather than the exception.

The name *Joe Notekabortsky* had been in his head all night long like a bad earworm, and he couldn't stop wondering how the guy connected to all of this. After an hour of research back at the hotel the night before, Dak hadn't found anything particularly intriguing about the mechanic.

He ran Notekabortsky's Auto Shop on Third Street just outside the little downtown square. The shop had been his father's, and when the older Notekabortsky retired, Joe took over, stepping into his father's footsteps after working at the place since high school.

The repair shop and gas station had been in business for nearly fifty years, so Dak surmised they did good, honest work.

As far as Dak could tell, the Notekabortskys were good folks and appeared to do their best to steer clear of trouble, which only begged the question as to why Joe's name appeared on a list at Julie Carlisle's place.

Was Joe connected to the Markhams? Baldwin? Or did he have

something else to do with Heather's investigation? Dak didn't have answers to that yet, but he hoped getting in a little early to meet with Joe would help clarify some things.

He stopped outside the auto shop and parked his car in a space next to the sidewalk that ran parallel to the street. Dak stepped out of his ride and took in the sight.

The old repair shop looked as though it might have fifty years ago, still sporting the same architecture Dak had seen in old gas stations growing up, or in pictures his grandparents had around the house.

Two garage bays occupied the left side of the shop, with the cashier's station just inside a glass door opposite two gas-pump lanes. Dak breathed in the tire- and gas-scented nostalgia as he walked toward the cashier's station. He loved the smell of a shop, even though he'd never spent much time in them growing up, aside from his grandfather's garage every now and then.

Dak spotted Joe Notekabortsky through the glass, standing just inside near a shelf stocked with motor oil and engine additives. Dak recognized him from a few pictures he'd found online, and he again wondered how the owner of the repair shop and gas station tied into the mysterious disappearance of Heather Markham.

He doubted the mechanic knew anything about what happened to the young woman other than what everyone else in town knew— that she'd vanished and that no one was saying a thing about where she was or who might have taken her. If the people of Dawsonville thought Baldwin was the one responsible, Dak knew they weren't going to say anything.

Notekabortsky, however, was on a list that predated—as far as Dak could tell—Heather's disappearance. If he was on a notepad at Julie Carlisle's home, that meant he was one of Heather's sources, and potentially a source that could help Dak track her down. If Joe was willing to help.

There were no other customers getting gas, and anyone there to get their vehicle looked at must have been waiting in a sitting area just inside the office on the right end, beyond the garage bays.

Dak pulled open the glass door to the sound of an electronic bell and stepped into the narrow cashier area. A door to the left led into the garage. The room smelled of decades-old grease, and Dak found himself again thrown back in time to his grandad's garage.

Another technician sat in a blue plastic chair next to the far window beside the register. The man was older, and Dak figured from the look of him that the guy had probably worked there for the better part of his career. His thick fingers looked like they could squeeze lemon juice right from the tree. They bore dark stains that might have either been from the morning's work or from days gone by where soap simply couldn't cut through the grime. The name tag on his light blue work shirt declared his name was Jimmy. A trucker hat on his head sat up high, boasting a white Chevrolet bow tie logo on the front. His thick salt-and-pepper beard dipped down to the top of his shirt where the first button was undone.

Joe, on the other hand, looked no less than twenty years younger. Standing at six feet two inches tall, Joe Notekabortsky was a big, strong man in his mid to late thirties. He wore the same uniform as Jimmy and sported the same work-stained hands. Dak figured the man to be at least three hundred pounds, if only a shade under that, and he carried the weight with huge, hulking muscles that strained the fabric of his uniform to its limits.

"What can I do for you today?" Joe said in a friendly tone as Dak walked in.

Dak gave a nod in greeting. "I'm looking for Joe Notekabortsky," he said. "Was wondering if he could help me with a problem."

Joe and Jimmy glanced at each other, then Jimmy answered. "Looks like you found him," Jimmy said, jerking a thumb at his employer.

Dak knew who it was from the images he'd seen and from the name tag on Joe's shirt, but he wasn't going to barrel into this place and demand to see the owner without at least a thin layer of propriety or social convention.

Joe continued to look at Dak with dark brown eyes under light brown hair that was swept to the side and was kept in place with the trucker hat on his head. One flap of his button-up shirt had come untucked and hung loose over the belt around his waist.

"What can I do for you?" Joe asked, his voice still just as friendly and sincere as the first time he spoke.

"Would you mind if we step outside and I show you?" Dak asked. "Sometimes these things are difficult to describe." He never shifted, never lost focus, and there was no way Jimmy knew Dak was doing his best to be discreet. For all he knew, Dak was there to have something checked on his car.

Dak risked a sidelong glance out the window and noted another car pulling into the full-service line of the gas pumps. It had been years since Dak had seen one of those relics to days gone by, back when no one filled up their own gas tanks.

He recalled those days, back in the eighties, when people rolled up to a gas pump and the tires ran over a tube that caused a bell to ding somewhere in the station. Immediately, a guy would come running out of the building and ask if they wanted a fill-up and whether they needed anything else. They'd usually wash your windows for free.

Dak's parents rarely used the full-service pumps, and Dak honestly couldn't recall a time when he had, either.

"Jimmy?" Joe said. "Would you mind helping that customer while I help this one?"

"Sure thing, boss," Jimmy said in a pleasant tone. He almost sounded glad to be getting the easier assignment, and he stepped quickly as he walked out the door and across the lane to where the gray sedan sat parked next to the first of two fuel pumps.

When the door was closed, Joe continued to watch his employee until he was certain Jimmy couldn't hear them. Then, he turned to Dak and locked eyes with him.

"What seems to be the trouble?" Joe asked, picking up a pair of black nitrile gloves from a nearby box. It seemed the mechanic was tired of getting his hands messy.

"Well," Dak started, uncertain as to how he should handle this. A voice in the back of his mind kept screaming for him to tell the truth. But the truth would be blunt, especially for a guy who was just starting his day at his dad's repair shop. It was unlikely Joe's mental preparation for a kidnapping inquisition was on the docket while the man sipped his morning coffee.

Joe sensed Dak's hesitation and urged him on. "You were saying you had an issue with your car?"

"Yeah. I did suggest that." Dak squirmed for a second. "I only said that because of the other guy sitting here. What I have to ask you is for your ears only." Dak tilted his head forward, giving Joe his most serious stare. "And I need our conversation to remain completely anonymous."

Joe, caught off guard as he was, didn't flinch. He blinked a few times, then nodded. "Okay. Want to go back to my office to talk?"

"That would be great. Thank you."

"Sure thing," Joe said. "Jimmy can handle the register for a while. The office is this way."

He motioned through a door in the back near the one leading to the garage bays. "Follow me."

Joe led the way through a corridor lined with fake wood panels that looked like they had been hanging there since the late seventies.

Dak followed Joe down the corridor, turned left at the end, and continued on until they arrived at an office in the back corner of the building. Joe walked through the open door and took a seat behind a wide, cluttered metal desk. Pictures of little league baseball teams adorned the walls, and after a quick inspection, Dak realized that the gas station had sponsored all of them.

Dak accepted an invitation to sit down in one of the two uphol-stered chairs opposite the boss and eased into the seat.

Everything about the place, from the furniture to the walls, told Dak that very little had changed in the last four decades, and maybe longer. Some of the stuff in this building, he realized, probably dated from way back, when Joe's father ran the place.

It took a second for Dak to rip his attention away from the decor and back on track, and by the time Joe steepled his hands atop his desk, leaning forward in a way that begged Dak to hurry up so he could get back to work, the visitor had already refocused.

"I'm sorry to bother you like this," Dak began. "I know you're busy, and you run a business, so your time is paramount."

"It's fine," Joe said. "You some kind of cop?"

"No." Dak twisted his head, searching Joe for the reason behind the query. "Do I look like one?"

"Not really. But I've never seen you in town before. That means you're either new on the force, or you're not a cop. We only have a handful of officers in Dawsonville, aside from the county and state guys who wander through now and then, although they tend to keep their distance."

Dak's instinct was to ask, "Why's that?" But he already had a hint to that answer. His guess was that Baldwin did everything he could to keep any cops not on his payroll out of the area. It was called damage control, and Baldwin was clearly trying to keep a lid on something— or a couple of somethings.

"Yes, I've noticed a lack of police presence here," Dak said instead.

"Pfft." Joe leaned back in his chair and folded his hands in his lap, rocking back and forth to a rhythmic squeak from one of the springs inside the seat.

For a second, Dak realized the creaking part was the only thing that hadn't been greased or lubed in the building

"There are more than enough cops in Dawsonville," Joe complained. "Try driving through here on a Saturday night with an expired tag or a headlight out, or through one of the six stop lights without getting pulled over for not stopping completely."

"Sounds like a small town where I grew up," Dak shared. "I got pulled over for having a headlight out, and three other cops pulled in behind me to help out. I figured they were just driving by and decided to stop in and see if their buddy needed help. I've heard from a few cop friends that's what happens now and then when you see a bunch of them behind one car."

"Maybe," Joe half agreed. "I think we just have too many here. It's not like we have a lot of crime going on."

The way he made the statement sounded like it fringed on sarcasm. Dak took the sliver and widened it to a chasm.

"Yeah, I suppose there are still some criminals here in Dawsonville." He watched the mechanic's expression cautiously for any signs he'd overstepped.

A chuckle from Joe disarmed Dak's concerns. "You got that right. Local cops, politicians, even one of the preachers from what I hear, but don't quote me on that. In fact, don't quote me on any of this."

"You don't have to worry about me running back to Baldwin with a report," Dak said, hoping to dissolve any of Joe's fears. "I don't work for him. He doesn't even know me."

"But he knows you exist."

"Maybe," Dak hedged, "but I doubt it. Outside of our brief conversation yesterday, I'm just an ordinary traveler passing through."

"So, Mr. Traveler, what could I possibly do to help you? You don't need car repairs. That much is evident."

"No, sir. I don't. I'm not here about a car. I'm here about Heather Markham."

He watched the mechanic's face pale at the mention of her name. It wasn't the kind of color someone's face turned when they were guilty; this was more like if they'd been caught misleading someone —perhaps outright lying or simply passing along information that wasn't entirely true.

"What would you like to know?" Joe asked, reservation in his voice.

Dak leaned forward, planting his elbows on his knees. "Did you know she went missing?"

Joe nodded. "I heard. Just like everyone else. Are you sure you're not a cop?"

"Definitely sure." He stopped for a second, letting his answer settle before going on. "What do you know about her disappearance?"

Joe sized up his guest, then answered. "I know about as much as anyone else in this town. I'm sorry, what did you say your name is?"

"I didn't. But you can call me Dak."

"That's an interesting name."

"I've gotten used to it." The response rolled off Dak's tongue. "You were about to tell me what you know regarding Heather's disappearance."

"Right," Joe agreed, getting back on topic. "Like I was saying, I know about as much as anyone else around here. She came back to town a week or two ago, as far as I remember. She came by here a few days before she disappeared. Of course, the local cops put me on their list of suspects because of that little fact. Pretty sure I'm still on that list, but I had nothing to do with her being missing. I didn't kidnap Heather Markham." He shifted nervously and looked over at the door.

Seeing it was open, Joe left his seat and shut the door before returning to the squeaky chair.

"Worried someone might be listening?" Dak theorized.

"Look, man, you're not from around here. You don't know how things are." Joe leaned forward, resting his elbows on the desk. "Baldwin runs everything. Owns everything. And everyone. He has ears everywhere. I heard a story about how he bugged a local cleaners, then when Baldwin heard the owner say something negative about him, the place was shut down within days."

"I've heard stories to similar effect."

"Yeah, well, nothing gets by him."

"And yet," Dak said, "here you are, talking to a stranger about it. For all you know, I could work for him. How do you know I'm not skulking around the town, looking for anyone who might betray the boss?"

Joe studied Dak for several seconds, then shook his head. "No, I know you don't work for him. Never seen you in town before. And on top of that, you came to me asking about Heather Markham. If you worked for Baldwin, you wouldn't be asking about her disappearance."

"Oh? And why is that?"

"Because," Joe said, "you'd already know he took her."

Dak nodded. "That's true." He felt silly for not connecting those dots. "So, working from the assumption that Baldwin kidnapped Heather Markham, I need to find out what she was working on, and how I can take him down."

13

For a dozen seconds, Dak stared at the man across the desk from him. An observer might have thought he'd just been told the identity of the gunman on the grassy knoll, but the truth was Dak wasn't that surprised by the revelation. He'd been working from the assumption that Baldwin was responsible for Heather Markham's abduction, but to hear Joe Notekabortsky say it out loud, in a way that left no questions in Dak's mind; that was something Dak hadn't expected.

"You're sure about this?" Dak pressed.

"Of course I'm sure." Joe crossed his arms and shot Dak a knowing glare. "That's why you're here. You know I know something. Since you're not with Baldwin, I have to wonder: How did you know? And have you told anyone?"

"No, I haven't told anyone. I don't know anyone. Not in this town, anyway. And the people I do know aren't aware of what I do."

"Which is?"

"We all have secrets, Joe. I'd prefer to keep mine to myself. Let's just say I bounce around, and I try to help people when I can." He crossed his right leg over his knee, folding his hands on top of his thigh. "I found out Heather was working on an exposé, some kind of investigation that would take down Baldwin's company."

"Pollutants," Joe said.

"So, you know what she was working on?"

"Look, man. I connect the dots. I'm not some conspiracy-theory guy. But when I see things, I put two and two together. It's not that complicated. People have been getting sick here in Dawsonville for the last four or five years now. Before that, nothing. And it all revolves around when plant number five was built by the Baldwin Corporation."

"Plant five?" Dak asked, making a mental note for later.

"Yeah. It's the newest monstrosity Baldwin slapped onto our beautiful landscape. Right after the thing went operational, people in town started getting sick, especially people who were downstream from the creek that runs through that property. Doctors aren't saying anything, but they know what's causing it."

Dak inclined his head, peering at his host with curiosity-filled eyes. "I don't understand," he admitted. "Rock quarries don't use harmful chemicals to process their stone, to make concrete, those kinds of materials. It's one of the few industries that doesn't actually do a ton of damage to the environment with chemical pollutants."

"They do plenty of damage to natural settings, though," Joe argued. "The land is never the same when they're done taking what they want. Wildlife habitats are destroyed forever. But yeah, I hear what you're saying. The process involved shouldn't use harmful chemicals. Which is why the issue we're talking about is so sinister."

"Which is?"

"Heather found out that Baldwin isn't just processing rock. He's gotten into the coal business, which involves different processes and chemicals. Those chemicals are the ones he's dumping into the water."

"Coal," Dak realized. That was the answer he'd been missing, the piece to the puzzle that could bring all of this together. "Where's he getting the coal?"

"Who knows?" Joe said with a shrug. "But I know where he wants to get it."

The realization hit Dak like a sledgehammer to the chest. "Hattie Markham's place." He breathed the words, afraid to be correct.

"Bingo. My guess is he found out that Hattie's farm has a mother lode of the stuff, which isn't exactly typical in this part of the country. Usually, the coal reserves are farther north...West Virginia, Pennsylvania, that area. Could be that one of his other properties has a bunch too, although he could be bringing it in from another state to process it and sell.

"If I was trying to illegally get coal to market," Joe continued, "I would go through a third-party distributor, one that another company already uses, if not simply going back to the source with it and reselling the finished product. But I'm not in the coal business. I work with other fossil fuels. At least until all the cars go electric." He huffed the last sentence.

Dak sensed his irritation in the words, not because he thought it was bad that the world was doing more to run a cleaner civilization, but because Joe would have to foot the bill for retraining all his technicians. Dak wondered if Jimmy would even bother. He looked like he was at the end of a long career, and likely would rather retire than learn how to work on electric cars and all their new intricacies.

"How is Baldwin getting away with it?" Dak asked. "Surely he has hundreds of people working that plant. You're telling me none of them is saying a thing about the coal or the toxic chemicals he's dumping into the soil and water?"

"You say something; you end up dead," Joe answered plainly. "As far as I know, he keeps the shifts pretty tight at Plant five. Skeleton crew. And he keeps them under lock and key. If any of them were to say anything about what's going on, they'd disappear just like Heather."

Dak caught the insinuation. "You think she's dead?"

"Maybe. Maybe not. I don't think Baldwin would be willing to risk losing the Markham property by killing Hattie's daughter. He's probably using her for leverage, to blackmail Hattie into selling."

"I figured the same."

"Anyone's guess how long that will last, though. Baldwin may get antsy, decide to kill her to send a message. He'd never do a second of jail time. That much I know. The guy has the best, most expensive lawyers around. Which is why, I suspect, Heather wanted to try using the media and the public-at-large to help take him down."

That part wasn't new information, but Dak said nothing. People didn't like a know-it-all, and so he simply nodded as if he didn't have a clue.

There were still a few questions, however, that needed answers. "Would you mind me asking what your relationship is with Heather?"

The question didn't faze Joe in the least. "We're friends. Went to high school together. We were in the same graduating class. She went off to college to pursue journalism. I stayed here to take over the family business. Heather trusts me."

"Seems like you're putting a lot of trust in me. And we've never met."

"True, but I got a call from Hattie last night. She told me someone new is in town and is trying to help find Heather. Seeing as no other people have come around asking questions like yours, I'm going to work from the assumption that you're the guy Hattie mentioned. And if Hattie Markham trusts you, that's good enough for me."

The statement surprised Dak, but the woman had made an impression on him, too. She was a hard worker, someone with integrity, one who didn't bend to materialistic greed or shy away from a fight. She stood her ground and for what she believed in. It was hard to imagine anyone not appreciating a person like that. They were, in truth, exceedingly rare these days.

"So, you're just friends," Dak tried to clarify.

"Sorry if you were looking for something juicier. I have a wife. Two kids. Not interested in trying to break up a good thing. Heather's a sweet girl. I'll always love her like a sister. Which means I'll do whatever I can to find her. If that means helping a total stranger, so be it. Way I see it, with most of the town too afraid to go against Baldwin, the only people we can trust are those from the outside."

Dak admitted it made sense, in a strange sort of way. He'd never been quick to trust anyone, especially strangers. He had one last question that needed answering, though he wasn't sure if Joe would be the guy to ask.

"You mentioned the chemicals that were poisoning the water and the local soil. What kind of chemicals are we talking about here?"

"Heavy metals," Joe said. "Stuff that you typically see in coal production. When folks started getting sick, I wondered what was causing it. I also noticed that most of the sick people were coming from the same side of town."

"Let me guess," Dak cut in, "the side where Plant five is located."

"Bingo," Joe confirmed with a click of the tongue. "Some of the landowners simply left town and never came back. They took their businesses, their farming, everything, and left. I suppose they chose to do that instead of going against Baldwin. Or maybe they threatened him, and he paid them to shut up and leave town. Now there aren't many people living in that area. He's run out most of them, except a few diehards who refuse to let go of their land. Baldwin is probably planning on fencing those properties off and allowing them to grow into forests as a cover for his operation." Joe stopped for a second, listened as if hearing footsteps approaching, and then continued. "I wandered into the woods over there by Plant five while I was hunting last year. Took a few soil and water samples and then sent them to a lab in Atlanta."

"What did the lab say?"

"Same thing I'm telling you right now. That there were unusually high levels of toxins in the soil and in the water samples. And that those chemicals are in line with what companies use to process and refine coal for fuel."

"You don't happen to have the names of a few of the people who were affected most by this, do you? I don't want to go knocking on the doors of people who have hit on hard times, or have experienced tragedy, but if I can help, I want to be as thorough as possible, but I also want to be sensitive to any pain these folks have endured."

Joe nodded absently. "Yeah, sure. I know a few names. Betty Coverdale is one you could talk to. She's a nice lady. Lost her husband two years ago. The guy was in his early seventies, plenty of good years left and in excellent health. Exercised all the time, ate clean, no vices that I know of except the occasional cocktail. Shame he passed. Don was a good guy. Another casualty of the Baldwin empire. Of course, Betty received a settlement to keep her mouth shut. She was determined not to take it, but then they started threatening her children and grandchildren."

Dak remained reverently silent until he thought it was okay to speak up again. "Does her whole family live here?"

Joe shook his head. "No. They moved out of town years ago. Betty and Don stayed because they'd lived here their entire lives."

"That's awful."

"Yep," Joe said, slapping his hands on his knees. "But there isn't much we can do about it. If you're looking to talk to someone around here about it, though, Betty would be a good place to get information."

Joe paused.

"I guess another one you could check out would be Mike Hamilton's place."

Dak wondered why Joe said the man's place and not the man himself, but he had a feeling he was about to get the answer.

"Mike died last year from an illness the doctors said they couldn't explain. Like so many other people in this town. They labeled it as something else, but those of us who aren't keeping our head in the sand know the real cause. The property is still sitting there, unsold. It's not even listed on the market right now. Not that any of the local realtors could move the place, not any with a good conscience, anyway. Even with the current inventory in the home market being so low, I don't think there are any agents in town who feel comfortable listing that property."

"At least they have ethics," Dak said. "I'll find the addresses for both of those." He changed gears, rolling his head to the side to stretch his neck.

"You know, Joe, you're lucky Baldwin didn't catch you on his land when you were out snooping around," Dak warned. "Your body might have been found at the bottom of a quarry."

"Or floating near the top," Joe added. "Like the guy they found the other day. Poor son of a gun. I wonder what he did to piss off Baldwin, or if he was just in the wrong place at the wrong time."

Dak rolled his shoulders then planted both feet on the floor. "Could be both." He wasn't about to give up his intel on the thief, much less Baldwin's motive for killing the man. Knowledge of the pistols wouldn't be useful to a guy like Joe, and besides, that information was on a need-to-know basis.

"Yeah, you're probably right." Joe reached across the desk and picked up a pen. He started fidgeting with it in both hands, cartwheeling it across his fingers the same way Dak had seen other poker players twirl chips while sitting at the card table. "I can't believe they actually had the gall to try and make it look like a suicide. Pfft." Joe shook his head. "How would someone shoot themselves in the head, and then drive their car over a cliff into a quarry?"

"Seems unlikely," Dak quipped.

"I just wish someone would take him out."

The confession caught Dak by surprise, but he kept quiet and listened.

"He's ruined so many lives in this town," Joe continued. "Some people left. The smart ones, anyway. Others..." His voice faltered. "What I've seen him do, to people, families, makes me sick."

"Why don't you leave? Why doesn't everyone leave?"

Joe stared at Dak as though the answer should have been obvious. "Because if we do that, he wins. And besides, this place is home."

There it is again. Home.

"These country roads mean something. To all of us," Joe explained. "Baldwin is a bully. Sooner or later, someone will stand up to him."

"You think so?" Dak asked.

"Yeah, you know, I'm a big guy, but I can't take out Baldwin and his goons. And his mansion might as well be a fortress."

Why does it always have to be a fortress? The thought would have amused Dak if it weren't becoming such a dangerous trend.

"Sounds like the man is a touch paranoid." Dak watched his reaction carefully.

Joe chuckled. "You could say that. I would be too if I'd screwed over thousands of people in this town. Lot of folks with guns around here. If Baldwin didn't have the cops on his side, I suspect there would have been a revolt by now, one that put Mitchell Baldwin in the ground along with those toxins he's been leaking."

The mention of the cops reminded Dak of his next stop, one that he didn't look forward to. Police made him nervous, especially since there was no way to know if Colonel Tucker was jacked into departments around the world. Tucker's extensive resources could easily reach into police precincts, though Dak doubted he was going that route, especially in a town like Dawsonville, where the cops' opinions and cases were already decided by Baldwin money.

Tucker didn't want to get involved with too many cops, though, and Dak had seen that truth play out in multiple nations. The former colonel wouldn't risk overreaching with legitimate law enforcement. Still, if Dak was going to find answers from the local cops, he'd have to pay them a visit, and that proposition didn't comfort him.

Dak decided he'd heard enough from the mechanic and stood to excuse himself. "I've taken up enough of your time this morning, Joe. But I really appreciate it." Dak shook hands with the man and found Joe's grip to be every bit as strong as his own. Not that he was surprised. A lifetime of hard work would do that. "Thank you so much."

"You're welcome." Joe stood, too, and met Dak's gaze.

"I have to wonder, though, why you're willing to take a risk on telling me all this. Like you said, you have a family. I would be concerned something could happen to them."

Joe nodded. "Yeah. I am concerned about that. But I'm also concerned that if someone doesn't step in and do something about all this, that we're just going to keep going down the same corrupt path we've been on all along. I can't uproot my family business and relocate to a new town like others. We're Dawsonville folk. This is where we're from. And it's where we'll die."

Dak didn't want to agree with that last sentiment, especially considering that it could come to fruition much sooner than Joe probably figured. For all he knew, Baldwin had written his name down next on the hit list. The fact that Joe and his business were still around meant that either he or his father had something on Baldwin, or that the man simply hadn't figured out a way to take down Joe's family.

"You're trying to figure out how the Notekabortskys have managed to stay out of Baldwin's crosshairs all this time. Aren't you?" Joe asked, reading Dak's mind.

"Seems like a valid question," Dak defended.

"It is. And you'd be right to want to know. We own this property, the building, everything in and around it—unlike most of the businesses in this town that rent from Baldwin. Even so, there are ways around that, things he could do to get to us. I guess most of the town thinks of us as a staple they can't afford to lose. In reality, we're just a gas station and repair shop. Baldwin came by a few times, inquiring about purchasing the place. Dad recorded the entire meeting, too. Those video recordings are in a safety deposit box. They're Dad's ace in the hole."

"So, if Baldwin ever comes after your business, or anyone in your family, he's done for."

"Exactly."

Dak considered asking Joe why he didn't take the proof to the authorities long ago but decided not to. That was a personal decision, and Dak figured he had a good reason for sitting on the evidence.

Then there was the other end of that story. Joe's father could have been bluffing about the entire thing. Dak knew it was just as likely no video existed, but Baldwin couldn't take that risk. A threat to take the evidence to the feds would be enough to keep him at bay, for a while anyway. But that was no way to live long term.

Sooner or later, men like Baldwin found a way around those who tried to subvert any threats. If he hadn't yet, it was only a matter of time. Dak got the impression Joe knew that.

"Thanks for the help," Dak said, turning to the door. "I appreciate it."

"Happy to."

Oh, one other thing." Dak stopped and faced Joe again. "You took a risk, letting me come here to talk to you. You didn't have to."

Joe shrugged. "Sooner or later, something has to give. Heather was trying to make that happen for the good guys. Right now, though, it looks like the bad guys are winning."

"Yeah, seems that way," Dak groused. "Well, maybe it's time for a change around here."

14

"Yeah, I'm at the place right now." The man behind the wheel peered through chrome-finished aviator sunglasses. His shaved head glistened from the humid morning air.

Across the street, a stranger walked out of the gas station and climbed into a car parked along the curb.

"Anything unusual?" Baldwin asked through the phone's speaker.

The observer kept the device pinned against his ear. "Some guy just walked out of the gas station. Looks like he was talking to Joe."

"What guy?"

"Don't know him. Never seen him around here before. Must be new in town. Or maybe just passing through."

Baldwin breathed audibly through the speaker. It was a labored, exhausted breath that made it sound like the man had just climbed a steep mountain. "What does he look like?"

"Tall. Probably over six feet. Maybe two hundred pounds. Athletic. Dark hair. Probably mid-thirties."

"What did he want with Joe?" Baldwin said the line almost as if he were asking himself.

"I don't know, sir. I'm just watching the place like you asked. But whatever the guy wanted, he wasn't there to get his car worked on."

"Why do you say that?"

"Because," the observer explained, "he's in a rental, first of all. Second, he didn't take the car into the shop. Didn't have the technicians look at it. He walked into the front office then disappeared into the back for fifteen minutes."

Another sigh breathed through the phone. "If he didn't go there to have a car repaired, or to get gas, then he must be a friend of Joe or his family. I don't think any of Joe's relatives, outside immediate family, are anywhere in the area."

"Could have been a friend. Like you said."

"Maybe."

The observer took a breath and then said, "You want me to follow him?"

Baldwin considered the offer for a few heartbeats. "No. Probably just someone asking for advice about a car or something. You said he's in a rental, yeah?"

"Yes, sir. Plate is a rental. And the company's sticker is on the bumper."

"Sounds like he's in the market for a new car. Probably just wanted to get Joe's opinion."

"It's possible," the observer agreed. "Maybe his car broke down on the trip and he got stuck near here. Decided to find the local mechanic and find out what he needed to do. It happens."

Baldwin huffed. "Happened to me more than once. I threw a rod in one of my cars when I was younger. Was on a road trip with friends. Had to get a rental and wasn't going to get a new car until I'd spoken to a mechanic." He seemed willing to let the stranger go about his day and diverted his attention back to Joe. "Keep an eye on the shop for another hour."

"Yes, sir." The observer wasn't sure what he was doing there, other than looking like some kind of creep staring at a gas station. So far, the men inside had paid him no mind, and he didn't think they would. He'd kept his distance and parked in the shade of a massive oak at the end of the street.

When Baldwin asked him to watch the gas station, all the man said was to look out for anything unusual. The stranger qualified, but apparently not enough in Baldwin's book to be worth much time or effort.

The boss often displayed eccentricities of that kind, sending his men out to watch houses or businesses. Most of the time, it was to make sure Baldwin's tenants weren't doing anything they weren't supposed to. But there were other reasons too.

Over the years, the people in town had grown tired of Baldwin's grasp on everything. The rumors had turned into gossip, and the gossip had bloomed into a near-rebellion. It was only a matter of time until everyone either left the town—turning it into an abandoned relic of yesteryear—or they banded together and went after the man.

The observer doubted that would happen. While the townsfolk certainly had numbers on their side, and even some guns, the days of uprisings were long gone. He'd never even heard of anything like that regarding a private land and business owner, not outside of Central America, anyway.

"What do you think, Jake?" Baldwin asked, bludgeoning the silence with his blunt tone.

"About the stranger?"

"No. Forget the stranger. I'm talking about Joe. You think he's up to something?"

Over the course of the last two years, Baldwin had grown increasingly paranoid. Jake had watched the man continue to spiral into a pit of swirling anxiety that left him jumping at every shadow, every perceived slight. More than two dozen men worked for Baldwin as part of his personal security detail. Most of them stayed at the mansion on the hill overlooking the city. The others, like Jake, were sent out on observation duty, to make sure Baldwin's grip on the town remained intact.

Joe was one that Baldwin had yet to corral. The truth was the boss had tried to yank the family business out from under the younger Notekabortsky, but much like Hattie Markham, Joe had managed to hold on to the gas station.

Jake didn't understand why anyone would fight so hard to keep a business that required so much time, work, and careful attention. He certainly wouldn't do it, but he was cut from a different cloth. Jake didn't have parents, not ones that cared about him. He had bounced around from one foster home to another, never really finding his place in the world and certainly never forming attachments to either people or things. After a short stint in the military, he found himself in the private security sector and eventually, in the Baldwin fold.

"Not that I can tell, sir. Just business as usual at the gas station." Jake had been on watch duty several times at the repair shop, but he'd never asked why Baldwin wanted him there. Jake assumed it was because Baldwin wanted the man killed, which wasn't a problem. Not for Jake. He'd killed people in the military—and after. Usually, the victims were the worthless dregs whom society could do better without. Even the one or two instances Jake hadn't been sure about the murders, he never felt a twinge of regret.

Today he decided it was time to pry a little. After all, employees who know the *why* of what they're doing are usually better at what they do.

"I know it's above my pay grade, sir, but what is it I'm looking for here?" He quickly added, "I know you've told me to watch Joe's patterns, when he shows up, drinks coffee, does paperwork. But if I knew what the reason was, it might help."

He clenched his jaw, hoping he hadn't angered his employer. Jake had only been with the group for six months, but he felt like he'd earned Baldwin's trust, as well as that of the men he worked with.

"That's not above your pay grade at all, young man," Baldwin said, cheerfully. His tone immediately disarmed Jake's fears. "It's only natural that you would want to know why you're doing what you're doing. I will say it's admirable that you didn't question it sooner. We could use more people in the world who just shut up and do their job without complaining or wondering why they're doing it. But we also need smart folks who do ask the question when it's appropriate. And right now, son, it's appropriate."

Jake waited for his boss to answer the question, but he only heard the man breathing through the speaker. He was about to ask if Baldwin was all right, but Jake's employer started speaking again before he could ask.

"Joe Notekabortsky is one of the few business owners that stands up to my authority," Baldwin began. "Everyone else understands how things work around here. Due to a few...unfortunate circumstances, I can't just kick the Notekabortskys to the curb. Some of the more traditional ways I deal with problems won't work with them. I won't get into the details about why, but just know that the reason I have you on observation duty is because we need to find something that they're doing wrong."

"Wrong, sir?" Jake didn't mask his confusion.

It was a fair question. Joe ran a simple gas station and repair business. Most of what they did was by the book, and from what Jake knew about the man, they ran a tight ship.

"Yes. Anything we can use against them. Sexual harassment of female customers, tax fraud. Heck, if we're lucky, he's running an underground drug ring out of that garage. Although I doubt it. Everything they do is clean."

"Nobody is perfect."

"Precisely, my boy," Baldwin snapped in agreement. "No one is perfect. We all have our secret sins. What I need you to do is find out what Joe Notekabortsky's are. The man has to have done something despicable. Find out what it is, and when you do, report back to me."

Jake already knew to do that. He'd been briefed before he'd been sent out to watch the shop. He only wanted a little more clarification. His superior had given instructions to report back with anything unusual, but Jake didn't know what that meant. In hindsight, his superior should have probably been clearer, but that didn't matter now. He'd heard it from the big man himself.

"I'll keep a lookout, sir. If he so much as spits out a window the wrong way, I'll know about it."

"Outstanding. Let me know when."

"I will, sir."

Baldwin ended the call and Jake set the phone back in the passenger's seat to his right. He watched the man who just left the shop drive away around the corner and refocused his attention on the gas station, watching like a hawk for his prey to slip up.

15

Dak stopped the car outside a gray rancher in a neighborhood full of homes that looked exactly like it, only differentiated by varying color schemes or the occasional detail on the façade such as shutters, door style, and window trim.

The biggest difference between this home and the others was the obvious lack of maintenance in the front yard, and Dak had a feeling the back didn't look much better.

Long vines climbed the walls next to the little porch at the front entrance. Weeds towered over the grass in the lawn, in the landscaped areas on both side of the sidewalk, and along the exterior walls. Giant azaleas lined the sidewalk, still displaying a smattering of white and pink blooms.

Some of the faded white shutters hung crookedly by dingy windows that looked like they hadn't been cleaned in years. A piece of paper hung from the glass on the front door, and Dak knew that the house had probably been condemned.

"No wonder no one wants to try to sell this place," he thought out loud. "I don't even know any flippers who would want to tackle this one."

Dak had a few friends who'd gotten into the real estate game; buying homes, fixing them up, and selling them for a profit on the back end. He didn't particularly like the practice, but that kind of business had become common over the years. The last thing Dak wanted to do was tear apart homes and try to rebuild them from the inside out. While he was handy enough to take on odd jobs around the house, Dak preferred not to mess with certain tasks—like drywall or electrical work. He'd done both but wasn't proficient in either. And certainly not as good as the licensed crews.

As he stared at Mike Hamilton's home, Dak wondered what the reaction would be from construction and landscaping teams as they assessed the needs of this property.

He wasn't here to do an appraisal, though, and Dak reminded himself of that as he climbed out of the rental, leaving the car parked on the street near the mailbox.

Dak had visited Betty Coverdale's place first, but no one answered the door when he rang the bell, and after a ten-minute wait and a quick look around, Dak determined no one was home and decided to visit the other location Joe had recommended.

In a way, he was relieved Betty wasn't home. Dak had never been good at talking to people who were grieving or who had experienced tragedy. While Betty's ordeal wasn't recent, Dak still struggled with bringing up the topic, and with a total stranger to boot. He didn't want to scratch at old scars, and randomly showing up on Betty's doorstep to bring up her late husband and the cause of his demise didn't seem like a great way to pop into someone's life.

Now he was at an empty home, and while it wasn't as emotionally stressful as visiting a widow, the house certainly exuded its own sense of loss and tragedy. The location felt like one of those abandoned places that were so popular on social media. Most of the time, when Dak saw those mansions, castles, and other types of structures, he wondered what would cause people to leave places like that. Often times, he found images of opulent homes that appeared to still be in good structural shape.

While this was no mansion, the house still looked like it had a good foundation, and the roof was intact.

Dak could see, however, that there was another reason the home was empty.

He looked away from it for a second, toward the Baldwin plant in the hills in the distance, the brownish-gray building jutting out just above the treetops. Dak noticed two other homes up the street that looked abandoned, though if they were, the owners appeared to have left recently. The lawns weren't overgrown to the level of the Hamilton place, and the homes looked like they'd been cared for over the years.

Nobody walked along the sidewalks, though, and no one in their yards mowing grass or tending to flower beds. The subdivision looked and felt abandoned, and Dak thought the sooner he got out of there, the better. He felt exposed out in the open on the side of the street. One thing he'd always known in the military was that you were only as good as your cover.

In this place, Dak figured it didn't matter much, at least not for the present. He hadn't been followed here from the gas station, though he'd considered it to be a possibility.

When Dak left the shop, he'd seen the man sitting in the car under the shady tree along the main street. Dak initially thought there was something odd about the guy, especially the way he was sitting in his car, doing nothing, both when Dak arrived and when he left. But the man hadn't followed Dak to this place, or to the other house he'd visited. So, Dak brushed it off as nothing more than a guy on his lunch break, or perhaps waiting on a friend.

After he'd inspected the area in front of the Hamilton place, Dak gave a last check around the neighborhood, slung his rucksack over a shoulder, and walked to the backyard through a chain-link gate on the left side adjacent to the garage. Once in the rear of the house, he found himself in a veritable suburban jungle. The back was even worse than the front, with overgrown shrubs, grass, and weeds in every corner of the yard. The fence in the very back was covered in honeysuckle that laced the air with its sweet scent.

Dak eased the fence gate closed and made his way to the steps leading up to a screened-in back porch. The screening had fallen away from the posts in a few places and dangled loose from the right corner of the screen door. Dak paused at the bottom to take inventory of his surroundings and then climbed the steps. He thought for a second that he'd have to reach through the torn screen and unlock the door, but the latch was unhooked.

He stepped onto the porch and walked over to the back door. It came as no surprise that the door was locked when he tried turning the knob. A quick look through one of the windowpanes revealed pretty much what he expected to find inside the home. The barren interior ahead was a narrow kitchen with a ceiling that didn't look like it was more than seven feet high. To the right, Dak saw the living room through an archway where the linoleum kitchen floor gave way to a gray carpet. The fabric displayed faded stains in the daylight pouring through the windows.

The hollow home again struck Dak with a creepy feeling, the kind that sends a shiver up the spines of even the most hardened warriors.

He retreated a step from the back door and panned the porch. The old patio furniture was still where it had been when the home's owner died. Two wicker chairs sat along the back edge with a coffee table in front of it that looked like it had been made from reclaimed wood, though Dak figured it was more likely original, and that it was just old. Like everything else here.

Even though he'd checked the back door, Dak didn't need to get inside the house. He came here to get samples—one soil and one water.

The water was probably shut off, but it was possible that one of the exterior outlets still had enough pressure to push out a small amount. The soil part was easy enough. Plenty of that in the overgrown back yard.

Dak made his way over to the porch door and paused when he noticed a security camera in the upper corner to his left, where the porch met the house. Dust covered the black, oblong device, and he couldn't see a light on that indicated it was active.

He continued out the door and down the stairs, then looped around the porch to the back wall, where he navigated through a couple of thick, double knock out roses to find the water hose outlet. The red paint on the knob had faded and chipped, but the valve still appeared to be functional.

Dak set his bag down, unzipped it, and removed a round plastic cylinder he'd purchased at a local drug store earlier that morning. He twisted the white lid off and held the cup under the spigot, then twisted the knob. For half a second, Dak wasn't sure if anything would happen. He expected the pipes to be bone dry, with no water running through the system since the homeowner passed. He felt a surge of hope, though, when the spigot gurgled, choked, and then spat out a short burst of water. The clear liquid quickly filled the cup to the halfway mark before sputtering out.

With his sample collected, Dak turned off the spigot and replaced the lid on the cup. He carefully set the sample down into the bag, securing it in an inner pouch so it wouldn't move around much, then grabbed the second cup and stood up.

From there, Dak walked out of the old mulch bed to the closest corner of the house and knelt again. He set his bag down and removed a spoon he'd taken from the hotel earlier. Dak used the spoon in a patch of dirt between the grass and the mulch bed and dug up four spoonfuls of soil until the sample cup was nearly full. Then he closed the lid and put the container in his bag.

As Dak stood up, his senses tingled, and he spun around toward the opposite corner where he'd come through the gate. No one was there. He frowned, puzzling at the sudden twitch that had coursed through his body.

His senses weren't usually off like that, but every now and then his mind tripped a false alarm.

He peered into the forest behind the house, scanning the trees and undergrowth for any sign of trouble. The only thing he noticed were a few squirrels and birds in the canopy's branches.

Dak shook off the paranoia and started back toward the gate. Halfway there, he froze. A man in a tight black T-shirt and matching cargo pants stood between Dak and the exit.

16

D ak stood perfectly still, and for a second, he wished his pistol didn't feel so far away. Holstered on his hip, the actual distance wasn't bad, but this guy had gotten the drop on him, and now Dak found himself in the precarious position of standing there with no weapon in hand—on someone else's property. Then again, the legal ramifications for shooting someone on their land was.... He stopped the thought right there. This wasn't anyone's land. Maybe the bank's, but Mike Hamilton was dead, and based on what Dak had learned in a quick search, the man's heirs didn't own the place either. He hadn't learned who the property belonged to, but he guessed a bank made the most sense. That was who usually took over foreclosed properties, unless it was owned by the state. Dak had heard of that as well, when governments took over homes or property that had been abandoned or condemned.

From the looks of the guy in Dak's way, he didn't believe the man was the owner or a representative from the bank. To him, the guy looked like someone who probably worked for everyone's favorite local tycoon.

"What are you doing here?" the stranger asked, brandishing a toothy smile that would have fit perfectly on a hungry tiger's face.

Dak stared at the man, assessing everything about him in seconds. The guy wore shiny aviator sunglasses on top of a perfectly angled nose. His tanned, cut face could have been carved by a great sculptor, and through the tight clothing, the man's well-defined muscles betrayed many hours in the gym. His spiked, black hair fluttered in the breeze.

"Hey!" Dak replied cheerily. "Just doing some evaluations on the property for one of the local realtors. They asked me if I could do a quick appraisal."

"Oh?" The man looked surprised. "Which one?"

Dak didn't know any of the local realtors, but he'd seen a billboard, and the name stood out in his head. "Geoff Samson," he said. "Works for Valley Realty Company."

"This is private property," the man said.

Great. One of these types.

Dak could already tell dealing with this guy was going to be a problem.

"Yes, that's true," Dak said. "I didn't mean to cause any trouble. Just trying to do my job, you know?"

The man took a menacing step toward Dak. The scowl on the man's face offered Dak an unspoken threat. "I'm going to have to ask you to leave." The gravelly tone in his voice seemed a bit much, especially because it sounded like the guy was trying to sound like Batman.

"No problem," Dak said, still putting on his best, nonthreatening smile. "I was just leaving anyway."

"And I'm going to need whatever you put in the bag."

Dak's expression soured. He looked down at the rucksack hanging from his shoulder then back to the goon he was certain worked for Baldwin. He didn't care for the man's tone or the smug look on his face. And he definitely didn't like the way the man was trying to sound tough.

"Yeah, well, that's a no-can-do on my end, partner."

"You can put the bag down on the ground," the man said, "or I can take it from you. Your choice."

Dak raised both eyebrows, a touch surprised at the threat but more so at the direct and overconfident way it was said. One of Dak's biggest pet peeves was bullies, and this guy definitely qualified. He probably picked on smaller kids when he was younger, and it was safe to assume he was a jerk to women, too. Dak had met a million guys like this one, even worked with a few in the military. They thought they could do no wrong, like they were God's gift to the world.

Some folks believed that the best way to handle a bully was to knock them down a peg or two, send them crying back home to Mama after taking them behind the woodshed for a little beatdown.

"Take it from me? No, I don't think that's how this is going to go down. I don't have a problem with you, but if you try to take my bag from me, and if you don't get out of my way, then I am going to have a problem with you. And you don't want me to have a problem with you."

The man stretched his neck, raising his head just a little higher, then tilted it to the left and right to crack the spine and loosen the muscles. He stepped forward, curling his fingers into tight fists. "I guess you want to do this the hard way then, stranger. I've never seen you around here before. You must be new in town. While you're doing some sightseeing, you may as well have a visit to the hospital. Or the morgue."

"Hmm. That's an interesting idea. But I have a lot on my plate right now, what with taking down your boss. I assume you're one of Baldwin's boys." He only paused to catch a breath. "By the way, I have to ask: your clothes?" Dak motioned toward the interloper. "Do all you henchmen shop at the same place? And do they sell anything other than black? Because I'll be honest, I would get so tired of wearing that same outfit all the time. And black in the summer? In the South?" He tossed his head to the side. "Forget that."

The man stalked toward Dak, even as he finished his sentence. "You got a mouth on you, boy. Time for someone to slap it off."

"Boy?" Dak asked, more confused than insulted. "I'm probably older than you, kid." He threw in the "kid" to antagonize the man.

"I told you to leave. Now you're going to. And it's going to hurt."

He stormed toward Dak, but Dak stood his ground, unmoving until the last second when the guy put out his hand to grab the bag.

That was his first mistake.

Dak shifted subtly to the left and snatched the attacker by the wrist. He jerked the man toward him, raised his knee, and drove it into the guy's midsection.

The assailant doubled over as the air left his lungs. When he did, Dak caught sight of the pistol in the back of the man's belt.

Dak grabbed it as the man stumbled forward, gasping for air. Looking at the gun as if seeing one for the first time, Dak put on a show of appearing curious. Then he chopped the man in the middle of the back with his elbow. The blow dropped the attacker to his knees, and he crawled forward in an attempt to get away.

"What's this?" Dak asked, holding up the pistol. He ejected the magazine, then the round in the chamber, before tossing the weapon in the mulch. "You won't be needing that right now. Actually," he said, pretending to have just received an epiphany, "maybe you do need it. Because you clearly don't know what you're doing."

The man blurted an obscenity as he clawed at the ground.

"That wasn't very nice," Dak cautioned. "You don't even know me. But that's fine. I have to ask, though: Are all of Baldwin's men as incompetent as you? Or are you some kind of overachiever?"

Dak received the same profane comment as before. "Okay, that's fine. No problem." Dak grabbed him by the collar and pulled his torso upright. Then he wrapped his arm around the man's neck and squeezed. "Now, I'm going to ask you a few questions, and I want you to answer honestly. Do I make myself clear?"

The man grunted for breath. He swung his arms around in a wild manner, trying to strike Dak in the head, groin, and just about any other vulnerable place he could find.

"First question," Dak said. "Who do you work for? Is it Baldwin?"

The man grunted as he squirmed. Spittle spewed from his lips with another profane offering.

"Baldwin it is, then. Next question. What is Baldwin doing that's polluting the water and soil around here?"

Dak received the same response from the man. "You know, you should really work on your people skills if you're going to be in the real estate business." Dak squeezed the man's throat a little harder, and he could feel the strength leaving the assailant with every passing second he lacked air. "You seem to be getting tired," Dak teased. "So, I'll ask one last question before you pass out."

Dak waited for a few seconds to let the man wonder if he had a chance to be released or not. He'd found in the past that doing so often caused the victim—if they could be called that—to seriously consider a change of heart.

"Where is Heather Markham?"

The answer came in grunts and gurgles, but it was more swearing —not the information Dak wanted.

"I said," Dak loosened his grip enough for the man to suck down a gulp of air, "where is Heather Markham?"

"Screw you," the man spat.

"Wrong answer." Dak tightened the noose, closing the airway again. "I know he has her. Where is she? In his mansion?"

"Go to—" Dak squeezed harder, and the man's last word cut off. Within seconds, Dak felt the man's muscles go limp. He let off the chokehold enough so that the man could breathe again. Dak had a bad feeling he should have killed the man and left the corpse there in the backyard, but there was the slimmest of possibilities that the interloper was some kind of property manager, or private security person assigned to watch the house. He didn't believe the man was innocent, or that the guy didn't work for Baldwin, but if Dak could avoid bloodshed, he preferred it that way.

He lowered the man down to the ground, checked the pulse to make sure he was still alive, and then set his bag down next to the unconscious assailant. He unzipped the front pouch, reached in, and removed a Sharpie. He popped the cap off, then knelt next to the man and pressed the marker to his forehead.

17

Tory walked with a determined pace down the corridor while rubbing his throat. It was still sore from the choke-hold the trespasser had used on him earlier at the old Hamilton house. The only thing that hurt more than his throat was his pride.

He passed some of the other guards, who looked at him with curious stares. Tory couldn't be certain, but he thought one of them snickered at him. He wrinkled his forehead in a confused frown but continued stalking down the hall, growing more irritated by the second.

Mr. Baldwin would not like to hear his report, or the fact that he'd been taken down by some random trespasser. Tory knew a tongue lashing was probably coming. He'd only been on the job for a month, but he'd seen his employer lambaste the other new guy, Jake, for doing nothing more than showing up three minutes late to a briefing.

The boss liked things the way he liked them, and he wanted everyone on the same page in his organization.

Tory felt a tightness in his gut as he marched down the long hall-way. Black chandeliers hung from the twelve-foot-high ceiling over-head, spaced out every twenty feet or so. The corridor seemed to stretch forever, and Tory recalled how overwhelmed he had felt the first time he visited this place.

The marble columns lining the wall, the expensive paintings between them, and the sculptures in the foyer and surrounding the circular dining room were all mere hints at the extraordinary wealth Baldwin possessed. And if those weren't enough, the 20,000-square-foot mansion confirmed just how powerful Baldwin really was. The white marble floors glistened with a shine Tory imagined never faded, and he wondered what it was like to live in a place like this.

He'd lived a minimalist lifestyle before then, working his way through high school and the first two years of college before quitting to pursue a career in private security. He was at his local gym one day in Charlotte when another member approached him about a job. Tory guessed the guy figured he was unemployed or in college because he was working out in the middle of the day.

The idea of quitting school was something Tory had been considering for months, and not just because he hated it.

He heard rumors about some of the girls he'd been with at parties telling other people that he'd forced himself on them. They were lies, of course. If they didn't want to hook up with him, then they wouldn't have come over to his place at such a late hour after a hard night of drinking. Not to mention the way they were dressed. They were practically begging for it.

Leaving the university and those rumors behind, Tory had accepted the invitation from the guy at the gym. It was only later he learned that Johnny was Baldwin's right-hand man. And it was Johnny who'd assigned him to monitor the security system at Mike Hamilton's old home.

At first, Tory had wondered why they were watching the place so closely, along with several other homes on that street. No one was living there, and the place felt deader than a ghost town in the middle of the desert.

But the pay was excellent, and he didn't have to study or deal with ludicrous allegations from coeds who were clearly out to bring him down. He'd been able to get a nice home in town with the money he made from his new career and was living a life he never imagined possible. Even though he loved his home, and it truly was a beautiful place—new construction with a full acre—that house didn't compare to this palace.

Tory didn't have wild dreams of living in a place like this. He was content with his setup. And working for Baldwin gave him a sense of power that he hadn't felt in a long time. He enjoyed being an enforcer, even though his official role was security. He and the platoon of men Baldwin employed for that job understood their mission—protect the boss. Sometimes that meant taking out potential threats.

Baldwin wouldn't be happy that Tory had allowed this stranger to not only get away but had mugged him in the process. Of course, the trespasser had cheated. There was no way Tory could have known the guy would be so adept, so powerful. No one could beat Tory in a fair fight. The second he'd lunged to grab the man and remove him from the property, he'd driven his knee into Tory's gut. A twitch of soreness reminded him of the incident as he rounded the corner into the next hallway.

He saw the huge oak doors at the end that blocked the way into Baldwin's study and nearly stumbled from the intimidation that thumped him in the chest like a baseball bat. The mansion was intimidating enough, but staring at the coming doors directly ahead of him, Tory's anxiety spiked. The imposing doors contained the most powerful man he'd ever met in his life, the man who paid him to get things done, and who didn't take failure well. Tory hoped that Baldwin would be merciful, tell him that it was okay, that they would handle the situation.

In hindsight, Tory wished he'd called the realtor's office to find out if the trespasser's story checked out, but he hadn't thought of it before coming here. As he approached the door, he figured it would be the most prudent thing to tell Baldwin that he'd actually made that call and confirmed that the man did indeed work for the real estate company. That way, maybe the boss would be lenient.

He stopped at the door, knocked twice, and waited.

"Come in," a familiar voice answered from the inside.

Tory pulled open the right of the two doors and stepped into the enormous study.

The room stretched sixty feet from left to right, with a massive stone fireplace built into the wall to the left. It contained a stack of logs ready to be lit, but as the weather had been warm lately, there was no need for a fire, not even for aesthetic purposes.

"Sir, I have some news for you."

Baldwin sat behind a giant desk to the right.

This guy doesn't do anything small, Tory thought.

The walls to the left and on either side of the fireplace contained tall bookshelves that reached to the ceiling. Brass ladders with those rollers on rails like Tory had seen in movies featuring big libraries stood on both the inner and outer wall. Smaller shelves occupied space against the walls wrapping around Baldwin's desk. Some of the tomes looked old, perhaps first editions.

Tory had never been much of a reader. Growing up, he'd been too busy for reading, and placed his interests in other things.

Baldwin was staring at a computer monitor on the right side of his desk—one of the newer 4K ultra high definition curved jobs that Tory had seen while walking around the electronics store in Charlotte. The screen was connected to a laptop where the boss's fingers rested on the keyboard. Baldwin's eyes darted back and forth between the bigger screen and the one on the laptop, and Tory didn't know if he was trading stocks, checking emails, or looking at the latest corporate reports.

Without acknowledging Tory with even a sidelong glance, Baldwin simply grumbled, "Have a seat." He didn't even point to one of the two brown leather chairs across from him.

"Yes, sir," Tory said and made his way across the walnut floor onto the multicolored decorative rug where the desk and two guest chairs sat. He lowered himself into the seat on the right and tried to relax. Looking down at the floor, he said, "This rug really ties the room together."

Baldwin said nothing, still intently looking back and forth between the two screens.

Tory decided silence was the best route with the man who was clearly uninterested in chitchat, and so he sat there waiting for the boss to speak again.

He waited another two full minutes before Baldwin finally tore his eyes away from the screen, sat up straight, flattened the striped button-up shirt he wore, and turned his attention to Tory.

The second he looked at the security guard, he scowled. "What in the world is that on your forehead?"

He leaned closer and then turned pale. His eyelids widened to the size of quarters, and he looked as if he'd seen a proverbial ghost.

Tory frowned and rubbed his head. He checked his fingers and noticed a slight smudge of black.

Baldwin stood up and walked around the desk to get a closer look. His face darkened when he could see the letters clearly, despite the smear of one of them on Tory's forehead.

"Son," Baldwin said, "have you looked in the mirror? I think one of your coworkers might have played a trick on you when you were sleeping? Did you have some of them over for a late night of drinking last night?"

"No," Tory shook his head and stood up. Bewildered, he took his phone out of his pocket and opened the photo app. He reversed the screen view and looked at himself. "I can't read it. It's backward. What does it say?" He tried to smother the burning fear swelling in his gut.

Baldwin's confusion came in the form of a thin line between his pressed lips, accompanied by narrowed eyelids. "It says, 'I'm coming for Heather.'"

"What?" Tory asked, the last remnants of color draining from his cheeks.

"It says, 'I'm coming for Heather.' What's this about? Is this some kind of joke? Who did this?"

Tory swallowed against the lump in his throat, but it wouldn't go down. "I...I..." He stammered, but the words wouldn't form.

"Spit it out, son. If this is some kind of joke, it isn't very funny.

Who did this? And why are you here? I was told you had something to report about the Hamilton place."

"Yes, sir," Tory said with a nod. Finally able to find his voice, he still stumbled over the words. "I got an alert that someone was on the premises over there. One of the security cameras notified my team. I was the closest one there, only a few minutes away, so I hurried over and..." He faltered again.

"And what? You better start making sense, son. And fast." Baldwin's tone soured; the irritation no longer masked.

"There was a man there on the property. Said he was there to do an appraisal for one of the real estate companies. I recognized the name of the company, and on my way here, I called and checked to see if he was legit, and they said yes." Tory hoped his boss couldn't see through the lie, but with every breath, he felt like Baldwin could see right through him.

Baldwin's nostrils flared, and he peered at Tory with flames in his eyes. "That doesn't explain to me what happened to your head."

"Oh. Yes, well, I was, um...Well, you see..." He couldn't patch together a believable explanation, and with every passing second, Tory could only find one way out of this. The truth, or at least part of it. "I told him that he had to leave, just like you instructed us. I told him he was trespassing on private property and that if he didn't leave, I would make him leave."

"And?"

"He had a bag. I think he might have taken something from the property. I don't know what. I told him to give me the bag and get out, or I would take it from him and force him to leave. He told me no, so I approached him to escort him off the premises. That's when he surprised me. I didn't see the attack coming, sir."

"And this...stranger is the one who wrote that message on your forehead?" Baldwin fumed.

"Yes, sir. I can't imagine anyone else doing it. I guess it had to be him. I swear, I didn't know it was there, sir. And that won't happen again. You have my word."

"Ah." Baldwin walked over to an elaborate bar to the left of his desk. The drink station's counter and shelves were festooned with various forms of liquor, ranging from vodkas to tequilas, whiskeys, gins, and rums. He took two glasses from a shelf and set them on the bar, then picked up a whiskey bottle and removed the corked lid.

"This stranger," Baldwin said, "what did he look like?"

"Tall, a little over six feet, I guess. About the same build as me. I've never seen him before, sir. So he must be new here. Probably came in to take a real estate job or something."

"I see." Baldwin finished pouring the drinks and turned around, one in each hand. He walked back over to where Tory sat up straight in the chair. Baldwin's guest looked nervous, as well he should have been. Baldwin enjoyed making others uncomfortable, even the people who worked for him. *Especially* the people who worked for him. He'd learned long ago that a good dose of fear kept the troops in line, along with a few generous bonuses here and there. Still, the latter without the former wouldn't work. It never had, at least not in Baldwin's market. Leaders had to be cutthroat or they would fall behind, and eventually lose to competitors.

He extended the drink he'd made for Tory, and his guest accepted it with surprise in his eyes.

"Thank you for letting me know about this, and so quickly." His eyebrows shot up, as if remembering to do something important. "Let me get you a damp cloth for those markings on your face."

Baldwin set down his whiskey and returned to the bar. Tory sipped his drink, feeling relaxation settle into his veins, more from relief that he wasn't going to be roasted over a fire for his screwup. Maybe Baldwin was an understanding guy after all. And the whiskey was incredible. The man spared no expense when it came to getting the good stuff, and Tory couldn't believe his boss was sharing it with him.

He stared at the picture on the wall behind the desk—a portrait of Baldwin standing in the woods with a hunting rifle. The painting depicted him in a plaid hunting vest, one of those caps with the fuzzy ear flaps, and a brown Labrador next to him in the forefront.

The faucet ran for a few seconds, then Baldwin spun around with a damp washcloth in one hand. The boss walked back to Tory and handed him the white fabric.

"Thank you," Tory said. He dabbed at his forehead, and then began wiping harder, pressing the towel against his skin.

He never saw the other guard silently enter the room behind him.

"Cheers," Baldwin said, raising his glass as he leaned against the edge of the desk, bracing himself with his left hand.

Tory was about to lower the rag from his face and raise his glass in toast, when the guard behind him grabbed the cloth and pressed it against Tory's mouth and nose.

Baldwin set down his own drink and grabbed the glass in Tory's hand before his guest could drop it. "I'll take that," Baldwin said, snatching it from the struggling man's hand.

Tory shook violently, kicking his feet and waving his hands around, clawing at the fingers that pushed the cloth harder against his face.

He suddenly felt strange, and a sort of weakness took over his body. He felt...drowsy. *But why would he suddenly feel...?* By the time the realization hit, it was too late.

He fought in vain to remove the damp rag from his nostrils and mouth, digging his nails into the man's hands in a last, desperate effort to free himself.

The hands covering his face only squeezed harder. The figure of Baldwin's disaffected grin blurred in his vision. *How has it come to this?* His swirling thoughts drifted to the man responsible for this, the stranger at the Hamilton house. This was his fault.

The figure of the man appeared in his mind's eye as his vision faded. *Who is he? I should have killed him when I had the chance.*

TORY'S EYES peeled open painfully. They felt like they'd been doused in sand, and every blink did almost nothing to relieve the irritation. His head throbbed, especially the lower back of his skull. He had no idea where he was, not that it mattered. Pitch black surrounded him.

He felt something hard against his back and started to roll over in order to get out of the uncomfortable position. His shoulder wedged against something above him, and in the haze, he found the low ceiling odd so close to a bed.

The second that thought passed through his mind, a surge of fear snapped Tory out of his drug-induced stupor.

Panic filled him. He moved his hands outward and immediately felt something hard against them. He raised his head and bumped it against the same surface that had barged his shoulder a moment before. He kicked his feet and they met the same resistance.

"Hey!" he shouted. The volume of his voice hurt his ears, and he immediately regretted doing it. Then again, how would anyone be able to hear him if he didn't yell? "Somebody help me!"

The darkness started to fade a little as his vision continued to clear. Cracks in the roof above allowed slim rays of light to stream into his confines. Only then did Tory realize what this was. The smell of lumber filling his nostrils confirmed the horrific suspicion.

He was in an old coffin.

"Mr. Baldwin? Hello? Someone? Anybody? Please! I'm sorry!"

"Tory?"

Baldwin's familiar voice sounded muted outside the pine box.

Everything rushed back to Tory's mind. He'd been in Baldwin's study. The boss had offered him a drink and a rag to wash off the message that... *the stranger. The man at Mike Hamilton's house had written a message. Something about Heather.*

"Are you awake in there?" Baldwin asked, taunting him.

"Yes. Yes, sir, Mr. Baldwin. I'm awake. Please. Let me out of this thing. I learned my lesson. It won't happen again. I swear!"

"Oh, there's no need to apologize, Tory. I know you won't let something like that happen again."

There was no mistaking what Baldwin meant by the comment. Tory didn't miss it either. This was an execution, and Tory started to feel like he was on the receiving end of the punishment.

"After all," Baldwin went on, "we can't have these carpetbaggers coming into my town and sticking their noses where they don't belong."

"I can find him," Tory groveled. "Just give me another chance. Please." He felt tears forming in the corners of his eyes. The heat inside the box stifled him, and he found himself gasping for air. Never before had he suffered the effects of claustrophobia, but now the walls of the box seemed to close in around him, which only heightened the panic coursing through him.

"Oh, that won't be necessary, Tory," Baldwin countered. "I've reviewed the surveillance footage from the Hamilton house. I've seen this man before. He was at the diner having breakfast. I sent a few of the boys out to hunt him down. If he's still here, we'll find him."

"That's good. That's good to know, sir. Please, let me out of this thing." Tory's desperate begging reached its peak.

"Tory, I guess you just don't get it, do you, son? I'm sure by now you've realized you're in a pine box. You do know what they make pine boxes for, don't you?"

Tory knew, and even though the answer was on the tip of his tongue, he didn't offer it to the man. Instead, he went on a tirade, kicking and screaming obscenities, hoping adrenaline alone could power him through the boards that trapped him inside.

"That's enough," Baldwin snapped.

Seconds later, Tory heard the sounds of shoes crunching against dirt and rock. He felt gravity shift as someone outside lifted the coffin. Shadows shifted and moved, blocking the sun's rays. Then the box twisted and Tory felt himself being carried.

"Guys? Please! You don't have to do this. Guys! Gary? Marcus? Someone? Please!"

"Put him in," Baldwin ordered.

"No! No! Don't put me in! I'll do anything!"

Suddenly, Tory no longer felt his back against the pine, and his face crunched against the ceiling as gravity disappeared. He couldn't even manage a yelp as the coffin fell. Then, the box hit the ground and he crashed back onto the bottom. What little breath he'd kept in his lungs left in a single huff.

His head struck the wood and instantly plunged him back into the hazy darkness from before. He could still see light, but it was dimmer now, and Tory knew exactly why. Within seconds, he heard shovels clinking against rocks. Then came the dirt splattering against the top of the coffin, blotting out the light in tiny fragments. Some of the clumps sounded like rain or hail striking against a roof. Others were more like baseballs thumping into the wood.

With every shovelful, the darkness enshrouded Tory within the grave. He screamed louder, the sound of his voice piercing his ears. "No! No! Let me out of here!"

His pleas fell on deaf ears and cold hearts.

He pounded his fists against the roof. Tory even twisted his body sideways, hoping that he could use leverage with his shoulders against the top and bottom to somehow pry the lid off. For a second, he thought he felt it give way, but those hopes were smothered with every pound of dirt tossed into the hole.

His throat felt as though a cat had clawed it—sore and raw. His hands hurt, and his head still pounded from the blow against the bottom of the box.

"Somebody," his voice creaked. "Please." Tory's strength left him a second before the last glimmer of light disappeared forever.

18

Dak waited in his car outside the coroner's building until everyone had left for the day. Then he waited another thirty minutes until the sun had set beyond the mountains to the west. The brick edifice that housed the coroner's office sat across the street from the town hall, inside which was also the local jail. Dak wondered how many criminals they really had in this cute mountain hamlet, outside of Baldwin, of course.

Under the cover of night, Dak walked around to the rear entrance and produced a key card he'd swiped while paying the facility a visit earlier in the day. Jeb, one of the custodians, had been kind enough to leave the ID sitting in one of the storage closets.

Dak's first dip into the place had been under the guise of a former military guy turned college student who had been required to visit a coroner's office for his studies in criminal justice.

The facility's head seemed to accept the explanation and was happy to give him a tour of the building, as well as explain the ins and outs of the job—which was more than Dak cared to hear, but he played along exactly as an eager college student would and did his best to look interested. That last part took an Academy Award-worthy effort.

Now, back at the scene, he had everything he needed to look for answers.

He pulled the black baseball cap down low so the cameras at the back door wouldn't get a good look at him, and then Dak swiped the key card. The green light blinked to life, and Dak heard the door lock click. He hurried into the building before it could relock itself.

Dak looked around the room and recognized a place he'd seen earlier in the day during his tour. The break room was really a conference room that had been converted to a place for the workers to eat. Two vending machines in the corner offered the usual processed snacks that would, ironically, eventually aid in sending the employees who ate from it regularly to their own visit to this place—as a customer.

He walked by the long, glossy table and stopped at the door to the hallway. Poking his head through, Dak saw what he expected—an empty building. That, however, was only half the battle. There was still the problem of finding the records he needed.

The man in charge of showing him around had done a good job pointing out where all the sensitive records were kept. The room known as the vault was nothing more than a 15x15 space surrounded by poured concrete that had been painted white. Lining the four walls inside the nondescript space were shelves of rolling file cabinets, three rows deep.

Dak recalled being impressed by the storage contraptions. They made efficient use of the limited space and were able to contain information from the last several decades, based on what the guide had said.

During his initial visit, Dak had also asked about how they kept the vault secured, which again, the man seemed more than happy to divulge.

He explained that they kept a key on site, and that he had one at all times, along with the woman in charge of information. Her desk sat just outside the vault, inside a lobby with a wide, long waiting room. Dak had wondered why a records department in a little town like this even needed to bother with a waiting room, but that question was for another time. Or no time at all. It didn't matter, and Dak found himself annoyed for thinking of it.

He moved calmly but swiftly down the corridor until he arrived at a glass door set inside a metal frame. The wall to the records room looked like one huge window, held in place with a frame that matched the door. Dak checked the door—it was locked.

It didn't surprise him, but it didn't exactly fill him with joy, either.

Fortunately, more than one way into the records department existed in the halls of the town coroner, and Dak remembered each one, including the one he hoped he didn't have to use. His eyes drifted upward to the ceiling inside the waiting room. A single square vent, more than large enough to accommodate him, blew fresh air into the room from the center of a series of tiles.

He walked around the next corner and turned left. Two doors occupied the wall to his left, each spaced out by twenty feet. At the end of the short hall, two more doors—these attached in the middle, opened to the outside. The red lights on an exit sign burned over the way out, casting an eerie glow into the dark space next to a set of stairs that led down into the bowels of the building.

Dak had no desire to see what was down there, and it was the one place the guide hadn't put on display.

The door into the records lobby was locked, but he guessed the second door wouldn't be since it led into a storage room. Dak checked the knob. It turned easily, and he stepped into the next corridor out of the main hallway.

He didn't want to linger out there because of the security guard on duty. Dak saw the man sitting in his white pickup truck in front of the building. He recognized the security company logo on the doors —not a name he'd heard of, but Dak had seen plenty of security guards, and their vehicles. They all looked the same.

Dak figured the guy spent half of his shift sitting in his car, probably perusing social media apps or shopping online for stuff he didn't need. The man would step inside every so often to make sure the place was as he left it on his last pass, but Dak didn't concern himself too much with the guard. The guy would be armed—of that Dak was certain—but usually these kinds of guards preferred to call the cops rather than try to saddle up and play cowboy. Dak didn't have any designs on dealing with the cops in this or any other town. That meant he needed to get in and get out quickly, without being noticed.

Dak hurried to the back door leading into the records lobby. He checked the knob and wasn't surprised to find it locked. He found it odd that the front door, and side door, to the records room were both double locked with the knob and a deadbolt. This back door, however, offered no additional security measures. On top of that, there was no steel plate covering the gap between the door's bolt and the receiver.

He'd noticed the absence of the simple yet effective security measure as he'd passed by earlier on his tour and filed the information in the back of his mind.

Dak took out the grocery discount card he kept in his wallet and slid the hard plastic through the groove between the door and the frame. He worked the corner of the card into the receiver and pried it up. The first two tries, the bar slipped back into the hole, but on the third, Dak managed to retract it far enough that he could keep the card between the two.

With no way for the lock to catch, he pulled the door open and slipped into a closet where the records room kept additional printer paper, stacks of reference books, boxes of pens, envelopes, and other supplies.

He walked through to the other side, opened the door, and stepped into the records lobby.

The room had an eerie feel at night with no one there. While he wasn't one given to irrational fears or superstitions, the place definitely felt creepier after hours than it had earlier.

Without wasting precious seconds, Dak moved over to the desk behind a counter that stretched from one side of the room to the other. The left side contained shelves full of books and files. The right, separated by a Formica gate, housed the records receptionist workstation, computer, phones, and the drawers where Dak hoped to find the key to the vault.

He bent down and pulled on the first drawer to the left. He didn't expect to find the keys inside what was obviously a deep file cabinet and wasn't surprised when that's exactly what he discovered inside. Files hung in dark green envelopes with hooks on each end clinging to rails.

He closed the drawer and checked the next, this time finding a collection of staples, two red Swingline staplers, pens, and an assortment of other small supplies all organized neatly within the limited storage space.

The next drawer he checked was the thin one that hung above the chair. When Dak pulled it out, his eyes flew over the paper clips, pens, and notepads. It took less than two seconds for him to spot the two brass keys nestled in a little divider.

He picked them up and was about to turn to the vault door when he caught movement in the hallway through the lobby windows. A circle of light bounced off the walls and danced on the floor in a slow waltz. Dak immediately recognized the rhythm.

The security guard was inside the building.

19

Dak ducked down, quietly rolling the chair out of his way. He crawled into the space under the desk, shut the drawer from beneath, and pulled the chair back in.

His pulse raced just as it had when he was a child playing hide-and-seek, desperately hoping that the other kids wouldn't find him. Back then, the stakes had seemed so high, but the reality was the only thing a kid had at risk was bragging rights, or the punishment of being the one doing the seeking in the next game.

Here, the risk was significantly higher.

Dak had seen the older man in the security truck, and he hoped it wouldn't come down to using force to get out of this place. The uniformed guard was just trying to earn an honest living. He didn't clock in to work tonight expecting to deal with a break-in, especially from someone as dangerous as Dak.

Before he caught sight of the man patrolling the building, Dak made the decision not to hurt him if at all possible. If he had to restrain the guard, or perhaps render him unconscious, Dak would, but for now he chose to hide rather than risk any kind of confrontation.

He sat on the floor, his legs pulled up close to his chest and the desk chair squarely in front of him, so close he could rest his chin on the seat if he wanted. Dak waited patiently, listening for the guard to enter the room.

Perhaps he won't come in here, he thought. *It's a records room, and if the rest of the building is adequately secure, this place would be as well.*

As he waited, Dak heard the jingling keys on the man's belt. The flashlight's beam penetrated the windows along the outer wall and sprayed onto the white walls Dak faced with his back to the lobby entrance.

He's looking in here, Dak realized. If the guard thought for one second that something inside the records room was amiss, he would come in and snoop around. Or maybe he didn't even have to think something was wrong. The man didn't need an excuse if checking every single room was part of his job.

The sound of the jiggling keys faded as the guard continued his steady gait down the corridor until he reached the corner.

The temptation to leave his hiding spot toyed with Dak, and he even considered it for a few seconds. He dispelled the notion, though, fully aware that the guard could simply opt for an easier entrance much as Dak had done.

He chose to wait, and sitting there in the silence of the dimly lit room, he listened for the sound of the guard to return.

The seconds ticked by, and Dak wondered how long he might have to sit there. His answer came in under a minute when he heard a key being inserted into the side door at the other end of the room.

The guard wasn't coming in through the back door, which brought Dak a whisper of relief since the guard would easily see him from the other end of the closet. The movie played out in Dak's head —the guard opening the door, spotting the intruder crouching under a desk. The man would try to call the cops. Dak would have no choice but to spring from his cover, wrest the phone from the guard's hands, and then either tie him up—and Dak hadn't brought any rope or zip ties with him—or knock him out. He hoped it didn't come to that, and Dak prayed that it didn't come to something worse, such as the guard pulling his firearm.

Dak kept his knees close to his chest as he listened. He heard the door open with a creak. The keys clinked when the man grabbed them out of the doorknob. Then again when he hooked them to his belt. The light shone on the floor four feet ahead of where Dak hid. It moved back and forth, then up the wall and onto the door leading into the vault.

Dak heard the guard's swishing as he drew near, then the man's breathing, and the whistling of a quiet melody.

He appeared in Dak's vision next. The black polyester pants, the matching New Balance shoes, and the blue uniform shirt probably came from the same uniform companies that made the outfits for the food service industry, custodians, and any other business that required a uniform of some kind.

The guard shoved old glasses up his thick nose. He looked to be in his mid-sixties, and appeared to be a little overweight, which Dak could understand.

The guy's job largely required a lot of sitting and almost no physical activity, save for his occasional casual stroll through the building.

The distance between Dak and the guard barely took up seven feet, and they were so close that Dak could smell the older man's aftershave.

The guard walked to the end of the work area, where a tall filing cabinet stood at the corner and a short entryway led into the vault. He reached out, checked the knob to make sure it was locked, and then turned around abruptly and walked back the way he came in.

It wasn't until the door closed behind the guard that Dak realized he'd been holding his breath, or at least breathing in an extremely shallow pattern. He let out a sigh of relief and then took several deep breaths.

Even with the threat gone, Dak remained under the desk for another three minutes before he felt confident enough to get out from his hiding spot.

Dak pushed the chair away and cautiously stood up. A quick check through the windows revealed nothing but a dark hallway, and not a sign of the guard or his flashlight anywhere. Dak assumed the man had gone on to patrol the rest of the building before heading back out to his vehicle for another hour or two.

At the vault door, Dak inserted the key, turned the knob, and hoped he'd been right about this being the correct one.

To his relief, the knob twisted easily and Dak pulled open the heavy door. The vault's interior lit up the second the door opened. Fluorescent lights overhead flickered to life, casting their sterile, hospital-like glow onto the shelves and cabinets.

He stepped inside and let the door close behind him. This entire room was fireproof, which was essential since it contained sensitive and important information.

Standing in the center of the room, Dak scanned the letters attached to the tops of the rolling files, and the ones connected to the stationary cabinets on the floor. He found the first name he'd wanted to locate and walked over to the shelves on wheels.

He found dozens of files stocked on the shelf and had to thumb through the tabs until he found the name he was looking for.

Hamilton, Michael D.

Dak took the envelope out of its place, walked over to a waist-high cabinet, and set the folder on the top. He flipped it open and noted a few details—birthday, day of death, age, and a few other general facts about the deceased.

He'd seen a few of these documents before and knew roughly what to look for in the section where cause of death was listed.

Dak thumbed through the paperwork inside the folder and located the cause of death determined by the investigator. There were some technical terms that Dak didn't understand, but he recognized the words relating to cancer and liver failure.

So, this victim had been safely swept under the rug.

Dak returned the folder to the shelf and switched to another section, the one with the capital Ms over it.

He searched through the many folders until he reached the one with the name he'd been looking for. Carefully, he slid the file out from the others and returned to the cabinet, where he set the documents down on the top and flipped the folder open.

Heart failure was listed on the sheet as the cause of death, but Dak continued scrolling until he noticed something odd.

Succinylcholine was written in the toxicology section. Dak's forehead wrinkled at the word. He'd never heard of it, but that didn't surprise him. His knowledge about nonexplosive chemicals was scant at best, but he made a mental note of it, and also took a picture of the page with his phone.

Dak heard a noise out in the lobby and froze. The second time Dak heard the muffled sound confirmed it. The phone on the desk was ringing.

He quickly folded the file and put it back where he found it, or at least as close as he could without going to the trouble of getting the exact alphabetization right.

The phone continued ringing incessantly.

Who is calling here after hours, anyway?

His immediate concern was that the guard would hear the phone and decide to answer it himself, even though Dak doubted that was part of the man's job description.

Dak twisted the doorknob and inched the door open. He listened for any sign of the guard's return, and was ready to retreat back into the vault if necessary. From there, hiding places within the vault were limited. Dak's only plan for that was to get behind the three rows of rolling shelves and roll the two front rows in front of him.

It could work, but he hoped things didn't come to that.

The phone rang two more times, and then the voice mail message picked up.

Dak listened to the woman's voice instructing the caller to leave their name, number, and a brief message, and the records department would call them right back.

After the beep, Dak heard a voice he'd heard before. It was the man from the diner. Mitchell Baldwin.

"Gina, it's Mitchell. Hope you're doing well. I just wanted to give you, Doc, and the others over there a heads-up that someone is in town snooping around. I'm not sure what they want, who they work for, or even who they are, but be on the lookout. He might try to come by there, though I doubt it." Baldwin huffed a laugh. "He probably won't come there, but just to be safe, I wanted to let you know. Y'all do a great job of keeping everything under tight lock and key. But a little extra vigilance never hurts. Have a good upcoming weekend. Thanks."

The call ended, and Dak narrowed his eyelids at the message.

Someone knew he was here, searching for answers. It was no mystery to Dak. The man who'd accosted him—or tried to—at the Hamilton house, had run home with his tail tucked between his legs to deliver a message to Baldwin. Dak wondered if the guy had even looked in the mirror and seen what he'd written. Part of him hoped the assailant hadn't noticed it, had walked into Baldwin's office, and had been lambasted.

Dak had written the message on the guy's forehead for a reason. He wanted Baldwin to know he was there.

One of the first rules of chess is to know what your opponent is going to do next and make them think your next move was your last. But this was more than chess to Dak. He'd written the message on the man's forehead to get under Baldwin's skin, to force him to come out of hiding. The message on the voice mail told Dak his plan had worked.

Now, Baldwin would begin scouring the city.

And Dak could whittle away at the tycoon's resources, one by one.

20

Heather sat in her prison, staring blankly at the television. It had been one of her favorite streaming shows back in her normal life, back when she'd been free to do whatever she wanted. She didn't miss the coincidence of that observation, either. Before she'd been imprisoned, free to do as she pleased, she'd chosen to watch this show, the same as she was doing now.

Her previous talk with Baldwin had been awful, and she'd spent every second since then wondering if her mother was okay or if the man had gone and made good on his threats.

Heather could only hope and pray.

She heard a commotion in the corridor outside her room and thought she heard Baldwin's voice. After pausing the show, she twisted around slightly on the couch, slinging her arm over the back so she could see the door.

Within seconds, the locks clicked and the door opened. Just as she'd thought, Baldwin stood there with his face burning red. The man fumed about something, but it was anyone's guess as to what had upset him.

He breathed as if he'd just run a marathon, and sweat dribbled down both sides of his face. He glowered at her, giving Heather the impression she'd done something wrong even though she hadn't left her prison apartment since arriving.

"What did you do?" he fumed. The question came with an accusing finger jabbed in her direction.

Her brow furrowed in confusion, and she shook her head. "What are you talking about?"

Baldwin searched her eyes for the lie he was certain she was telling, but he found nothing there, which only heightened his own bewilderment.

He composed himself, flattening his shirt and jacket. His face, however, still betrayed the anger inside him.

Baldwin stepped through the door and turned to one of his guards. "Stay there," he barked and eased the door shut. Then he turned to Heather and loosened the tie around his neck, twisting his head back and forth as if stretching.

"No, I suppose you wouldn't know what I'm talking about," he demurred. "But let's ask anyway."

She puzzled over his odd behavior, the furious demeanor, but also felt a surge of fear. There was no telling what this man was going on about, or what he would do to get the answers he sought.

On top of that danger, Baldwin had a reputation as a man who enjoyed the company of women—whether the women enjoyed it or not. Rumors floated around the town regarding his various tastes. Heather found the notion revolting. But now, she was alone in a room with him, with his personal bodyguards watching the door.

No one would interrupt if Baldwin was here to have a little fun at Heather's expense. While she knew how to defend herself—thanks to her upbringing—she had no misgivings about being able to keep the larger, stronger man from having his way with her. She grimaced at the thought and fought away a shiver that rippled across her skin. Heather found herself involuntarily retreating from the man as he stalked toward her, then stop just short of the sofa.

"I suppose it was your mother's doing," Baldwin said thoughtfully. "She was rather adamant that I had kidnapped you, and that I return you to her at once."

"You did *kidnap* me, you lunatic."

"Dear, dear. Name-calling? Is that what it's come to? Heather, listen. I'm going to be frank with you. Your mother can have you back the second she signs over your family's farm to me. It's that simple. You get to go home, change clothes, sleep in your bed, and all of this goes away."

Rage burned in her gut, and she found herself angrier than she'd been before. "Except that my bed will be bulldozed into the ground, along with the farmhouse, the barn, all of it. You want to destroy everything the Markhams have built up for over a century."

"What have you built?" he roared. Heather pushed against the couch cushions to try to inch farther away from him. "Your family has built nothing. You're just a bunch of worthless farmers. Your kind are a dime a dozen."

"Farmers put food on your table. Farmers helped build this country," she fired back.

"Oh. How nostalgic." He put up his hands in a fake show of appreciation. "That's a marvelous history lesson, darlin'. But I don't think you realize how little I care about that nonsense. I built a company that has changed the world, provided materials for people's homes, roads, neighborhoods, businesses. What do your people do? Your answer is you grow food? How noble." He took another menacing step toward her, and Heather's eyes couldn't help but fall toward his waist.

She hoped he didn't notice the glance. The last thing she wanted to do was give him the wrong idea, that she somehow wanted him to try something.

He apparently missed the look. "Who is the man your family hired? Give me a name, and I'll consider going easy on you."

It was her turn to search him for answers. She peered into his black eyes, trying to find a conclusion that made sense of what he said, but all she found were more questions. "What man?"

He pushed aside his frustration, albeit with considerable effort. He collected his thoughts and drew a long breath through his nose. "Your mother, or someone around here, has brought in a man who has been snooping around my properties. Now I have reason to believe he attacked one of my men. This sort of intrusion will not stand, Heather."

"Man?" She said the word as if it were foreign to her. "I seriously doubt my mother knows anyone like the person you're describing. Perhaps your men have seen a ghost, Mr. Baldwin."

He inclined his head and peered down at her over his nose. "You think that's funny? You think it's funny that some brigand is here in my town, running around, attacking my men, trespassing on my land?"

"I do. I truly do, Mr. Baldwin. I think that hearing about this stranger who's managed to put such a bee in your bonnet might be exactly what this town needs. Sounds like you have yourself a boogeyman to take care of, Mr. Baldwin. I wouldn't stand around here chatting with me all day about it."

He took another short breath, and she could tell the man was trying to collect his thoughts, or perhaps come up with something clever to say that would really stifle her.

"Miss Markham, I don't think you need to concern yourself with this supposed boogeyman. And I don't believe in ghosts. Whoever this stranger is, he's going to have to answer for what he did."

"Which was?"

"He threatened me," Baldwin said plainly. "And I don't take kindly to threats, Miss Markham. I don't take kindly to them one little bit. The last person who threatened me is dead. And the way they died, I assure you, was quite painful. So, if I find out that your mother found a way to bring in some kind of private eye or, heaven forbid, a mercenary, then I'm afraid she is going to be both out of luck, and out of the money she spent to hire them. My men will kill on sight."

He thought for a second, looking pensive as he directed his gaze to the wall to his right, as if it would remind him of something. "I suppose the best I can hope for is this rogue showing up on my doorstep. It would be a pleasure to watch him die on my front steps. Of course, the boys would have to dispose of the body, but that's nothing new to them. That sort of thing happens now and then. I have plenty of land, though, and more than enough places to dispose of...unwanted garbage."

She didn't miss the gist of the threat. The man made it blatantly clear that he was happy to take out her and her mother, too, when the opportunity arose.

Still, Heather summoned her courage and defiantly glared at her uninvited guest. "You will never own my land, Mr. Baldwin. We aren't selling. And if you lay a finger on me, my mother will make certain you pay."

He snorted at her as if a mouse had just threatened him with its tiny teeth.

"I guess we'll have to see about that, now won't we, Miss Markham." He turned and walked over to the door, stopped, and swiveled around to glare at her one more time. "Of course, I know how this little movie ends, darlin'. I don't lose. And I'm certainly not going to lose to some out-of-towner who thinks he can just walk in here and push me around. When he's dead, and I take his head to your mother on a plate, maybe then she'll change her tune about selling the family farm."

He jerked open the door and stepped outside, leaving Heather to her thoughts and the show she'd paused.

Outside, Baldwin fumed, but he didn't say anything to his guard until he and the other men were several paces down the corridor. Then he stopped and rounded on the guard.

"I don't think the girl knows anything, Johnny," Baldwin confessed. He put a thumb to his chin and thought hard. Then he looked Johnny in his icy blue eyes. "I want you and the boys to find this rogue. Whoever thinks they can come into my town and push me around has another thing coming."

"You want us to kill him?" Johnny asked.

"Dead or alive is fine by me, although I would prefer alive. This is one that I want to kill myself. It's time to send a message, Johnny. The people around here are getting too bold. They haven't had a good scare in a long time. Sounds like maybe we need to change that. You and the boys spread out, see what you can learn. And if you see anyone that you haven't seen before, they're an immediate suspect. You understand? Keep it on the down low as much as possible, but I want you to question any visitor in this city who meets the description of that stranger. He's here somewhere. We just have to root him out. Once we do, I should have more leverage than I need with Hattie Markham."

"Yes, sir."

Baldwin resumed walking but only made it a few paces when he stopped and faced Johnny again. "Oh... and get that useless Sheriff Meachum involved. I'm sure he can afford to take a couple of his guys off traffic duty to help us out."

21

Dak sat facing the door in a little coffee shop called Wired. *Clever name,* Dak thought.

He knew that the message he'd sent Baldwin would cause a chain reaction of events. The tycoon's response would be predictable. At that very moment, Dak figured there were at least a dozen of Baldwin's goons scouring the town, checking every stranger who met his description.

It would be nice, Dak thought, if he could give it some time, let Baldwin stew in his own insane paranoia about a guy who came into Dawsonville, threatened him, then disappeared.

Unfortunately, time wasn't a luxury Dak had in his back pocket. Heather Markham's life was in jeopardy, even though Dak still didn't believe Baldwin would harm her until Hattie handed over the farm. Still, the two women were on borrowed time, which meant, so was he.

Dak took a sip of his coffee, keeping the trucker hat pulled down low over his forehead. He knew that sooner or later—sooner knowing his luck—Baldwin's men would come around asking questions. The last thing Dak wanted was to bring anymore of the locals into the bucket of trouble he was stirring.

That didn't mean his level of patience could manage. It was a difficult thing to wait, especially with such dire circumstances weighing heavily on Dak. But he had to formulate a plan, and every detail needed to be addressed.

His first concern centered around the police. Dak couldn't simply start eliminating cops left and right. There were, as he understood it, good ones and bad ones on the force. The last thing he wanted to do was take out one of the good guys.

Then there was the issue of Baldwin's henchmen. He had a few dozen men in his employment. Dak had spent the previous night at his computer, perusing the dossiers of some of the men Baldwin hired; information provided by his friend Will, whose knack for digging up buried intel had proved extremely useful since Dak began his new life as Boston McClaren's relic runner.

Most of the men working for Baldwin had some form of military training, or martial arts as was the case with some of the henchmen. One had been a college football player but blown out his knee. The man, name of Johnny Arenson, now served as Baldwin's enforcer—or head of security. Dak knew what that meant. You could paint a barn whatever color you wanted, but at its core, the building was still a barn no matter how much you wanted to call it something else.

Arenson, like many of Baldwin's men, kept skeletons in their closets, which Dak figured Baldwin exploited when recruiting. Guys who'd committed crimes, done despicable things, were kicked out of the military or civilian jobs, all seemed welcome under the Baldwin umbrella. He always did a routine criminal background check, just to make sure he wasn't hiring outright thieves or murderers.

He didn't have information on all of the men working for Baldwin, but Dak had enough of the puzzle pieces to make some guesses as to the backgrounds of the rest of the Baldwin entourage. They were a motley bunch with a stack of misdeeds against them.

Dak imagined what the recruitment of those men had been like. Conversations over drinks, Baldwin brings up a few missteps by the guy he wants to hire, and then gives him the whole "You've got nothing to lose" pitch, along with making a financial offer that the men would never find anywhere else. The world wasn't exactly teeming with billionaires looking for hired guns with bad reputations.

Or maybe it was. He didn't personally know any billionaires. The one's he'd seen in the headlines for most of his life didn't appear to be inherently evil, though everyone had their secret sins they kept hidden in the cupboard.

Some of the men would be difficult to deal with, particularly the one named Johnny, but his primary reason for researching Baldwin's men wasn't so he could gauge the talent or abilities of the enemy. This case involved a kidnapping, the murders of innocent people, and a man who would do anything to keep his iron grip on the empire he'd built.

Dak knew some of the men he went up against would end up dead. Back when he was in the military, clearly defined lines guided him and the men on his team. There were never any misgivings about the task they had to do. The mission left no room for gray areas, and his commanding officers likewise made it easy to understand what they were supposed to do.

His team included the good guys, and the ones at the other end of their weapons were the bad. Dak never regretted pulling a trigger during his time in the military. Here it was different. The last thing he wanted to do was take an innocent life, ending the journey of some poor soul who simply wanted to work a security gig and happened to stumble into Mitchell Baldwin's life.

Dak had yet to come across one of those, which made him feel a little more at ease with the task ahead.

Reading the dossiers relieved him of any guilt regarding what he knew he had to do. Even so, he still knew it was going to be difficult, and he'd have to be careful with how he handled things. Fortunately, Dak had a plan.

First things first, he would finish his coffee and biscuit. Once he found Baldwin's men, and observed how they were going about their hunt for the mysterious stranger, Dak could make his move.

He figured Baldwin would send men out to the regular places first: the diner, the two taverns in town, the cafés, hardware stores, and eventually back again. There were only so many businesses in Dawsonville. Which meant Dak would have to be strategic. Fortunately for him, Dak excelled at that sort of thing.

While he'd decided to get a place to stay in the neighboring town, Dak had no intentions of lying low in Dawsonville. The plan was simple. He would put himself in plain sight. That way, the innocent civilians of Dawsonville wouldn't be caught up in any trouble, and they would have something that every good politician wished they had—plausible deniability.

He knew that by merely eating breakfast here at the diner, someone would come around looking for him, and when they did, he'd have a full house of witnesses who'd be willing to say which direction he went in exchange for a little leniency.

Still, Dak preferred to handle things directly if he could. And just like a good fishing hole, all it took was a little patience before you got a bite.

He sipped his coffee, looking over the mug's rim to the door to the building next to the coffee shop. Through the glass, the occasional car or pickup truck drove by. Pedestrians intermittently walked past the diner on their way to nowhere in particular.

Dak wondered how long he'd have to wait before Baldwin's men started making an appearance in the local shops. Those thoughts didn't serve a purpose, though, and Dak again had to remind himself of the importance of patience.

He was in the right place. All he had to do was sit and wait. How long didn't matter, although Dak knew he couldn't stay in the diner all day. He had a plan for that, too. There were several eateries in the town square; all would be adequate locations for him to wait for his quarry. Sooner or later, they would show up.

Dak had poked the proverbial hornet's nest.

He finished his biscuit, dabbed his lips with a napkin, then slid the white ceramic plate away from the counter's edge. A quick check on his watch told him it was twelve minutes past nine in the morning. If Baldwin's goons didn't show up soon, he'd leave and go to the next fishing hole, repeating the process until they finally appeared.

Dak slid a twenty-dollar bill across the counter, wedging it under the plate so he could leave at a moment's notice, without having to worry about paying his tab. He hefted the mug to his lips again and peered out the window, scanning down the street to the left, then through the park in the center of the town square. His eyes darted back and forth with the sight of every new pedestrian or car that appeared in his vision.

He was about to give up and make his way over to the next spot—a pastry shop down the street—when he noticed four men walking down the adjacent sidewalk. The men wore similar clothes and carried themselves with a determination, an air of confidence, that Dak hadn't seen in the other people's faces or in their gait.

That's them, Dak thought.

He felt the stir of battle energy rouse in his gut, an old familiar feeling he used to get just before combat. A combination of nerves, fear, and adrenaline, the sensation had always served him well. Some of the women and men he served with often wondered if he was fearless. Dak always explained it the same way. He felt fear just like anyone else, but his sense of fear kept him alive, prevented him from making stupid mistakes in the heat of battle. He'd blown it off as luck just as often as not, but deep down he knew caution was one of the biggest reasons he was still alive.

The four men split up, each taking a different business to step into. Each of them disappeared for a minute or two, then returned to the sidewalk to meet the others. Dak took the last swig of his now lukewarm coffee and stood up. He walked by the cash register, thanked his server for the meal, passing her an easy smile as he did so, then left the diner and stepped out onto the sidewalk. He peered across the street corner to where Baldwin's men marched by other businesses.

Dak picked up his pace, chewing up the concrete at his feet with long, purposeful strides.

He reached the next corner, checked both ways, then crossed and hurried to the next intersection, where he waited at the stop light. Dak faced the four men on the other side of the street. He continued waiting until one of them looked at him, nudged the guy who was apparently the leader, and then motioned toward Dak.

The one in the middle inclined his head slightly. Dak couldn't see their eyes through their sunglasses, and they couldn't see his either through his own aviators, but he knew their reaction was surprise.

Dak held his ground for a few more seconds. Then, as a pickup truck drove by, he took off running down the sidewalk away from the town square. The truck only distracted the men for a few heartbeats, but it gave Dak a head start, and he didn't need much.

He sprinted down the empty sidewalk and didn't look back over his shoulder until he was beyond a couple of closed businesses—more casualties from the Baldwin regime.

Dak quickly turned down an alley he'd scoped out before, running between the brick building on the left and another defunct shop built from white painted cinder blocks.

He ducked behind a dark green dumpster and waited.

Dak had spent a few hours doing recon in the little town. It hadn't taken him long to get a feel for every nook and cranny in the place, and he knew this alley would serve as a good location for his first encounter with Baldwin's men.

He'd been correct in thinking they would be out looking for him. Now it was time to give them a little taste of their own medicine. He knew the four men would have seen where he went. And with no other way out of the side street, they would assume he'd either hidden in, or behind, the dumpster.

The henchmen didn't disappoint. Dak heard the footsteps as the men trotted to a stop. He crouched in his hiding spot, waiting for the men to appear. He didn't have to wait long.

"We know you're in here," one of them said.

Dak assumed it to be the leader.

"Our boss wants to have a talk with you. Seems you've caught his attention. And not in a good way."

Dak stood up from behind the dumpster and sized up the four men. They carried pistols, but they wouldn't be stupid enough to fire those unless they were desperate. Without suppressors, the firearms' report would be loud enough for anyone in the square to hear. Baldwin had connections, and the best lawyers money could buy, but discharging a firearm in a place like this would have unavoidable consequences.

If the men were going to use their weapons, they'd have to be judicious. Dak had a feeling they'd use something that made a little less noise, like the knives strapped to their belts.

The men he faced all looked to be younger than Dak, and he imagined they did nothing other than work out at the gym and run errands for their boss, or occasionally do what their titles suggested and work security for the Baldwin properties.

"Hello, fellas," Dak said cheerfully. "Seems like I took a wrong turn."

Dak made a show of looking around the alley, as if truly confused. "I was looking for the coffee shop. Y'all don't happen to know where it is, do you?"

"You took a wrong turn, all right," the leader of the group said. He took a step forward, an initial move in corralling the stranger.

"Yeah, so, like I said, if you could show me to the coffee shop, I'd be much obliged."

The leader shook his head, and the other three fanned out, effectively blocking the only potential exit to the street.

"Our boss wants to have a little talk with you," the leader said. "Because of you, we had to put one of our own in the ground."

So, Baldwin killed one of his men. Dak knew it had to be the guy he'd bumped into at the Hamilton house. He'd also suspected Baldwin might handle the man's fate the way he had, by executing him. Dak doubted the tycoon did the deed himself. He likely ordered one of these goons to do it, which was also why the leader had said it the way he did, about having to eliminate one of their own.

"Boss? What boss? I'm not looking for work, if that's what this is about. I'm just passing through. I already have a job."

"No, idiot," the leader said, still drawing closer to Dak with every threatening step. "He wants to speak with you about the trouble you're causing around town. Mr. Baldwin isn't happy with the message you sent him."

"Message?" Dak pretended to try to think of what the guy could possibly be talking about. While he put on the show, he also calculated every possible attack that would come from the four men. "Baldwin?" Then Dak's eyes widened, as if struck with an epiphany. "Oh, I think I've heard of him. He's the one that owns the gravel companies and all that stuff. Maybe you guys could help me out. I heard he's been dumping pollutants into the water and soil here, and I was curious if you guys happen to know why."

The men circled around Dak now, with two closing around behind him, cutting off any route to the back wall.

"Mr. Baldwin doesn't like people asking too many questions around here. Especially people from out of town."

"Sounds like kind of a jerk, if you ask me. I hope you guys are well paid. What are the benefits like? Because if this Baldwin wants me to come work for him, he needs to understand I need full health coverage."

"You got that right," the leader agreed. He left no room for confusion about what he meant.

Dak put on a bewildered expression, then lighted his face to pretend he just got the punchline. "Oh, I get it. Because you guys are going to beat me up. That's a good one." He pointed at the leader with a limp finger. Seriously, though, I'll just be going."

He started to walk by the leader and the man to his right with long brown hair pulled back into a tight ponytail.

They blocked Dak's path, Ponytail extending an arm to the side, while the leader shoved Dak backward.

22

"Whoa," Dak complained. "Take it easy, man. I don't know what this is about, but I think maybe you got the wrong guy."

"The boss said to bring you in dead or alive," the leader said, drawing the long knife on his hip. "We can do that in pieces, if you prefer."

"Not the alive part," Dak corrected. "Not without a lot of mess, anyway."

The leader furrowed his brow for a second, then reset to his default menacing expression. "You think you're funny?"

Dak shrugged. "Not really. I think maybe my ex-girlfriend thought I was."

"Dead it is," the leader said and stepped forward with the knife brandished. "Get the plastic bag, Ted," he said over his shoulder without so much as a half glance backward.

The second the leader was within Dak's sphere, he felt the two behind him drawing closer. He knew their plan of attack. The two goons at his back would grab him, hold him there or pin him down on the ground, while the leader did his thing with the knife. Dak doubted the man would actually kill him there in the alley, what with cars and people randomly passing by on the street. Then again, since the pickup truck that drove by a few minutes before, Dak hadn't seen anyone else go by on the street or sidewalk.

Dak could almost smell the steel of the knife blade. The leader inched closer, waving the knife around, left to right. The intent in the man's eyes told Dak more than his words ever could, and he knew how this fight was going to have to end.

"So," Dak said, still sensing the men behind him getting closer, "your boss is sending you guys out in groups of four? He should have sent you more help."

The leader shook his head. "The rest are in groups of five. We're one short."

Dak knew what that meant. The man he'd beaten up at Hamilton's house would have been assigned to this yahoo.

"Say hello to him for me," the leader said, and he lunged forward with the tip of the knife aimed at Dak's throat.

"You first," Dak replied. The aloof look in his eyes switched off like a light, instantly replaced by the eyes of a wolf with prey right in front of razor-sharp teeth.

The man stabbed, thrusting the blade forward. Dak stepped back and ducked down to one knee, dipping between the two men behind him. He made the move so quickly, the men couldn't react fast enough to keep him from grabbing them both by the ankles. Then Dak pulled forward, kicking his right foot up into the air and rolling onto his back. The tip of his boot struck the leader's hand, knocking the knife free in a single blow, while the other two men instantly lost their balance with Dak pulling on their heels. They tumbled down onto their backs on either side of Dak, while the leader grabbed his wrist.

The knife clattered to the ground several feet away. Dak rolled back up to his feet. The leader, angrier than ever, foolishly rushed forward without a weapon, other than the pistol at his side. The enemy would only use that weapon as the last resort, which he would if that didn't make sure that the man couldn't get to it.

The leader jabbed at Dak's face, but he deftly stepped to the side and drove his elbow into the leader's nose. He wrapped his arm around the man's neck, twisted, then pulled him backward to the nearest wall.

Dak already knew what Ponytail's reaction would be. The man drew his pistol, as did the two men on the ground who clambered back to their feet. Now, though, Dak had a shield.

He clicked his tongue and shook his head as he drew the hostage's pistol. "Nuh-uh-uh," Dak warned, pressing the muzzle to the leader's temple. "You pull those, and your boy here gets it."

"Don't listen to him," the leader protested. "Shoot him now."

"Not smart, son. From the looks of these two, I'd say they're just as likely to hit you as they are to hit me. You willing to take that gamble?"

The man didn't respond, and Dak squeezed his neck tighter. "Now, if y'all want this to be a fair fight, you'll drop those guns and kick them over to me."

Ponytail and the other two exchanged glances, then gave an agreeing nod almost in unison.

"No!" the leader barked. "Do not put your weapons down! Do you hear me?"

They didn't listen and instead did as the stranger ordered. The three dropped their pistols and kicked them over to Dak.

"That's more like it, boys." Dak teased. Then he shoved his prisoner forward. The man went sprawling onto the ground and turned around on his tail in time to see Dak scoop up the three pistols.

Then he stood and watched Dak eject the magazines from the weapons and toss them in the dumpster, then the pistols as well after ejecting the rounds in the chambers.

Within seconds, all the weapons were rendered impotent and safely disposed of in the dumpster.

"Now," Dak said with satisfaction in his voice and on his face. "That makes things a little more fair, doesn't it?"

"Except there are still four of us and only one of you, idiot," the leader spat. "You should have kept one of those guns for yourself. Now there's nothing to stop us from killing you."

"You're a pretty linear thinker, aren't you? Kind of an AB guy, yeah?"

The leader picked up the knife lying at his feet and snarled. "Stand back," he ordered the other three. "He's mine."

The man rushed forward, slashing and slicing at the air in a metallic blur. Dak tracked every movement as the man advanced. He watched the blade as it whipped and cut dangerously back and forth. The leader drew close enough that Dak could feel the breeze from his movements.

Then, when the man was within a single stride, he lunged, hoping to slash through Dak's neck and end the fight in one blow.

Instead, Dak surged and spun toward the guy's left arm, in the direction the blade was moving. He used the attacker's momentum, allowing the man to overswing. Then, when the assailant was off balance, Dak grabbed his wrist, continued spinning, and forced the man's hand to continue its looping trail. At the last second, panic swept through the leader's eyes. The knife point sank deep into his throat, and the eyes widened farther at the pain, and at the realization.

The long blade went through the man's neck and out the other side, the tip dripping red. The leader still held the handle of the weapon that had ended his own life. He stumbled backward a few paces, eyes still staring in horror at the man who'd killed him. Dak had seen that look before, the vacant stare of wondering how this could have happened when the opponent believed he had every advantage he needed to win the fight.

Then the leader dropped to his knees. He gurgled a few times, coughed once, and then fell on his face.

The other three stared at the body of their comrade on the ground and then raised their eyes to the enemy. Each drew their knives and spread out.

Without a word, their coordinated attack came hard. The men surged forward as one to avenge their fallen comrade.

Dak had faced these odds before, and worse.

He picked the one he would take out first—the one farthest to the left—and charged. With the dumpster to Dak's right, he could hem in the other two while eliminating the one on his left flank.

The man quickly assumed a defensive posture as Dak surprisingly went on the offensive. He tightened his stance even as he moved forward, keeping his left fist ahead of the blade.

Dak feigned a jab at the man's face, which the attacker attempted to defend with his weapon. Dak pulled back the fist and punched him with a quick roundhouse to the jaw. The blow carried significant force behind it, and the assailant's head snapped to the side. In the split second it took for the guy to recover, Dak jerked the knife blade across his throat, opening a deep gash in the man's skin.

Without stopping to watch the second henchman die, Dak spun around in time to block a downward stab from the third man—a blond guy with hair cut like Dolph Lundgren. At the same time, the fourth goon went low, thrusting his blade toward Dak's abdomen. Before he knew what happened, the stranger kicked his foot hard into the base of the weapon, sending the man's fist upward toward his chest. With so much power behind the kick, the attacker couldn't stop the knife from plunging into his chest. Dak shoved the other guy back, stepped closer to the wounded man, and used both hands to drive the blade deep into the attacker's torso.

Dak kicked the man in the gut, dropping him to his knees, then backward against the wall.

The last opponent tried to recover, resuming his attack with renewed vigor. He grunted as he swung the weapon wildly back and forth, forgetting any training he may have had with the knife.

Dak jumped back from the first swing, then again, and again. The attacker never stopped to wonder what his opponent was doing. For Dak, the strategy was simple: he'd eliminated the overwhelming odds and now only had to let this last guy wear himself out a little.

The dance didn't last long.

With every sloppy lunge, the assailant used more and more energy, chasing Dak around the alley until, frustrated, he raised the blade too high. Dak snapped into motion, kicking the man in the groin with the bone of his right foot. The wind left the man's lungs, and he doubled over, nearly dropping the weapon.

Dak grabbed the man's wrist, twisted it, and wrenched the blade from his grip. Then he wrapped his own forearm around the guy's neck and pushed the knife tip into his ear, just far enough to open a tiny cut inside the appendage.

"Don't move," Dak warned. "You fight it too much, or struggle, and this blade will go through your brain. You understand?"

The man nodded, but quickly stopped as he felt the cold steel slice through another portion of skin.

"See what I mean?" Dak asked. "Now, I want to know what Baldwin is doing. Why is he dumping toxins into the soil and water here in Dawsonville? From what I know about it, there shouldn't be anything like that used in processing gravel."

The hostage's lips were pressed together, as if he feared even speaking would cause the knife to slip and drive through his skull.

"I don't know," the man muttered.

His long ponytail tickled the skin on Dak's neck. "What conditioner do you use? Your hair smells wonderful."

"What?"

Dak pushed the knife a few millimeters deeper.

"Ah!" the man shouted.

After a quick shush, Dak continued the interrogation. "Now, I want you to pay close attention to what I'm saying. Okay? Don't bother nodding. You'll only hurt yourself more. Just say yes."

"Yes. Yes. Just don't kill me. Please."

"That's better," Dak said, appreciating the man's cowardice, and his desire to continue living. "Now, I'm going to ask you again. What is Baldwin dumping into the water here?"

"Please," the man begged. "I just work security for him. I don't know what he's doing at the facilities. I swear. You have to believe me."

"I don't have to do anything," Dak snarled. "Against my better judgment, though, I'll give you the benefit of the doubt on that one.

But I do think you know the answer to this next one. Where is Heather Markham?"

Ponytail breathed hard for several seconds, contemplating the consequences of his response, and what it could cost him.

"I'm getting impatient," Dak added, twisting the knife tip slightly against the man's ear.

"Okay. Okay. He's got her. At his mansion. She's being kept in a basement."

"Basement?"

"Yeah, man. She's there. I swear."

"And she's healthy?" Dak pressed. For all he knew, this guy was telling the truth about Heather being at Baldwin's in his basement, but that could have meant she was dead and buried on the property.

"Yes. She's alive. And unharmed." Ponytail blurted.

"Good. That's good." Dak had already made up his mind regarding killing the man or setting him free.

Dak shoved him forward. Ponytail stumbled and fell onto the ground, rolling to a stop on one knee. Dak rubbed off the knife handle and tossed it to into the corner where the dumpster met the wall.

Ponytail glared at Dak like a predator who'd just cornered his prey. Dak knew that would be the man's choice. He'd seen it before. Give a little mercy, and they'll turn on you.

"You don't have to do this," Dak warned. "You can pick up your chips, leave the table, and go cash them in."

The enemy stared at Dak with a lost glaze in his eyes. "You don't get it, do you?" he said, shaking his head from side to side. "We don't get to just walk away. Failure isn't an option for Baldwin."

Dak passed a glance over the bodies on the ground. "Sure looks like one."

Ponytail glowered at him. He stood and produced a switchblade from his pocket. The sharp knife popped out of the handle. The sun glinted off it as he turned it back and forth.

"How retro," Dak said.

The enemy sprang from his kneeling position and charged. He

slashed in wide, diagonal arcs. Dak retreated, jumping back three times. Ponytail switched his grip and tried to slice Dak across the abdomen, but Dak sucked in his gut, threw both hands forward, and narrowly missed the knife's point.

Ponytail quickly countered, switching to a backhand attack in an attempt to drive the blade into Dak's side. Dak spun, barely twisting away from the knife as it scraped across his T-shirt, then he chopped his forearm down onto the attacker's. It was more than enough.

Dak used his other hand to grab the assailant's wrist. Using his legs to gain even more strength, he shoved the knife upward while pushing the man's head down toward the blade.

The assassin found himself in an impossible battle between pushing his hand down and pulling his head back. The fight lasted less than a second.

Dak shoved his head down into the knife, sinking the blade deep into the enemy's left eye.

Ponytail screamed at first, a deep, haunting shriek that echoed off the brick walls around them. But as the knife's tip burrowed into the victim's skull, the voice cut off. The resistance Dak felt from the killer's muscles weakened, and his head started to twitch. Dak finished the job with a last shove, sending the weapon in all the way to the hilt.

With a final shudder, the attacker's body went stiff for a second then fell limp.

Dak looked up from the body, peering out toward the street. Miraculously, no one was there.

He didn't take the time to check the bodies or make sure he'd left no evidence that could connect him to the killings. Instead, he hurried back to the edge of the sidewalk, checked both ways, and walked out onto the empty sidewalk.

No cars came down the road toward the town square, and the business across the street was closed and boarded up.

He walked down the street to his left, away from the town center. At the back of the building, Dak cut to the right and crossed the street, continuing on a one-way access road behind the row of businesses.

A line of trees, bushes, and a dingy white picket fence separated the first few shops from a neighborhood adjacent to the town square. The fence cut away from the buildings, angling to the backyard of a matching white rancher home that looked like it had been built in the fifties. A corroded chain-link fence took the place of the shorter picket one and set the boundary for an adjoining yard to another home.

Dak walked briskly but not too fast. People tended to notice fast movement, especially from someone they'd never seen before running along a back alley to local businesses. A person just out for a stroll, however—local or not—didn't tend to raise any eyebrows.

He reached the connecting street at the other end of the row, looked both ways, then turned right and walked back toward the city square.

People smiled at him, nodded politely, and continued on their way just as they would have if he were a neighbor they see all the time.

Dak finally took a deep breath when he neared his vehicle, and exhaled when he was safely behind the steering wheel.

He started to turn the ignition, then froze. Two cops stood on the other side of the street, on the corner, and they were looking directly at him.

Act natural.

Dak didn't need the reminder from his subconscious, but it was there nonetheless, ringing in his ears as a warning.

Normally so full of certainty, Dak found himself in the unusual position of not knowing what to do next.

He sat there, waiting for something to happen. Then the two cops pointed at him again and crossed the street.

They ambled through the intersection as if they didn't have anything better to do, though their eyes never wavered from Dak and his car. They walked straight toward the sedan, and then at the last second, worked their way around it and stopped on the other side, where an elderly man sat on a bench outside the barber shop on the corner.

The cops started talking to the guy, who greeted them with a smile and handshakes.

Dak felt a flutter of relief in his belly and started the ignition. He drove out of the parking spot and onto the town square's main street, then took the first right out heading back toward his hotel.

He hoped a kid didn't find the bodies in the alley, but there'd been no way to handle disposing of them in an efficient way. If he'd stuck around, he could have been caught. Figuring it was a school day, the odds of an adult finding the bodies were way higher.

Satisfied with his assessment, Dak accelerated away from the town. Once the dead men were found in the alley, the heat would really get turned up, and Dak's next move would require some planning.

For now, he'd eliminated a quarter of Baldwin's hired goons. It was a good start, but now the stakes were higher, and Dak would have to be vigilant if he were going to survive this.

23

Baldwin's face burned red. He didn't notice the surrounding countryside, the farms, the suburbs, not even the outskirts of the town passing by outside his window. He faced straight ahead, stewing as he stared at the back of the headrest in front of him.

He'd divided his men into shifts to handle finding the stranger. The nineteen remaining guards split up into groups of five with the exception being Tory's former group, each taking a different time of day and different locations in town to watch for the man with the dark hair.

Chance Morton headed up team one, and his was the first out on patrol after Mr. Baldwin had instructed Johnny they would be aggressively investigating a person of interest in the area—a stranger with dark brown hair, a muscular, athletic build, and maybe a little over six feet tall.

Mr. Baldwin hadn't been great with the description, but Chance and the other team leaders were familiar enough with most of the people in town that they would recognize a stranger if they saw one.

That's what he believed.

All that changed the second Baldwin got the call from Sheriff Tom Meachum.

A busboy at one of the restaurants in town had stepped out back to grab a quick smoke when he found the bodies of four men who'd apparently been violently murdered in the alley behind the business. The young man, who was actually a twenty-six-year-old guy from Houston named Raul, had rushed back into the restaurant to alert the manager.

After that, the expected chain of events followed. The restaurant manager called the police, and when Meachum's men arrived on the scene, Baldwin was immediately contacted.

His attention focused on a single point surrounded by a swirling, bubbling vortex of thoughts and memories. None of those other things tried to steal his focus, rather, they all pointed to it.

In his mind, Baldwin saw the face of Tory with the message from this brigand written in black marker. Some of the other thoughts came to him as voices, reminding him of his past wrongs. Others appeared as ghostly faces, never directly in his field of vision but always in his periphery.

Baldwin didn't feel guilty about anything he'd done in life. He was glad to be afforded immunity to such weakness. He'd never have achieved much if he walked around feeling guilty for being competitive, for taking what he wanted, and for outworking his rivals.

No, it wasn't guilt that racked his mind. It was fear.

He'd always heard the saying "The tallest tree falls the hardest," but by that comparison, Baldwin was a sequoia.

He didn't have any illusions about being immortal. Baldwin knew that someday, just like everyone else, the proverbial bell would toll for him, and everything he'd ever built would be passed on to someone else. It bothered him, but the future was unavoidable. He'd forged a tepid peace with it.

But that didn't mean Baldwin was happy to let some outsider wander into his town and start causing trouble.

In fact, this guy had done more than that.

Meachum's concise report over the phone described the situation as "pretty bad." Baldwin had rolled his eyes. *Of course it's bad, you nitwit. Someone killed four of my men.*

The SUV stopped just outside the alley where two squad cars sat angled inward toward the center lines, blocking the way into the square. Several other vehicles—two ambulances, a fire truck, and two white SUVs with government plates—occupied space on the street between the two police cars, and two more on the other side near the crosswalk. A collection of curious onlookers had gathered. Two young cops stood guard over the crime scene.

The second Baldwin stepped out of his vehicle, he spotted the sheriff.

Tom Meachum towered over most of the people in his department, and in the town for that matter. At six feet six inches tall, he'd played basketball for the state runner-up team in high school. After a pedestrian career in a Division II university, Meachum returned home to Dawsonville, where he joined the local police force. It took him just under five years to leverage his legend into being elected sheriff. Of course, Mitchell Baldwin had helped make that happen, and also made certain his boy Meachum stayed in office.

Most of the time, Tom ran unopposed. In the last twenty years since he'd become sheriff, only twice had someone been foolish enough to think they could challenge the incumbent.

Both times, the opposition lost in a landslide.

Some people questioned the validity of those elections, wondering if some kind of tampering had been involved. But with no one else in at least some position of local influence or power challenging the results, there was nothing the average citizen could do. Plus, it wasn't like zero people voted for the challengers. Baldwin was certain to make it look like the other guys had a fighting chance. The truth was, on both occasions, the tally had been much closer than anyone realized.

In the first instance, Meachum had actually lost the vote, much like he had during his initial election. In both cases, it was Baldwin's influence that pushed Meachum over the top. The young man had ambition, and he also knew who ran things. While his first opponent talked about cleaning up the town, making life better, Tom focused on preaching how great Dawsonville already was, and how they could continue improving on the things the previous sheriff had done to make the town both safe and enjoyable for all.

As it turned out, Meachum would have won the second challenge fairly, but why risk it? Baldwin had rigged the vote just in case, and the result was an easy win for the sheriff.

At forty-nine, Meachum still had several years left to serve his master, though he hadn't taken good care of himself. The skin on his face hung from his cheeks and jaw like loose tapestries. He wore a wide-brim hat, and more than filled out the dark blue uniform all the other city cops wore.

He'd put on considerable weight since his basketball days. Too many hours at a desk job, he'd complain now and then, though no one really believed he hated the gig. Meachum's job was simple, at least as far as Baldwin was concerned.

Keep that man happy, and everything else would be fine.

Tom didn't have to worry about elections or scandals, though he certainly dipped his toes into troubled waters now and then, most often with the ladies in town. But they knew not to protest too much when it came to his advances. With his badge came power, and that authority was backed by the most powerful man in the region.

People didn't often tell Tom Meachum no, and they certainly didn't more than once.

The sheriff turned at the sight of the black SUV pulling up, and quickly finished his conversation with a CSI tech standing a few feet in front of him. Meachum waved to Baldwin as the man approached.

The cop watching over the yellow tape didn't need to be told to allow the man to pass through. All the cops in the department understood the order of things, although the new kid seemed to have trouble catching on.

Kip Landers was one of those do-gooders, a by-the-book sort of cop who didn't know what was good for him. The kid had good intentions, Meachum had to admit, but got in the way more often than not, and the sheriff had to gently redirect Officer Landers every time he made things difficult.

At one point, Meachum had considered requesting a transfer for the kid, perhaps to Charlotte or Asheville, anywhere but Dawsonville. But eventually, Meachum was convinced he could turn Landers into a useful ally, and so he'd skipped the idea of sending him away, instead choosing to try to mold him into the image Baldwin wanted for all his cops.

Both the sheriff, and Baldwin, put on their grim faces as they met just inside the yellow line.

"Morning, Mitchell," Meachum said in a somber tone.

"What in the Sam Hill happened, Tom?" Baldwin replied, forgoing the pleasantries. He'd been working in his office when the call came through, and with several multimillion-dollar deals pending, wasn't about to waste any time.

Meachum shook his head, as if full of regret. "This way." He motioned toward the alley, where several people milled around collecting evidence. One held a plastic bag with a bloody knife in it. Two more wheeled a gurney toward one of the ambulances, a body bag atop it as the wheels bumped and rolled on the rough surface.

Baldwin barely paid the corpse any mind, instead surveying the grisly scene before him with analytical eyes.

Two more workers zipped up another bag, sealing the lifeless face within. Baldwin recognized the dead man, along with the other two who still lay in the alley where they died.

He spotted Chance's body on the ground, covered in blood from a knife wound.

Maybe I should have sent them out in larger groups, Baldwin thought. He stared at the body as he spoke. "Anyone see who did this?"

"No," Meachum said, sincere regret filling his voice. "Unfortunately, no one saw a thing."

Baldwin counted to three in a vain attempt to quash his boiling anger, but it did nothing to push back the tide. "How in heaven's name did no one see anything, Tom? This person killed four of my men. And we have reason to believe he did something to Tory, too." He passed off the lie about Tory without even blinking.

"Yes, we're still looking into that. It's possible, likely even, that the group who did this might be targeting your men."

"It's not a group," Baldwin corrected. "One man did this."

"One man?" Meachum looked dubious, casting a questioning glance at his benefactor. "All due respect, sir, I have trouble believing one guy could take out your men like this. They're trained, most of them former military."

The sheriff was well acquainted with Baldwin's security team; after all, he'd helped handpick them. That wasn't to say he got attached. Meachum didn't care about any of Baldwin's men on a personal level, or Baldwin for that matter. The sheriff's only concern centered around keeping himself in the lifestyle to which he'd grown accustomed. The steady flow of money coming in from the tycoon took care of that.

Baldwin remained calm, though Meachum could tell he'd said the wrong thing, or perhaps crossed a line with a man unaccustomed to that happening.

"A word, in private, please," Baldwin said and motioned back to the opening in the alley.

He led the sheriff back toward the street, around the corner, and back beyond the line of police tape. Baldwin rounded the back corner of the building, and Meachum followed close behind. The second the two were out of sight, Baldwin spun around and drove his right fist into Meachum's gut.

The cop doubled over, gasping for air. He dropped to his knees, desperate to fill his lungs.

"Don't ever contradict me in public, Tom," Baldwin warned with a shaking finger and a flushed face. Then he flattened his suit jacket and put on a dignified expression. "Get up," he ordered, sans sympathy.

Meachum rolled onto his side, and the air managed to find its way back into his chest. He breathed heavily for a minute, while Baldwin looked around as if embarrassed of the scene.

"I said get up, Tom. I didn't hit you that hard."

The sheriff crawled to his feet. Anger boiled in his eyes, but the man didn't have an ounce of dignity, much less the courage to stand up to Baldwin. The billionaire made Meachum. Before that, he was nothing. Baldwin made sure to remind him of that every now and then.

"Sorry, sir," Meachum said sheepishly. "Won't happen again."

"Good. Now, I can understand why you would think a group did this. You're right about our men being good. That means someone better killed them. Especially if he's working alone."

For the moment, Meachum seemed to forget the humiliation of being sucker punched. "You think someone is coming after you?" He tried not to sound hopeful, but the truth was, Meachum knew only one man stood between him and being the most powerful person in Dawsonville. For now, he was nothing more than Baldwin's puppet.

Baldwin's usually stone face cracked. It was only for a second, but Meachum caught it. He didn't let on, instead pretending he hadn't noticed.

"I don't know for certain," Baldwin admitted. He looked down the line of fences behind the businesses. "But it's possible."

"Who would be stupid enough to do that?" Meachum asked. Deep down, he concealed a flicker of hope, and the seed of a plan sprouted in his mind.

"I've made enemies through the years. That's no secret. It's also the price you pay for success." Baldwin narrowed his eyelids. "I need you to find this stranger. I wouldn't be surprised if he lured my men into that alley."

Meachum's head twisted in the direction Baldwin mentioned. "Lured them?"

"It's possible. Sending them out in packs might not have been the best idea. I'll be sure to tell Johnny to change his strategy, use smaller groups or maybe patrol individually. I'll have them dress more casually, too."

"Probably a good idea," Meachum said and hoped he hadn't just earned himself another punch to the gut. His abdomen throbbed as a reminder of his previous transgression.

The comment didn't seem to annoy Baldwin. "I also want you to offer a reward for anyone who has legitimate information about this guy."

"Okay. I'll have Sherri write it up immediately. How much do you want to offer?"

"One million," Baldwin said, as if the sum were no more than a bag of nickels.

Meachum's eyebrows climbed up his forehead. "Okay, then." He cleared his throat. "That amount is going to get us a lot of, um, false leads too."

"Deal with it," Baldwin gruffed. "I don't care if you have to personally answer a thousand calls a day. I want you to find out who this man is. And when you do, I want him brought to me. Alive, preferably."

The last detail caught Meachum by surprise. "Alive?"

"I didn't stutter. I want to find out what this man wants, and who hired him. When I find out it was Hattie Markham who hired him, then you'll have all you need to lock her away."

A sly grin swept across the sheriff's face. "With her in prison for conspiracy to commit murder, her land will be forfeit."

"And I'll be able to buy it at auction for pennies on the dollar." Confidence oozed from Baldwin's eyes. Despite the bodies of his security team being carried out of the alley around the corner, he didn't look worried at all. "Hattie should have taken my generous offer when she had the chance." He inclined his head and glanced out toward the street, then back to the sheriff. "See to it that you have that reward offer issued by the end of the day."

"Will do, sir. I'll get on it right away."

Baldwin nodded, and without saying anything else walked back to the waiting SUV and climbed into the back.

Sheriff Meachum watched the vehicle drive away. He wore a look of appreciation until the SUV disappeared at the next street. Then, the wolf pulled away the sheep's clothing and bared his teeth.

He'd put out Baldwin's reward offer. And he'd make sure that every lead went through him.

24

Dak sauntered into the hotel room and nodded to the manager. "I'll be checking out today," he said. Dak guessed the guy was in his late forties, maybe early fifties.

The manager reeked of stale cigarettes. He wore a Jack Daniel's T-shirt with big holes dotting the fabric, and stonewashed jean shorts. Black hair formed a rim around his bald head. Dak figured the most activity the guy saw was when he stood up to leave or to get lunch.

"All right," the manager said, as if Dak's departure was of no consequence.

Dak reached into his pants and pulled out five, one-hundred-dollar bills.

He counted the money and placed it on the counter. "I expect some folks are going to come through here looking for me. Baldwin's guys." A spark of concern flashed through the manager's eyes. "You're in no danger. In fact, you can help me out. When they or the cops come by, they'll probably ask if you've seen me. I want you to tell them you did. And that I stayed here but left."

"They'll want to know where you're headed, too, I suppose," the manager drawled.

"Most likely, yes. So, I want you to tell them you heard something about Asheville."

"Okay," the manager nodded.

Dak scooped up the bills, then stacked them in front of the man. "That's yours. Thank you."

The manager looked down at the money in such a way that it almost seemed like he didn't believe it was real. *Could this really be his lucky day?*

"Anything else you need me to do?"

"Nope. That's it. Just be sure to tell them you heard I was heading toward Asheville."

"Sure," the manager said. "Whatever you want, man."

"Thanks," Dak said, then turned down the corridor toward his room.

He knew that the second the manager was offered a reward of any sum, he'd happily spill the beans about the stranger heading toward Asheville. The manager would hope he'd receive some cash for the information, and Dak had little doubt that Baldwin would employ the old-school tactic.

As an extremely wealthy person, Dak wondered how high the offer would be. He'd threatened Baldwin directly with the note on one of his guard's faces. Now Dak had eliminated four more of Baldwin's men.

After climbing the stairs to the second floor, Dak proceeded down the hallway to his room. He entered, checked everything in seconds to make sure no one had disturbed his things, and then quickly collected the few things he'd left there. A tan rucksack carried his clothes and hygiene necessities, and a small black book bag housed his laptop and tablet, along with a few other electronics.

His eyes swept the room twice before deciding he'd retrieved everything, then Dak left the hotel room, walked to the other end of the corridor, and descended the stairwell. He knew the manager probably called the local cops the second Dak disappeared down the hall. If the reward hadn't been offered yet, it would be soon, and Dak had intentionally planted the seed in the manager's mind.

He usually read people pretty fast, and this hotel manager was someone Dak knew couldn't be trusted.

The man probably ran more than one illegal operation out of his shady hotel. People like the manager were greedy, ready to sell their souls for a little more cheddar. The second Baldwin's men walked through the door, the manager wouldn't be able to tell them soon enough where the stranger was headed.

Dak figured the man might well be on the phone at that very moment, calling the cops or Mitchell Baldwin—though it would be easier to reach the former.

At the bottom of the stairs, Dak turned right and slipped out the door at the end of the long hallway. He didn't see the manager behind his desk at the far side of the building, and listen as he might, Dak couldn't hear him either.

He wasn't going to stick around to see what happened, though. The plan was set in motion. Dak had to stay a few steps ahead of Baldwin's people if he wanted to survive, and if he wanted to complete his mission.

He stepped out into the sunlight and marched over to his car.

The drive to the next town took less than twenty minutes, and Dak was pleasantly surprised to find the hotel he located there turned out to be much cleaner and in better shape than the one he left—only reaffirming his decision to make the switch.

Not that he had much choice.

Once he was checked in, and in his room, Dak unpacked a few of his things and then collapsed on the bed to rest for a few minutes. There was little chance of a nap, or any kind of real rest—he had too much on his mind, and too many plans to go over.

Even if he believed Baldwin only had twenty guards, give or take a few, Dak knew that those numbers could change at any moment. Baldwin was a man of nearly unlimited resources. If he needed to hire more goons for his squad, he could do it without batting an eye.

But that would take time, and Dak knew the man was too bold, too overconfident that his current allotment of resources and manpower could handle this issue.

Maybe he was right. It was possible that Dak had jumped in over his head with this one, but based on what he'd seen from the first five henchmen, he liked his odds.

As he considered the next move, Dak found his eyelids getting heavy. It had been a hard couple of weeks—months, really. Now all of it was catching up to him. He shook his head and rolled back up to his feet. No time for naps or resting right now. A case needed to be solved. And on top of that, he needed to get the pistols from Baldwin. His primary reason for coming here had taken a backseat to the more serious issues going on in Dawsonville, but that didn't mean Dak was going to forget about it.

He walked over to the desk, took out his laptop, set it on the surface, and flipped it open. He waited several seconds for the screen bloomed to life. When it did, Dak clicked the email icon at the bottom and a list of emails appeared in the center of a box in the middle of the screen.

He saw the one from Tara near the top and clicked on it.

Dak had sent the soil samples to Tara and Alex, the two lab techs who worked for the International Archaeological Agency in Atlanta. While identifying toxic chemicals wasn't necessarily something their job entailed on a regular basis, they had the equipment, and they were the only people he could trust to handle the task.

He read through the first sentence, a short greeting from Tara Watson.

Hey, Dak. Good to hear from you again.

We ran the analysis of the samples you sent the other day. Really interesting stuff. We discovered an unusually high amount of lead in the samples, as in a toxic level of the stuff. Not sure what's going on in that town, but I would imagine if that kind of pollution is in the soil and water, you probably have a lot of sick people on your hands.

Dak read through the rest of the email. When he was done, he stared at the page in silence. "Lead?" He said the word out loud in confusion. "Lead doesn't have anything to do with the production of gravel and concrete."

Dak's suspicions were proving correct. Baldwin was up to something other than the construction materials business—but what?

He put his hands on his hips for a second, thinking about the implications. The fact that there was a high concentration of lead in the water and soil meant Baldwin was making something other than his usual product. Dak knew of a few items that required lead for manufacture. Batteries still used lead. Weights and ammunition were a few others he could think of.

But which one of those would be the most profitable?

That was the question Dak had to answer.

Over the course of the last year, electric vehicles, lawn equipment, and other items had increased in popularity as a result of growing environmental awareness. Electric cars were being manufactured, or designed, by pretty much every major automobile manufacturer on the planet.

Was Baldwin trying to get in on this new market as the wave of momentum carried it higher than ever before?

Dak considered the other viable option—ammunition.

Rounds of nearly every make and variety were in short supply. They had been for over a year as more and more people hoarded ammunition. Some simply wanted to make sure they had enough for the various hunting seasons. Many, however, had started buying up bullets out of fear. Some were afraid of social unrest. Others worried about the rising crime epidemic in many of the larger cities across the United States.

Dak assumed bullets would be more heavily regulated than batteries, and thus would be prohibitive to anyone looking to carve out a niche in that market. Still, that didn't explain why there was such a high concentration of lead leaking into the soil and water in Dawsonville.

He'd have to do a little more snooping around before he found the answers. And Dak knew that Baldwin's men would still be on the hunt.

After thinking about the question for a minute or two, Dak

walked over to the refrigerator and picked up one of the courtesy water bottles left by the hotel staff for patrons.

He removed the lid, took several drinks, then set the bottle back down. The question kept ringing in his mind. *What is Baldwin up to?*

Then Dak remembered he had something else he needed to look up.

He returned to the computer, eased into the seat, and began to type.

It didn't take him long to find the answer to his search.

Succinylcholine, the compound found in the body of Mike Hamilton, was hardly an innocuous substance.

The source he found online said that succinylcholine is a paralytic. The article, written by an anesthesiologist, went on to say that if someone were given the compound—without breathing assistance—every muscle in their body, other than the heart, fasciculates, and mimics what doctors call a grand mal seizure. Then the body shuts down, including the diaphragm, and eventually the heart.

People under the effects of succinylcholine are left completely aware of what's going on. The heart is still pumping blood to the brain and the rest of the body...while the victim slowly suffocates. Dak imagined it to be a horrific way to go, and as someone who'd seen more than his share of death—dealing most of it—he still grimaced at the thought.

The article went on, saying that unless someone steps in and starts breathing for the victim with either a mask or a tube, they would die.

Another interesting component to the compound was that it wears off quickly. In just a few minutes, the person who'd been administered the substance would—if assisted—wake up feeling extremely sore, like they'd just completed an intense workout. This is due to their body's muscles all firing at the same time for several seconds.

Further reading relayed the last tidbit of information Dak needed. The article said that the drug didn't have to be given via IV, rather, it could be simply jabbed into a major muscle, and that five to ten milli-liters of the stuff would be enough to cause the victim to expire.

Dak sat back in the chair and exhaled.

The information in front of him, combined with the toxicology report from Mike Hamilton's death, painted a clear picture.

As Dak suspected, Mike Hamilton was murdered. He wasn't sure how long the man would have lived anyway. With the amount of lead present on Hamilton's property, Dak doubted he would have survived much longer.

But why was Baldwin dumping lead?

Whatever the reason, Baldwin and his company weren't being regulated for it, and the town of Dawsonville and its people were suffering the consequences.

Dak knew the best way to prove what was going on was to get onto Baldwin's property and survey the location to see if he could find proof about what was happening. Heather must have figured it out, too. It would make sense that she'd learned of the lead Baldwin was dumping into the city and tried to take him down through an exposé at her paper. Unfortunately, the brave young woman had been caught in the act, and now Baldwin was holding her captive.

It was surprising, at least a little, that none of the people in Dawsonville had reached out to the feds to bring them in on the case. Dak knew why the cops had done nothing to solve the case of the missing reporter. They worked for Baldwin. The more Dak thought about it, the more he wondered if the Dawsonville police were inten-tionally keeping the feds from finding out about the missing woman. It was certainly possible, and a detail potentially worth addressing, unless bringing in the feds to conduct an investigation might end up bringing more harm than good to the young woman.

He sighed. That was the whole ball of yarn right there. Anyone who wanted to risk making a move to save Heather Markham would actually be putting her life in more danger by doing so.

Dak rubbed his eyes. The scenario made his head spin. It was difficult to understand how an entire town of people had simply coughed up their freedom and personal sovereignty to stay put. He couldn't wrap his head around it. If it had been him, he would have packed his bags a long time ago and left, and encouraged as many people as possible along the way to do the same.

Let Baldwin have his little town. There were always plenty more around the next bend.

This thought process wasn't getting Dak anywhere; he had to refocus.

He took a swig from his water bottle and entered a few new words into the search bar. Several links appeared on the next page and he clicked one four spots down. A picture of the Baldwin headquarters appeared on the screen, along with a list of locations for their manufacturing facilities.

If Dak was going to get any leverage against Baldwin, he'd have to go deeper. Getting into Baldwin's home would be tricky, and bloody, but getting into the man's corporate headquarters?

A plan formulated in Dak's mind.

25

Mitchell Baldwin stepped out of the SUV and searched the front window of the Notekabortsky filling station. The sun dipped toward the mountains in the west. Behind the closed garage doors, the empty bays sat quietly in the darkness. A fluorescent light glowed in the cashier office where Baldwin found the face he wanted.

Joe stood inside, behind the cash register, looking at his cell phone. Baldwin glanced back at Johnny, who stood by the door to the SUV. "Sweep the back; make sure everyone is gone."

Johnny nodded without saying a word and waited until Baldwin walked toward the front of the building before making his way around to the rear.

Joe noticed movement in front of his station and looked up from the phone. Baldwin didn't miss the irritated expression on the proprietor's face.

Baldwin ignored it and waved at Joe, smiling at the gas station owner as he would an old friend who he played golf with on Sundays.

The billionaire opened the door and stepped inside with the energy of a man ready to make a deal. In a way, that wasn't too far from the truth.

"Hey, Joe," Baldwin greeted cheerfully. "How you been?"

Joe slid the phone into his right-front pocket and looked over at his guest. "Mitchell," Joe replied. "What can I do for you? Trouble with your SUV?"

Baldwin snickered at the question. "No, despite your warning against buying that model, it still seems to be holding up well. Although I have been looking at the newer ones. This year's version has a new body style." He huffed. "Of course, that's how they always get the retail buyers roped in. Isn't it?"

"Pretty much," Joe agreed. He turned, clearly disinterested in the conversation, and picked up a clipboard with several sheets of paper stacked on it. He removed a black ink pen from the clip and began checking off a list.

Baldwin shifted, twisting his body slightly so he could see outside. He watched the quiet city falling asleep before his eyes. Only a few cars lined the central square, and even fewer people walked the sidewalks. Most of the businesses had already closed for the day, with the gas station being one of the last ones still open.

"Yeah, but I did it anyway. Like a sucker. I don't know what it is. You love the design when you initially buy the thing, and you think it looks so good, and so much better than the previous design. Yet we thought the same thing about the previous design, and its relation to the design before it. The whole thing is a vicious cycle."

"Yep. It definitely is."

"I mean, I love this current model. It's beautiful." Baldwin motioned to the vehicle through the window. "But somehow, the newer ones are so much sexier."

"That's because it's new," Joe offered. "We always want the new thing, even if it isn't necessarily better."

Baldwin chuckled and nodded. "Yes, I suppose you're right about that. Seems how we humans are wired."

"Did you have something you needed me to take a look at?" Joe asked, looking up from his checklist. "Or did you just come by to say hello?"

Baldwin's head bobbed absently. He pointed a finger at Joe and wagged it. "Can't get anything past you, can I, Joe? You like to get right down to business, and I appreciate that. I prefer to dispense with the pleasantries as well."

"Anytime you can get to the part where you do that, I'd appreciate it. It's dinner time, and I'm pretty hungry. My patience level drops when I haven't eaten in a while. And I haven't eaten since lunch. I'll let you do the math on how much I'm feeling like having this conversation with you right now."

The visitor's fake grin faded, and he replaced it with a set jaw and a leering gaze. "Very well, Joe. You probably think I'm here because I want to make you another offer on your station."

"Don't you?"

"You've made it quite clear that you have no intentions to sell this place, to me or anyone else."

"Especially you," Joe said, letting his eyes fall back to the clipboard before he could catch the scathing glare from Baldwin.

"Be that as it may, I didn't come here to make an offer on your gas station. That ship has sailed, and I'm at peace with it. Besides, I don't think one person should own all the businesses in the world, or even a small town like Dawsonville."

The last statement caught Joe by surprise and he looked up from the clipboard, almost involuntarily. He searched Baldwin for deceit, which didn't take long to find. Dishonesty dripped off the man like sweat in the dead of summer.

"Okay, Mitchell," Joe relented. "What did you come here for if it wasn't to make another offer?"

"I need information, Joe." He stared at the mechanic, meeting Joe's questions.

"Information? That doesn't seem like you, Mitchell. You have all your goons, your technology, your money. I doubt I have any information you don't already have."

Baldwin put his hands out as if in offering. "And yet, here I stand, Joe." Mitchell turned and paced slowly to the other end of the office, stopping at the far side before spinning slowly toward the street and once more gazing out at the square. "I know you and I have never really gotten along, Joe."

"That's an understatement."

"Yes, well, your father should have sold this place to me a long time ago. That goes for you, too."

"What," Joe said, "so you could build one of those mainstream gas stations here? With the thirty pumps and a huge convenience store selling all sorts of overpriced crap? Sorry, Mitchell, but this gas station is a part of my family. Always has been. Always will be."

Baldwin nodded. "I know. And as I said, I'm not here to make you an offer. I'm looking for someone."

"Oh?"

"Yes. A man. I heard he came into your shop the other day, early in the morning."

"Not really narrowing it down there, Mitch. Lots of men come in here in the mornings. Would you care to be a little more specific?"

Baldwin allowed the barb, deciding it wasn't worth getting angry over, especially since he was already furious. Instead, he concealed his wrath under a smooth response. "He's probably a little over six feet tall. Dark hair."

"Still not helping me out much. And I have to say, it's more than a little creepy that you posted one of your guys outside my place of business, Mitchell. Seriously? That's twisted, man. Do they just sit in a car all day watching my shop? Gotta be boring. If you preferred, you could just have one of them sit in here." He motioned to one of the chairs sitting next to the long window that ran the length of the other half of the office. "It's air conditioned. And when I get here first, the coffee is good."

"Thank you for your generous offer," Baldwin sneered, "but I'll pass. I make it my business to know the business of others in town. Especially those who might do something...foolish."

Joe tilted his head to the side. He looked back at Baldwin with curiosity in his eyes and confusion filling his cheeks. "What are you talking about? Foolish?"

Baldwin took a step toward the shop owner and crossed his arms.

"So, you didn't hear what happened earlier today? What am I saying? Of course you heard. This town is small enough you could hear Old Lady Winters drop a packet of sugar in the morning from the other side of the county."

"Ah," Joe realized. "This is about the men who were killed in the alley today."

"My men," Baldwin snapped. "Four of them, all murdered in cold blood."

"I doubt it was cold blood. In fact, if I had to guess, I'd say your men instigated the violence. And we both know they were armed. Your men are always armed."

For several seconds, Baldwin didn't say anything. He knew Joe was correct, but he remained unwilling to concede the point. Instead, he continued forward with his line of questioning.

"Four of my men are dead," Baldwin stated. "And one is missing. I have reason to believe that this rogue visited your station in the last two days. I want to know who he is, where I can find him, and what he wants." He thought of the expression on Tory's face just before he died.

Joe's right eyebrow arched upward. "I can't be certain, but if someone is picking off your men, I'd say they're coming after you at some point. Looks like they're working their way up the totem pole, so to speak."

"Yes," Baldwin demurred. "So it would seem."

"Has your boy Sheriff Meachum been able to turn up any leads? The cops should handle something like this. Then again, I guess we're talking about the same crew who can't seem to find Heather Markham."

Joe watched Baldwin's reaction when he said the name of the woman. It was the first time the visitor had flinched since arriving, and while he quickly recovered, returning to his normal, stoic self, Joe didn't miss it.

"Of course, you don't know anything about that, do you?"

Baldwin blinked slowly then sighed. "I can see that coming here was a waste of time, Joe. I thought perhaps you could help me solve a crime. Four of my men are dead because of this vagabond, and you crack jokes."

"I'm not joking, Mitch. My advice to you is give Hattie her daughter back. Maybe if you're lucky, she'll not press charges." Even Joe knew that was outside the realm of possibility. While he wasn't certain Baldwin had the young woman, or even had anything to do with her disappearance, that uncertainty was a mere blip on the radar compared to how sure he was of Baldwin's guilt for all the heinous things he'd done through the years.

Baldwin's eyelids narrowed. His nostrils flared with each breath. "Shame about Heather," he said with manufactured sincerity. "Sweet girl. I hope they find her soon. I heard she was out for a jog or something while visiting her mother." He looked down at the ground, regret darkening his face. "Awful. To think what those kidnappers could be doing to her, or did to her. I just hope she's still alive."

Joe watched him talk, unimpressed. "Yeah, so you can stop with the Oscar clip you're putting on here, Mitchell. I don't buy it for a second. I know you took her. Why you don't have the feds breathing down your neck right now is beyond me. I know you have reach, power, connections, but you're not immortal. And you're not beyond the law. One of these days, someone is going to get to you."

Baldwin's jaw set firm, and he raised his head to meet Joe's accusing gaze. "I hope you don't mean that, Joe. I know we've had our differences. You didn't want to sell the station, and I admire that. Takes guts, or maybe a little stupidity, to turn down the money I offered, but you stood by your principles."

"What would you know about principles?"

The jab bounced off Baldwin like a paper ball. "I know plenty, son," he replied in a haunting grumble. "Plenty. I know enough to not shake a hornet's nest. And I know when to take a good deal when it's on the table."

He turned and paced three steps back to the door. He stopped and looked across his shoulder at Joe, who stood there watching, his eyes devoid of emotion.

"So, you don't recall seeing this guy I asked about?" Baldwin added, throwing out one last line.

"Sorry, Mitchell. Like I said, the guy you described could be anyone. I see a bunch of those types every day. Strangers passing through, locals, you name it. If he was here, I don't remember it."

Baldwin pressed his lips together and nodded, as if accepting the answer as sincere. "Okay, then. Thank you, Joe. I appreciate it. Sorry I took up your time. I'm sure you need to finish up your work for the day and get back home."

All he received for his statement was a slight nod from the mechanic. Baldwin pulled open the door and walked out into the night.

Joe watched him get into this SUV. The vehicle pulled away, turning out of the station to the right, then again at the next intersection.

When Baldwin was gone, Joe finished his checklist, then switched off the lights in the front office. He walked through the maze of hallways to the back of the building. When he reached his office, he set down the clipboard, turned off the computer and lights, and went out the back door.

He turned his back to the small lot behind the building where his pickup truck was parked next to an assorted collection of vehicles needing various repairs. The moon glowed brightly in the sky, and the cool evening air smelled of honeysuckle.

Joe inserted a key into the deadbolt at the top and turned it. He removed the key and was about to lock the doorknob when he heard a muted pop. He grimaced at the sudden pain in his back. Joe spun around to face a masked attacker holding a pistol. Smoke dribbled upward out of the suppressor muzzle.

The attacker raised the weapon and was about to fire the head shot when Joe flung his keys desperately at the man's face. The muzzle popped again, but the assassin's shot went low, striking Joe in the upper-right side of his chest.

The shot knocked Joe backward against the door, then he fell onto his face. He breathed heavily as the gunman approached. The masked killer stopped, hovering over Joe for a second before raising the pistol again to put the last round through the back of Joe's head.

Suddenly, a pair of headlight beams swung around into the back parking lot. The gunman, caught off guard by the lights, turned and sprinted away, leaving Joe Notekabortsky on the ground to bleed to death in the moonlight.

26

Dak pulled into the gas station early the next morning, hoping to get there in time to catch Joe before he started his busy day. What he found, instead, was more like a funeral.

Flower wreaths hung from the windows of the gas station front office. And more bouquets occupied space on the ground. The place looked like some kind of makeshift shrine to a fallen hero.

Dak parked his car along the street and walked across the front lot, past the gas pumps, and to the office, where three of the technicians loitered inside, all with hands in their pockets as they talked, somber expressions on every face.

"Morning, fellas," Dak said as he stepped into the narrow room. He immediately sensed something wasn't right.

His initial instinct told him that someone had died, based on the arrangements outside. Add to that the devastated, drained looks on these work-hardened faces, and it was an easy conclusion to reach. The last thing Dak realized was the face missing from the collection. Joe wasn't here. His first thought was that Joe was probably in the back office working on bills or some other form of paperwork.

That thought only lasted a couple of seconds.

"Where's Joe?" Dak said. Concern filled his voice as he met the eyes of the men in the room.

One guy, a gruff-looking technician with a long, thick, reddish beard touched the bill of his trucker hat and answered. "Someone shot Joe last night as he was closing up the shop."

The words hit Dak in the chest with the power of a blacksmith's hammer. "What?" He wasn't sure he'd heard correctly, and while he didn't want to push such a heavy statement, Dak had to know.

"Last night," a skinny technician with a clean-shaven face answered to Dak's right. "He was the last one here, as usual. Looks like he was closing up shop for the day. Someone snuck up behind him and shot him in the back, then in the chest. Least that's what the cops are saying."

One of the men grunted at the mention of the police.

Dak's concern might as well have been written in bold, black ink all over his face. "Who did this?"

"No one knows," the skinny guy said. "The security camera in the back didn't get a good look at the shooter because they wore a mask. He just appeared out of nowhere. Shot Joe in the back and then again one more time. It's a miracle he survived."

A splinter of hope pricked Dak's mind. "Did you say he survived?"

The technician with the thick, lumberjack beard near the register nodded. "Barely. He's in a coma right now. Medically induced. But it looks like he might make it. His condition is stable for the moment."

"That's good to hear," Dak said. "That he's alive," he added quickly. If Joe were unconscious, though, he wouldn't be able to help identify the attacker, not that he could anyway. According to these men, the shooter wore a mask. "Do they have someone watching him at his hospital room?"

"Yeah," Skinny said. "They have a cop stationed outside the room. Twenty-four-seven from what I understand."

A ripple of fear shot through Dak's body. "The regional hospital?" he asked with urgency.

"Yeah, about ten minutes from here," the bearded man answered.

Dak didn't need directions. He'd passed the hospital a couple of times, making a note of it as he did many of the other landmarks.

"Thank you," Dak offered and hurried out the door.

He rushed back to the rental, climbed in the driver's seat, and sped out of town. Dak didn't see the black sedan parked up the sidewalk pull out behind him several seconds later. His focus remained locked on getting to the hospital. For all he knew, Joe could already be dead. It depended purely on which cop had been stationed there to watch over the man.

If it were one of Baldwin's guys, Dak feared the worst. It was all he could do to hope that there were at least a few good cops on the force, and that one of them had been stationed with Joe first.

Dak sped toward the hospital, the seconds flying by at Mach 4. Every stop sign seemed to put him between two other vehicles with drivers who couldn't decide which car should go first. He even caught the only two red lights he recalled between the downtown square and the hospital.

Finally, after an excruciating nine minutes, Dak whipped the car into the parking lot outside the regional hospital and into an empty spot near the front of the building.

He slammed the door shut as he took off toward the entrance, running at full speed until he reached the sliding doors.

A doctor in blue scrubs and a white lab coat stood outside the entrance, a cell phone pressed to his ear. He didn't seem to notice Dak as he slowed down then picked up his pace again to pass through the automatic doors.

He nearly skidded to a stop at the information desk. The young woman behind the desk smiled up at him, her eyes squinting behind tortoiseshell glasses. "Can I help you?" she asked. Something about the way she made the offer almost sounded flirtatious.

"Yes, ma'am. I'm looking for the intensive care unit," Dak said, figuring that would be the most likely place to find Joe.

"Sure. Are you friend or family?"

"Family," Dak lied, understanding the protocol. He did his best to be honest all the time, but there were circumstances that required less truthful approaches, like when a person's life was in danger.

The receptionist accepted the answer and directed Dak down the hall to three elevators, told him which floor to go to, and how to find his "relative."

Dak arrived on the fourth floor of the hospital with a ball of nerves in his gut. He hoped he wasn't too late, but as he stepped out of the lift and into the hall, he saw no signs of panic, no concerned faces—at least no more than usual for a staff working the ICU.

He'd been in those places on a few occasions, and Dak never enjoyed revisiting those memories. Maybe it was a reminder of his own fragility as a human being. Maybe his empathy racked him, too.

Either way, he didn't like being there, but he didn't have a choice. Dak knew he'd inadvertently caused this to happen. Perhaps he was being too hard on himself and truly didn't shoulder any of the blame, but he couldn't help feeling like it was his fault.

Dak ignored the man sitting behind the nurses' desk and immediately saw the cop standing by a closed door at the end of the hall. He'd never seen a private ICU room before, which was probably safer in some regards but more dangerous in others, especially when considering the absence of witnesses.

Fortunately, the cop still manned his post, though Dak knew all too well the man could have slipped into the room, administered a deadly drug, and returned to the hallway without anyone noticing.

Banishing the thought, Dak strolled hurriedly down the corridor toward the young man in uniform.

The cop saw Dak approaching and straightened up his stance. "Is he okay?" Dak asked, the urgency in his voice echoing down the hall.

"Yeah," the cop responded, turning to face Dak. "Restricted access, though. Family only, sir."

"Yes, sir. I know. I came in from out of town. We're just worried that whoever did this might not be done."

The confused cop frowned at the comment. "What?"

Dak stopped short of the door, and he noted the cop's hand

hanging on his belt close to the pistol on his right hip. "Has anyone else been by to see him?" Dak pressed. "Anyone other than family? Any friends or other locals who came by to pay a visit?"

"No," the cop shook his head. The name tag on his shirt read "Mills."

"Have you been the only one on duty since he arrived at the hospital, Officer Mills?"

The cop's eyes danced around like the answer should have been obvious. "Yes. Actually, my replacement will be here any minute. I'm beat."

That's a relief. Maybe.

"Can we go in and check on him?" Dak asked, trying not to look too hopeful.

"Sure," he hesitated. "But I'm going to have to go in with you. And I'm going to need to see some ID."

"Of course," Dak said. He took out his wallet and produced a driver's license.

"Carl Everhouse?" Mills sounded befuddled at the name. Then he laughed. "I hope you're in real estate with a name like that."

Dak chuckled. "I get that all the time."

"Sorry. I'm sure you do."

Dak put his wallet away. "Between Joe's side of the family and mine, there's no shortage of jokes at reunions."

"I bet." The cop turned and opened the door, easing it open quietly so as not to disturb the patient.

Sounds of beeping machines and monitors filled Dak's ears. His eyes immediately went to the display of Joe's heartbeat. It was still going strong, and when Dak shifted his vision to the man in the bed, he could see Joe's chest rising and falling—albeit with a tube sticking out of his mouth.

"You want a few minutes with him?" Officer Mills asked.

"Sure, if that's okay," Dak said.

"No problem. I'll be right out here if you need me."

"Thank you."

Dak let the cop ease the door shut. He couldn't believe the man had glanced at a fake driver's license and accepted his story so easily. Then again, this was a small town. Dak doubted Mills even considered the notion that someone might try to come finish off Joe, even though the cop's presence there was proof that someone had at least taken that into account.

With the door closed, Dak padded over to the bedside and looked down at Joe. Tubes ran from machines to his left arm. Wires also connected to various devices.

"I'm sorry this happened, Joe," Dak said. He'd heard that people in comas could hear when visitors spoke to them. Even so, Dak felt silly doing it. "I'm going to find who did this, Joe. I'm going to make them pay."

Dak didn't tell the unconscious man who he believed was responsible, and he didn't feel the need to. If Joe were awake, he'd know. He'd probably agree, too.

Voices at the door distracted Dak from his vengeful thoughts. He heard one man say something to Officer Mills. Mills responded cordially, as if greeting a friend or colleague. They spoke for a minute or two, and then Mills told the other man goodbye.

Mills had informed Dak that his shift was about to end. For a second, Dak wondered if he should step outside and let the new guy know he was in the room. Then he figured Mills would do it, but as the conversation ended between the two men, Dak realized Officer Mills must have either forgotten to mention it or didn't think it important enough to let the newcomer know about his presence.

Dak decided to take a risk and retreated into the bathroom, closing the door nearly all the way but keeping it open by an inch so he could hear if anyone else entered the room. He stood there for nearly five minutes, waiting in the darkness and feeling like an idiot for every second.

He hoped the new guard was one of the good guys, as Mills appeared to be, but there was no way to know.

As it turned out, there was a way.

Dak heard the door to the hospital room open slowly. At first, he expected to see a doctor in a lab coat or perhaps a nurse coming by to check on the patient's vital signs.

Instead, Dak saw the new cop enter into his view. The man, with graying hair and a belly protruding over his belt, tiptoed over to the bed and stared at the patient. Then he glanced back toward the door, as if making sure he'd closed it.

Dak knew he had because the sounds of activity from the corridor beyond had vanished a second before the interloper appeared.

The cop turned back to Joe. Dak watched as the man produced a syringe from his pocket.

So, that's how they're going to do it.

Dak wondered if the man might try to simply smother Joe while he slept. That sort of thing happened from time to time, from what Dak heard. But in this instance, they were going to use a drug, probably injected into one of the tubes connected to Joe's wrist. Dak would have put his life savings on the chemical in the syringe being the same one he found in the toxicology report for Mike Hamilton.

The cop removed the cap from the needle and flicked the metal one time as he'd probably seen doctors do on television.

Then he shifted and took hold of the tube.

Dak nudged the door open. He already knew it wouldn't make a sound because it hadn't when he initially closed it. He crept the eight feet from the bathroom threshold to the cop, reaching the plump man just as he was about to stick the needle into the tube.

"I wouldn't do that," Dak warned.

The cop twisted his head around, the color draining from his fleshy face. His eyes widened at the sight of someone else in the room. Instinctively, he started to whirl around and reach for his gun, but it was too late for that move.

Dak was on him in an instant. He grabbed the man's right hand and forced the needle toward the thick neck just above the cop's collar.

"Baldwin put you up to this? Is that it?" Dak taunted, forcing the syringe ever closer to the flushing target.

"Stop," the cop whimpered, realizing he was overpowered. He

pushed back as hard as he could, but he was no match for Dak. "I'm just doing what they tell me to do."

"And what they pay you to do," Dak added. He looked at the tip of the needle, regarding it casually as if the struggle on his end were nothing more than reading the Sunday paper.

"Please," the cop begged. His eyes crossed as he stared down at the needle approaching his neck.

"What's in the syringe," Dak checked the cop's name tag, "Officer Lipscomb?"

"Nothing. I swear." The man's face and neck jiggled as he vigorously shook his head in denial.

"Oh, now we both know that's not true. I can see the liquid in there. Looks clear. I wonder if you're the one they sent to eliminate Mike Hamilton. Were you?"

Sweat dribbled down the sides of the man's red face. Dak applied more pressure on the syringe, careful not to allow the plunger to depress fully.

"I don't know what you're talking about. Please. Let me go. I won't tell him. I'll leave town. You'll never see me again. Please, just don't kill me. I have a family."

Dak flicked his eyes to the man's left hand. "I don't see a ring." Then he shoved the needle into the man's neck just below the jaw. Dak pushed in the plunger, injecting the cop with whatever he'd brought in for Joe.

He held the syringe in the man's neck for several seconds until he felt the strength leave the cop's muscles. Then Dak let go and watched the assassin fall to the floor next to the bed. Lipscomb's eyes stared up at Dak, blinking now and then as if by their own will. He still breathed, but soon that would become more difficult, and the would-be killer would be the victim of his own designs.

Dak glanced back at Joe, who still lay there on his back, the machines beeping and whirring along the same cadence as his breath. He didn't want to leave Joe alone in the hospital, but when the nurse came in and found a dead cop on the floor, news would get back to Baldwin within minutes.

The hospital would go into lockdown, and Dak hoped someone honest would be put in charge of Joe's well-being. At least with one corrupt cop off the list, the odds had just tilted a little more in Dak's favor.

Still, he knew things were escalating quickly, and he would need to move even faster.

27

D ak walked over to the door and pulled it open, careful not to let the latch make a sound. He looked through the narrow opening to the left toward the end of the building, then inched it open a little farther so he could poke his head out and look the other way. No sign of any hospital staff in either direction, but he knew that could change in an instant.

He didn't want to risk passing the nurses' station again. The guy behind the desk had already seen him once, and Dak didn't want to give the nurse a second chance to get a good look at him. Without having done some recon beforehand, he had no idea if there was a staircase to the left at the end of the hall, but he knew that was his best bet. If there wasn't one there, he'd have to go back out the way he came in.

Dak pulled the door open wide and was about to step out when a doctor in a white lab coat walked around the corner. The young man's eyes stayed glued to a chart as he walked down the hall. Dak retreated into the room and carefully closed the door.

He listened closely with his ear pressed against the door's surface and heard the clicking of the doctor's shoes as the man walked by. When the sounds faded, Dak pulled the door open again and slipped outside. He saw a door in the corner ahead with a placard next to it on the wall. The image featured a stick figure descending stairs. Relief filled Dak's chest as he neared the door. Then, around the corner, a nurse appeared in light blue scrubs. Her long black hair draped over her shoulders, and she stared at a chart the same way the doctor had as she walked along—except she looked up when she caught sight of the figure moving toward the stairwell.

The young Asian woman smiled back at him, and Dak nodded politely, returning the smile while at the same time reaching for the bar on the door to push it open.

The nurse turned the corner and continued down the hallway toward the nurse's station, or perhaps to one of the rooms. Dak budged the door open and disappeared into the stairwell.

His feet flew down the stairs, taking some of them two at a time. Dak reached the first landing, grabbed the post at the corner, and whipped himself around to the next flight. He knew he was in a race against time, and at any second someone from the hospital staff would walk into Joe's room, find a dead cop, and sound the alarm. Questioning why there was a syringe sticking out of the cop's neck would come after the fact.

The initial reaction would be panic, followed shortly by someone on staff collecting themselves enough to alert the authorities. Then they would lock down the hospital, and Dak would be trapped inside.

Even in a small regional hospital like this one, Dak knew there would be a plethora of places to hide, but with a murder, the cops—and Baldwin's men—would scour the entire facility until they found the killer.

Never mind the fact that the late Officer Lipscomb was going to be the one doing the killing until Dak had stepped in.

Dak landed on the next platform and continued around the corner, heading downward, expecting to hear Klaxons blaring from every angle.

The piercing sounds did not come, and with every step toward the bottom, confidence swelled in his gut.

He reached the second floor and kept going, pushing faster,

though careful not to stumble or fall on the steps. Growing up, and even now, Dak had more than his share of clumsy moments. He'd fallen down the stairs more times than he could remember, and that didn't count the number of times he fell going *up*. At least going that direction, the fall didn't usually hurt as bad as tumbling downward.

But he wasn't going to fall this time.

Halfway down the last flight of stairs, Dak spun around the corner and was about to take the next step when the dreaded sound of the Klaxons began.

The terrible noise pierced his eardrums, blasting out of horns hanging from the walls by the doors to each level.

Dak didn't panic, instead hurrying up his pace, leaping down the steps and using the rail to balance and slide down to the bottom. When his feet hit the concrete base, he reached out and grabbed the door handle, praying in his mind that it was unlocked.

He pushed down on the handle's button with his thumb, grasped the handle with his fingers, and pulled.

Relief poured into him when it opened easily, but Dak wasn't out of the woods yet.

He poked his head through the door and noted the right edge of the receptionist desk just down the corridor and beyond the wall's corner. He imagined the woman fielding more calls than she could handle while the alarms continued to blare.

Dak didn't know the hospital's policy on how to handle a murder, but he assumed they would initiate a lockdown procedure, which was what he'd heard of at other facilities. Schools, he knew, used active-shooter drills to do everything they could to keep students and teachers safe from a threat.

He left the stairwell and started to make for one of the exits fifty feet away, but noticed a cop in uniform running back toward the desk.

Officer Mills, it seemed, hadn't left the building yet.

He ran around the corner, talking into this radio. More cops would be on the way, and Dak didn't like the idea of taking them all on in this setting. The guy at the nurses' station would identify him easily, and it wouldn't take much for the authorities to pin the crime on Dak.

Guilty as he was, Dak had killed Lipscomb to save Joe's life.

Somehow, I don't think that's going to matter in this town, he thought.

There was no way for him to get out of the building without being noticed. *Unless....*

He noticed a door ten feet away to his left and hurried to it in two huge steps. He twisted the knob, hoping it wasn't locked. Like the other doors he'd encountered so far, this one was also open, and he stepped inside and away from the noise, grateful that this room was apparently the only place in the building without a Klaxon built in.

Lockers lined the walls on all four sides. Most were closed, but a few doors hung open, and one of them contained exactly what Dak needed.

He rushed over to the locker and removed the lab coat from the hanger, slipped it on, and slid a mask over his face that he found on a shelf inside the locker.

Satisfied with his minimal disguise, Dak turned and exited the room less than a minute after entering.

He returned to the overwhelming alarms blasting throughout the building, and no sooner had he stepped out of the building than Dak saw the cops pulling into the parking lot outside the main entrance.

He remembered seeing an exit sign beyond the elevators and quickly rounded the corner into the hallway without the receptionist seeing him. She was too busy answering calls and staring out through the front entrance at the swarming police.

Passing a nurse and a doctor who both hurried down the hall, he walked briskly toward the rear of the building, doing his best not to look like he was in a hurry.

Dak saw the exit sign at the end of the long corridor. He felt as if every single step was thirty feet, and that weights were tied to his ankles, slowing down his progress.

The painful Klaxons continued screaming, and Dak wondered if the same kind of alarms were used in the newborn units or in parts of the building where patients sensitive to loud noises were housed.

Finally, after what seemed like an eternity, Dak reached the exit. He started to grab the bar and push the door open when a uniformed cop appeared on the other side of the second set of double doors.

The man pulled on the handle, but the door wouldn't open.

He looked through the glass and saw Dak standing there. "Hey, can you let me in?" the cop asked.

For a second, Dak hesitated then realized that the young cop had no clue who he was, probably figuring him to be one of the hospital staff. At least the disguise worked, anyway.

Dak shoved open the door and immediately went to the next. He pushed the second one open and painted a sense of urgency on his face. "So glad you're here, Officer. Fourth floor."

"Thanks, Doc," the cop said as he charged by into the building. Dak watched him lumber down the corridor. He kept a hand on the butt of his gun as he ran. Dak knew the drill. Small town or huge city, cops understood the danger of entering a crime scene, especially one where someone had been murdered. They trained for this all the time, and he would check every corner and cranny of the hospital until the suspect was discovered.

Little did the cop realize, he'd just let the killer walk right out the back door.

28

Baldwin stared at the screen with the intensity of a man terrified for his life. He read through the paragraphs, paused at the end—unbelieving of what he was seeing—and then read it all a second time.

The image of the dark-haired man glared back at him. He wore sunglasses in the picture, taken from a security camera in London, but there was no denying it was the same guy Baldwin had seen at the diner just a few days before. He never forgot a face, not one that didn't belong, and he recalled walking out of the diner that morning thinking that this guy was definitely an outsider.

Baldwin had let it go the second he laid eyes on Hattie walking toward him down the sidewalk. Understandable considering the furious, intent look in her eyes as she stormed toward him.

She'd tracked him down to the diner that day, though that feat was hardly a difficult one. Most people in town knew Baldwin took his breakfast at the same time, and typically at the same place, on certain days. The diner happened to be the day he'd bumped into Hattie, and the stranger.

He looked at the attached paragraphs and scanned over them a third time.

Dak Harper, former Delta Force operator, served the American military with distinction, earning more than a few honors during his years in the service. He'd been active mostly in the Middle East, though he'd served a few stints in other parts of the world.

Baldwin couldn't believe some of the things he was reading, especially in the confirmed kills category. Having never served in the military, much less special operations, Baldwin still recognized a trained, professional killer when he read his dossier.

After being wrongfully accused of a number of crimes, Harper had dropped off the map until his name was cleared. And even then, he only reappeared occasionally, like in this security camera photo. Baldwin wondered why, if the man had been cleared of any wrongdoing, he would still be on the run.

The answer, for Baldwin, came in the form of the disgruntled CO from the last place Harper was stationed.

Colonel Cameron Tucker's handling of the situation with Harper had put the nail in the coffin on Tucker's career in the military. Baldwin wanted this Harper character eliminated, and he figured Tucker probably felt the same way.

Baldwin clicked on another icon on the screen and looked over the details. He preferred not to peruse the filth on the dark web, both because of the vile nature of the content and because of the security risk. Fortunately for him, he ran the most advanced systems on earth to protect against any form of cyberattack. Baldwin wasn't about to let some two-bit hacker slide a virus into his personal network.

Johnny sat in the chair to the right, angled so he could turn toward the door at a second's notice. "What do you think, sir?" he asked after remaining silent for several minutes.

Baldwin's eyes didn't leave the computer monitor. He kept them focused on the face of the man who'd been causing so much trouble for him. Finally, he pried his gaze from the screen and faced the bodyguard.

"This is good intel, Johnny."

"An old buddy of mine scrounged it up. Owed me a couple of favors, so I made the call. I knew if anyone could find out who this guy was, it would be him. I also had a feeling our problem is probably former military, which turned out to be the case. My contact said he recalled hearing the story about this guy, though he never met him in person. They were in the service at different times and served in different places. But he heard the stories."

"How he was wrongfully accused of betraying his team?" Baldwin asked.

"That," Johnny nodded, "and what happened afterward."

Baldwin's interest piqued, and he lifted both eyebrows. Folding his hands under his chin, he leaned forward. "What happened afterward?"

"You won't find it in that dossier. Actually, you won't find the details about it anywhere. This is an urban legend kind of thing."

"Fine," Baldwin said with a twist of his head. "I don't care. Myth. Fact. I want to know everything I can about this guy."

Johnny bowed his head. "Dak Harper disappeared for a few months after the ordeal in Iraq. When the army lost track of him, Tucker did everything in his power to find him but could never locate Harper. The guy vanished like fog in July."

"Then what happened?"

"One of his former teammates disappeared. The local police think it was a mob-style hit. The guy had a gambling problem. Owed a bunch of money to one of the rings there in Miami. His name was Carson Williams. Big dude. Built like a linebacker. The cops' hypothesis is that he owed someone a gambling debt he couldn't pay, so they killed him."

"Did they ever find the body?" Baldwin asked, his face stoic.

"Nope. I figure it's probably in the ocean off the coast of South Beach or whatever other beaches are down there."

Baldwin took a long breath then exhaled slowly while nodding. "And you don't buy the story about the gambling ring killing him." It wasn't a question.

"Not when you add in what happened to the other men from his team. One of them worked for a cartel down in Mexico. From what I heard about the incident, someone attacked the cartel leader's mansion. Took out everyone. The guards and the leader, along with all his lieutenants. Then there was the Colorado killing. Sniper from Harper's team was killed there. Another guy was taken out in Kentucky. The last one was found dead on a farm in Turkey. So no, I don't think the gambling ring killed Williams. It's obvious Harper was behind all the killings and disappearances. It was payback for what his team did to him in Iraq. They ruined his life. I know what I would do to the guys I work with if they tried something like that with me."

The dark statement didn't affect Baldwin in the least. He knew what his head of security was capable of, and the things he'd done in the past—even some of them for him. He thumbed his chin for a few seconds then turned his attention to the cigar humidor to his right. He flipped open the walnut-colored lid and pulled out two thick cigars. He cut the caps off both, then reached the first cigar over to a lighter that sat on his desk, doubling as a paperweight when he wasn't smoking. Baldwin pressed down on a golden lever and a flame sparked from the top of the glass containing the fuel.

He held the cigar over the flame, turning it with his fingers until the entire tip glowed bright orange. He passed the cigar across the desk to Johnny, who took it with a grateful nod.

Baldwin repeated the process with his own cigar, and when it too glowed to life, he jammed it in his mouth and began puffing. Thick, white smoke encircled his head and hung in the air like his own personal fog. Johnny puffed less aggressively, but soon too had the hazy halo around him.

"All of this is good information, Johnny," Baldwin said as he stood. He walked over to the nearest window and looked out into the night. The forest on the hillsides surrounding his mansion seemed darker than normal, and ominous clouds loomed on the horizon to the west. "But we still don't know why he's here. Is he a mercenary now? Did Heather Markham hire him?"

"We questioned her about that, sir. I don't believe she knows anything about this guy."

Baldwin smoked his cigar with tight lips. He nodded absently, watching a cloud that strayed from the pack. "Yes, I don't think she has the connections to do something like that. Or the guts. Her mother, on the other hand..."

"It's possible, but I also don't think this was Hattie's doing."

Baldwin's shoulders lifted then fell. "Well then, who did it? Susan from the diner? Or was it Joe Notekabortsky? It wasn't you, Johnny. Someone knows something." His voice escalated as anger fueled it into a rage. "And speaking of Joe." He spoke through teeth clenching the cigar. "What happened there? He's supposed to be dead. How did that idiot Lipscomb screw it up?"

Johnny merely offered a knowing glance through the fog around him.

"Yes, of course," Baldwin said, bobbing his head. "Harper. He must have been at the hospital. Not sure how he got in. They're only allowing family members."

"Hospital security is largely based on the honor system, chief. You walk in. They ask if you're a family member. You say yes or no."

Baldwin rolled his eyes, nodding absently. "Yes, yes. I know that. But you're right. It's a lax system. Especially in a Podunk town like this one." He sighed in frustration. "You know he's going to come for me. It's only a matter of time." He glanced over at his desk, where the two pistols sat in the open case. He hadn't taken the time to frame them in a shadow box yet, having considered putting them in a more private place for fear some random guest might recognize the weapons.

A thought occurred to him, but he dismissed it immediately. Still, it pressed on the back of his mind. Baldwin couldn't help but note that the troubles with this rogue Harper coincided with his acquiring the pistols.

It had to be a coincidence, but one he noticed just the same.

"We should be able to get something from the security footage at the hospital," Johnny offered, interrupting Baldwin's thoughts.

"What's the point," Baldwin huffed. "We know it was him. No reason for us to go snooping around, especially with feds coming into town to have a look. Let them figure it out. I doubt they'll find anything, though. He wouldn't be that sloppy. I bet they don't discover anything that links this Dak Harper fellow to the murder.

And now the feds are watching over Joe, too. So, there's no way we can get to him. Not yet."

Johnny waited before speaking up again. He wanted to give the boss a second to process everything, and to calm down. When it felt right, he said, "What do you want us to do next, sir?"

"What do I want?" Baldwin growled. "I want you and the others to find this guy. He's not stupid enough to stay here in town. So check the other areas around us. He might be in one of the nearby towns, holed up in a hotel. Tell the boys to fan out and check every nook and cranny within a fifty-mile radius. I doubt he's beyond that."

"And you don't think he's left the area entirely?"

"No," Baldwin said definitively. He turned and faced the window again, watching as the storm swelled, seeping across the sky like a liquid monster to consume the moon. "He's not going anywhere until he gets to me."

29

Johnny stopped outside the hotel and stared at the front office. The manager for the night shift loitered next to the front door, taking a smoke break for what was probably the tenth time in the last hour. The woman bore the look of someone who'd had a rough life and was just trying to get by to the next day. Her half-curled blonde hair sprayed out in strands over her spray-tanned shoulders. Her denim jacket and matching stonewashed jeans made her look like she was ready for the Poison world tour. In 1987.

She stared at Johnny with an absent regard, more interested in her cigarette than the man sitting in the vehicle in front of the lobby.

He climbed out of the SUV and walked over to her, putting on the most disarming smile he could muster. "Hi," he said energetically. Being friendly, even cordial in the slightest, wasn't his thing. Johnny regarded people who walked around smiling all the time as idiots. And whenever he saw one of those Be Positive-type bumper stickers, he wanted to throw up. Still, he could fake it when necessary.

"I was wondering," he went on when the woman didn't respond with more than an annoyed look under her brow, "a friend of mine is supposed to be here this week, and I believe he's staying in this hotel. Dark hair. About my height. Goes by the name of Dak Harper."

She stared back at him, her vapid eyes portraying the truest disinterest he'd ever seen. "Don't know that I've seen that name here."

Johnny lowered his head, still forcing the stupid grin across his lips. "That kidder. He sometimes uses other names when he travels. Likes to pretend he's a spy or something ridiculous like that. No idea why. Sometimes, I think he's just messing with me. Any chance there might be a guy here with the description I gave you?"

Her head rolled to the left and she raised a finger, pointing to a window on the first floor. "Room one-eleven," she said.

"Thank you," Johnny offered with the least amount of sincerity he could muster. He walked back to the SUV, got in, and drove around to a parking space on the opposite side of the lot from the hotel. He could have parked close to the door, but Johnny wasn't stupid. He knew the man inside the room was beyond dangerous.

Johnny stayed in his vehicle, keeping room III straight ahead through the windshield. He took out his phone and dialed a number, then pressed the device to his ear while he watched the hotel manager finish her cigarette.

It took two rings before Johnny heard, "A little late for a nightcap, isn't it, Johnny?" Sheriff Meachum's voice scratched like sandpaper on metal. From the sound of it, the call woke the man up. No surprise just after midnight.

"Sheriff, I found the guy we've been looking for. Comfort Palace in Austel. First floor. Room one-eleven. I'm sitting here now."

"Wait a second," Meachum protested. "Did you say you found the suspect? In Austel?"

"Yes. I suggest you and your men get over here as quickly as possible." He heard a rustling sound in the background.

"Now, hold on."

Johnny rolled his eyes at the sheriff's disbelief.

"How the Sam Hill did you find him?"

"I'll explain when you get here. I need every man you can spare, Sheriff. This suspect is extremely dangerous. Probably armed, too.

We won't get another chance at this. If he gets away now, he may not pop up again."

Johnny didn't necessarily believe his own words. As his employer stated previously, Harper wasn't going to leave town until he got to Baldwin. Johnny was done wasting time trying to figure out who hired him, or how they found Harper in the first place. He could have come from a posting on the dark web for all Johnny knew. He'd seen some things like that before, even heard of private security guys and former military personnel going to the dark side to make some serious cash.

"You're sure he's still there?" Meachum asked. The sound of a belt buckle rattled in the background.

"The suspect's rental car is in front of the room. Lights are out. He's there. I need every guy on our side you can get here. Leave Mills out of it. I don't trust him."

"I don't trust him either," the sheriff agreed. "He's new, and we haven't had a chance to break him in yet."

Johnny saw the manger finish her latest smoke break and go back into the office. He took account of the five other cars in the parking lot and noted that most of the other lights in the hotel windows were out.

"Get here as fast as you can. I'll keep watch until the cavalry arrives."

"You calling your guys, too?"

"What's left of them. See you in a few."

Johnny didn't wait for the sheriff to say goodbye. He ended the call and scrolled down to the third number on his recent calls list, pressed the screen, and returned the phone to his ear.

A man answered on the other end of the line in an English accent. "What's up, Johnny?"

"I found him. Get to the Comfort Palace in Austel. Room one-eleven. Cops are coming too. We're going to take this guy down tonight."

"I'll be there in twenty."

Johnny ended the call and set the phone down on the center

console charger, then reset his focus on the door to Dak Harper's room. He knew his men would arrive before Meachum and the rest of the department he rounded up at this late hour. There would be a few guys on duty, but most of the Dawsonville cops would be at home in bed. Fortunately, Dawsonville was the county seat, which meant jurisdiction wasn't going to be an issue. Johnny didn't anticipate an arrest being made, despite Baldwin's orders to bring the man in alive. That command felt like more of a guideline than an actual request.

If, when he and the rest of his team breached the room, Harper was asleep, Johnny had no issue with apprehending the man and taking him straight to Baldwin's mansion. The cops would help, and wouldn't argue about not taking him down to the local jail.

There would be no talk of charges or a trial. This would be old-school justice, and there was nothing that could save Harper from that.

The nuisance would probably face a similar fate to that of the thief Baldwin had dumped in the quarry, though Johnny had a feeling Baldwin would want this guy to suffer far more than Merritt Wheeler.

He waited for ten minutes before he started to look around for the reinforcements. It only took another five minutes before the first of his team arrived, the man he'd spoken to on the phone.

Gil was short, three inches shorter than Johnny. He shaved his head, almost obsessively, and spent much of his time in the gym working out. Stocky and brutish, the crew nicknamed him "Bull." Hailing from North London, he'd been with Johnny's team since the beginning and was one of the first men Johnny brought on when he took the gig with Baldwin.

He climbed out of his SUV and walked over to Johnny's ride seconds before the first police cars showed up. The cops poured into the parking lot, tires squealing and engines revving. Johnny took a deep breath and sighed to keep his stress down. *If Harper had been asleep before, he probably isn't now.*

Not that it mattered. There was nowhere for the suspect to go. The hotel didn't have any back doors to the rooms. And based on what he'd seen, the windows didn't open. Harper might be able to crack the windows by firing his weapon, then break through, but by then it would be too late.

Even so, Johnny knew enough to cover all his bases.

"Head to the back of the building and watch the window for room one-eleven. I'll send three more guys to you when they arrive. Cover that end over there," Johnny said, pointing to the right. He knew from a previous visit to this place that a concrete retaining wall in the back blocked off any potential escape into the hills behind the building, leaving only the pavement that circled back to the parking lot in front. "Meachum's guys will handle the front door."

Gil looked over his shoulder at the cops parking their cars in a semicircle around room 111. He jerked his thumb at them. "You sure about that?"

The cops leaned over their vehicles, pointing their pistols at the door.

"I'll be out here with the rest of our team. I doubt he'll be able to get through their setup here, but just in case, we'll be ready."

Two more SUVs pulled into the lot, followed closely by Meachum bringing up the rear.

"Typical," Johnny muttered. "Always the last one to the party."

Gil nodded with a chuckle. "I'll be around back." He trotted off to the right and disappeared around the corner of the building before Meachum parked his car in the spot next to where Johnny stood.

The sheriff got out of his vehicle and put a wide-brim hat on. He walked over to Johnny and indicated the hotel with a tip of his head. "So, he's in there, huh?"

"Yeah," Johnny said. "Looks that way. Gil and the boys will cover both ends of the building in case this guy tries to go out the window in back. He'll stumble right into a kill box."

Meachum nodded. "Good work. Just make sure your guys don't get in the way."

Johnny felt the temptation to roll his eyes, but he resisted. "I'll make sure," he acquiesced, inspecting the sheriff's group with a careful eye. "These guys are all on the same page, yeah?"

The sheriff knew what Johnny meant. "Yeah. All these guys are with us and Mitchell. Nobody outside of this group will know about this little operation, per the usual. Now," he said, turning his attention to the hotel room, "let's root this animal out." He walked toward the door.

"You're going to do it yourself?" Johnny asked, surprised the sheriff would throw himself into harm's way. Usually, he let other people handle the dirty work unless it was an easy situation.

Meachum glanced back over his shoulder with a stupid grin on his face. "If you think I'm going to let someone else get the credit for bagging this killer, think again."

This time, Johnny did roll his eyes.

Three more of Baldwin's men exited the SUVs close by. The henchmen hurried over to Johnny, who told them to split up. He sent one to join Gil and the other two around to the left side of the building.

Their team had been cut in half, and Johnny had to keep the others back at Baldwin's home. Just in case.

Meachum marched toward the door, motioning for some of his men to surround him as he approached the building. At the entrance, Meachum drew his pistol and held it up high near his shoulder.

While he watched, Johnny couldn't ignore a little voice deep down inside telling him something was wrong.

It was too easy, and he knew it.

A highly decorated Delta Force operator wouldn't be caught asleep by a bunch of county cops. Johnny spun around quickly and rushed to the back of the truck. He flipped open the back door and retrieved a long case, opened it, and removed a sniper rifle. In seconds, Johnny was back at the front of his SUV with the rifle resting on the hood, cradled in his hands. He watched the front door through the scope and waited.

He couldn't believe Meachum was so foolish, thinking he could simply barge through the door and take down the dangerous Harper. From the looks of it, the sheriff didn't even have a plan. He'd just woken up, thrown on his clothes, and rushed over here.

Johnny kept his eyes glued to the door, waiting for Meachum to go in.

When the sheriff was ready, he put his back to the doorframe and rapped on the door three times with the back of his hand.

"Harper? This is the sheriff!" he shouted. "We know you're in there. We have the area surrounded. Come out with your hands up, or we will break down the door. It's up to you."

No response. Johnny wasn't surprised. He assumed the suspect would go down fighting. All he needed was to see the man's face in his scope and the battle would be over before the sound of the rifle report reached the cops' ears.

Sheriff Meachum knocked on the door again. This time harder.

Johnny wondered if Harper was waiting inside to spring a trap. It's what he would do if he were the one inside the room.

Or would he? All of this was too easy. That thought kept cracking like a whip in his head. Something about this was off. Harper had taken out half of Baldwin's security unit like they were Cub Scouts.

Before he could shout out a warning to Meachum, the cop nodded to the two men with the battering ram. The two surged forward, slamming the heavy cylinder into the cheap hotel door, which caved with almost no protest. Meachum and the three others charged into the room with guns extended.

The blast came only a half second after the flash consumed Sheriff Meachum and three cops. Johnny winced at the explosion. Within another two seconds, Johnny knew exactly what happened.

Harper had set a booby trap in the hotel room, and based on the lack of collateral damage to the building, the only answer was some kind of an improvised, shaped charge, or perhaps a homemade claymore mine.

"What was that?" Gil asked, immediately concerned.

Johnny responded without hesitation. "Harper set a trap."

He didn't need a confirmation from Gil to know he was already on his way to the back. Johnny kept his rifle trained on the door as he left his position and moved forward. He kept the weapon steady, and his movements fluid, checking to the left and right of the building in case Harper was perched somewhere in a sniper nest. With Gil and the others on the flanks, Johnny doubted that was the play. Still, better to be careful.

He reached the first victims of the blast and immediately knew the deputy was dead. Several bloody holes littered his body, and he lay still on the pavement. Two more matched that description. Johnny found the sheriff last, his face and body torn apart by shrapnel. From a quick inspection of the carnage, Harper had used ball bearings with the explosive. The cops that survived the blast were still badly wounded.

Johnny lowered his rifle as he approached the door. He dropped the weapon next to one of the injured cops and drew his sidearm as he entered the hotel room. He switched on the flashlight attached to his pistol and pointed the light around inside the hazy bedroom. Nothing but a foggy dust lingering in the air.

Remarkably, the hotel room had remained largely intact. And there was no sign of Harper.

30

A shiver crawled over Dak's skin as he stood outside the fence that wrapped around the quarry. He peered through the chain links to the top of the facility just beyond the edge of the trees.

Dak wondered what was happening twenty minutes away at the hotel where he'd laid his trap. He prayed one of the good guys on the police force hadn't been there, and immediately thought of Officer Mills, whom he'd met in the hospital. Mills had impressed him as a decent kid, and the fact he'd been at the hospital earlier on his shift told Dak that the cop was now probably at home in bed.

He had bet on the fact that Meachum would only use men who were on the take with Baldwin. Dak would have never planned the trap if he suspected Meachum might bring an innocent man in on something like that. It wouldn't make sense to. Someone like Mills, if Dak's read was correct, would protest, and likely wouldn't go along with the plan.

It was a huge risk, but it was one that Dak felt confident enough to take.

With most Baldwin's forces diverted to the hotel, including the cops on his payroll, Dak knew it was his best chance to get a look at what Baldwin was really up to out here.

He made quick work of the fence with some bolt cutters, then crawled through the hole and scrambled to his feet on the other side. He cinched his rucksack tight to his shoulders and marched into the forest.

Dak picked his way through the trees and underbrush. It took him less than five minutes to reach the other side of the forest, where he found a clearing that gave him a clear view of the processing plant.

A dull hum from the facility filled the cool night air. Overhead, clouds rolled in, and thunder clapped in the distance. Dak knew he didn't have much time. The facility didn't work around the clock, so the only people that could interrupt his investigation were the guards working the night shift. He wasn't too concerned about them. Baldwin reserved the best for his personal security detail, though now he was down to half strength with them.

Dak pushed ahead, walking down a little knoll until he heard the sound of running water. Following the trickling sound, he located the stream in short order and followed it toward the processing facility until it turned toward the forest on the other side of the clearing. It was there, at the bend in the creek, that Dak discovered the source of Dawsonville's pollution.

He bent down and studied the pipe spilling chemicals into the water, the fresh air tainted by whatever Baldwin was dumping.

The pungent odor assaulted Dak's nostrils, and he stood up straight again to escape the stench. Peering toward the building, he knew the only way to find out what was really going on was to get inside.

The samples he'd collected at Mike Hamilton's contained heavy metals, often the result of acid drainage at mines. But this wasn't a mine. Not in the traditional sense. While Baldwin's company did mine rock, it was a different process, and as Dak had learned before, prepping stone for construction didn't involve any harmful chemicals or processes.

Whatever was spilling into the stream wasn't natural. That much was certain. And it was definitely more than just dirty water.

Dak turned and looked back toward the town. A dull halo of light hung over it. Somewhere down there was Mike Hamilton's place, and everyone else Baldwin had screwed over, or worse.

How many people had he killed, sickened, or driven away? Dak didn't want to know the answer to that question, but his resolve to make Baldwin answer for it burned within him.

He faced the building again and marched toward it, carving a path through tall grass until he reached a gravel area on the perimeter. The crunchy surface gave way to pavement, and he knew that there were probably security cameras watching from the corners of the towering structures.

Until now, he'd worn the bandanna around his neck, but now that he was on site, he pulled it up and tugged the matching black hat down over his forehead. Even if the security personnel here saw him on the video feeds, they wouldn't be able to identify him. Dak's plan was to get in and out as quickly as he could. Getting caught wasn't an option.

He stopped outside a gray metal building that reminded him of a structure he'd seen in a bizarre movie—*Mosquito Coast*. Detached from the main processing facility, it was the closest in proximity to the stream, and by default made the most sense for him to check first.

At first glance, the building offered nothing out of the ordinary. It looked like most of the other structures on the property but with a few subtle differences. Several conveyor belts above connected other smaller buildings to the main building, where it appeared most of the rock processing occurred.

This structure, however, had none running to it. The four-story metal cube stood alone, and it looked newer than the other buildings on the property. Dak knew it didn't house offices due to the lack of many windows, along with its nondescript nature. Across the way, about a hundred yards from where he stood, Dak saw the building where most of the managers and office people worked.

This has to be it, he thought.

A single door at the corner of the building looked like the only way in, though he figured there had to be one on the opposite side, considering fire safety codes and things of that nature.

Dak lowered his rucksack into his right hand and pressed his back against the wall to approach the door, staying out of view of a security camera positioned just above the doorframe. When he was close enough, he reached out and grabbed the latch. As he expected, the door didn't budge.

"Locked," he muttered.

Looking up to the top of the building, he surveyed the wall for anything that might give him a way in. If he were going to find out what Baldwin was really up to, Dak needed to see what was going on inside that building.

He walked around the corner, down the length of the building, and to the other side, where he found another door. Dak repeated the process, shuffling along the wall until he reached the entrance so the camera wouldn't detect his presence. Just like the one before, this one was locked.

"Nobody's home," he said. "Guess I have to do this the hard way."

Dak had anticipated this. He didn't for a second think he could simply show up at the quarry and walk into any facility he desired. Especially *this* facility. Whatever secret Baldwin was hiding down there, the man would have taken extra precautions to protect it. Although Dak had to admit he was more than a little surprised to see no one guarding the building. If Baldwin were doing something illegal in there, he should have had more guards watching over the place. Two locked doors didn't seem like much, and from what Dak could tell, each one only featured a single deadbolt and a couple security cameras above them. Not the easiest lock for him to get through, but he could do it.

He set down his rucksack and took out a palm-size black leather pouch bound by a strap tied in a knot. The little bag contained a piece of putty composed of a compound that, when ignited, would burn hot enough to melt steel. Just as importantly, it worked quietly.

With the pouch open, Dak pulled out the material and was about to press it into the seam between the door and the frame when a voice interrupted.

"What are you doing over there?" a man snapped. The voice sounded crotchety and irritated, full of decades of broken dreams and beaten by life.

Dak dropped the compound and twisted his head in time to be momentarily blinded by a flashlight. He put up his right hand while shoving his left into the gear bag. He felt the subcompact pistol's box suppressor and ran his fingers down to the grip, wrapping them around it and fitting his trigger finger into place. He didn't draw the weapon, but like a coiled snake he was ready to strike in the blink of an eye.

"Paul, we have a problem down at building five," the old man said.

A flash of lightning illuminated the old security guard's face for half a second. Dak used the moment to draw his pistol and aim it at the old man.

"Lower the flashlight," Dak ordered, using the calmest, most disarming tone he could summon.

"What do you think you're doing?" the guard pressed.

Dak knew in an instant he didn't want to kill this man. His swept-over hair was so gray it was nearly white. The man stood a few inches shorter than Dak, and several pounds heavier, with a belly hanging down just slightly over his uniform's belt.

"Look," Dak said, "I don't want to shoot you. Okay? But I need to get into this building."

The older man frowned, his bushy white eyebrows tightening beneath his wrinkled forehead. A dim orange light hanging from the top of the building made his face look like a strange ghost caught between the land of the dead and the land of the living.

"I don't want you to shoot me, either." His eyes drifted to the right, to the camera over the door. "But they're watching, and if I let you in there, I'll lose my job. My wife had health problems, and I'm not qualified to do anything else. So, why don't you put down the gun, son, and walk away. I'll tell them you were too fast for me."

Dak breathed evenly, keeping the gun trained on the older man while he considered the issue. The guard could have been lying. Dak couldn't rule out that possibility. For all he knew, the older guy could be trouble. Unfortunately, Dak didn't have time to try to hash out whether the old man could be trusted or not. His finger tensed on the trigger, and Dak lined up the sights with his target.

With an exhale, and a flash of lightning, he squeezed.

31

The pistol's report sounded like a loud click, barely audible to the guard who stood a scant twenty feet away. His head snapped to the side in time to see the security camera above the door explode into a tangled mess of wires, plastic, and circuits. Dak held the weapon out at arm's length, a thin trail of smoke drifting out of the barrel. A gust of wind blew the smoke away in an instant.

Dak directed his attention to the keys on the guard's belt. "You think I could borrow those keys for a second?"

The guard didn't say anything for a second. "I just called for backup. They're going to be here any minute."

"I'm aware," Dak replied. "Please. Open the door. I am trying to help the people of this town. I need to know what Baldwin is doing in there."

"They make gravel here. It's not that interesting. And there's nothin' valuable in there, unless you're looking to steal some gravel machinery." The older man huffed. "And it's all pretty heavy or bolted down."

"I'm not here to steal anything," Dak said. "Like I said, I'm trying to help the town. Baldwin has been dumping pollutants into the water. I saw it down at the stream over there." He pointed in the general direction of the spring he found earlier. "People have been dying. I'm sure a lot of others have been sick."

"Pollutants?" The guard sounded genuinely confused. "My wife got sick a while back." His face darkened in the orange din.

He pressed the button on his radio and twisted his head to speak. "Cancel that," he said. "Trespasser ran off. I think he headed back toward the main gate."

Dak felt a twinge of surprise ripple through his body.

"They're heading to the front. That should buy you some time," the guard said, pointing to an earpiece with a wire dangling from it that connected to the radio on his shoulder.

The guard walked toward the door, his left hand reaching and plucking the keys from his belt.

He spoke with a distant sadness as he inserted the key into the door and unlocked it. "None of the doctors could figure out what it was. By the time they figured out it was heavy metal poisoning, it was too late. She died within hours of learning the cause. I never could figure out how it happened, or why it wasn't me that went. I got sick, too, but never felt as bad as her. After she was gone, I couldn't stay in our home any longer. I sold our house and everything we owned except pictures and a few things that meant something to us both. I wanted to leave Dawsonville, but there were too many memories."

"Memories can be a two-way street."

He hummed a chuckle. "Yeah. You got that right, kid."

Dak appreciated the sentiment of being called kid, despite the fact he was far from it. "What's in this building?"

"Like I said," the guard replied, "stuff for making gravel, concrete, all that. I assume."

"Assume?"

"Never been in this one. We were told not to worry about checking inside unless there was an emergency. They told us there's nothing but machines in there."

"But you've never seen them?" Dak clarified.

The guard shook his head. "Nope. I do as I'm told around here, for the most part. But if you think there's something in there that's making people sick, and that might have hurt my wife, then I want to know what it is too."

Dak could only imagine the man's pain, losing his wife to a mysterious illness. He'd lost a few of his military brothers in combat while in the Middle East, and some family members to natural causes, but nothing like what this man described.

The guard pulled open the door and held it for Dak. "After you."

"Thanks," Dak said. "What's your name?"

"Bob. You?"

Dak removed his mask. "Dak. Nice to meet you, Bob."

"You too." Bob's eyes wandered down to the pistol in Dak's hand. "You're pretty good with that thing."

"I've had a little practice."

"Heh. I don't think I want to know what you mean by that."

"Probably not," Dak agreed as he walked into the dimly lit building. Bob followed him inside and pulled the door shut. Dak looked over his shoulder at the man, surprised he was joining him for the tour. "You not staying outside?"

"Nope," Bob answered. "I want to see this for myself. Maybe it's part of getting that closure all my friends keep talking about."

Dak couldn't argue with that, and he wasn't about to tell the man what to do. Especially since he'd earned the right to see what was really going on here.

The two men looked around the room. The place reminded Dak of a glorified boiler room, with pipes everywhere, a metal staircase to his right, and big machines he'd never seen before. A massive cylinder to the left with a gauge on it sat against the wall. On the far end of the room, several steel drums occupied a space along the opposite side of the building.

"What's in the barrels?" Dak wondered out loud.

"That a rhetorical question?"

Dak walked across the room to the hum of machines. He stopped at the steel drums and inspected the sides. With a scowl, Dak kicked the side of one with the tip of his boot. It rang hollow, the sound echoing through the room.

"Doesn't look like anything out of the ordinary," Bob said. "Although I don't think I've seen those kinds of barrels in the other buildings."

"If there's anything in here, it'll be downstairs in the basement."

"You think so?'

"I guess there's only one way to find out." Dak glanced over at the wall to his right and indicated the huge sliding bay door. If Baldwin were bringing in something illicit, the workers would use that entrance to carry the goods in. A service lift to the left of the door allowed easy transport of the cargo down to the lower level. He knew it could just be more rock that the company brought in, but that didn't explain why there were no conveyor belts running to the building.

The two men made their way over to the stairs and began their descent. They rounded the corner at the first landing, then continued down until they reached the lowest level.

They stood at the bottom for several seconds, surveying the space with wide eyes. "I have no idea what this is," Bob said in a mesmerized voice.

The vast basement stretched hundreds of feet in every direction, taking up twice as much space as the floor above. A foul odor permeated the underground area, assaulting the men's senses as they scanned their surroundings.

No workers toiled in the basement, which Dak found surprising. Baldwin struck him as the kind of guy who would force his laborers to work long hours with few breaks, even on a weekend night like this.

Dak spotted several huge steel bins off to his left, close to a machine stuffed with pipes, gauges, valves, wheels, and all sorts of mechanical components. He stopped at the first bin and looked into it.

Bob joined him and stared into the pile of rubble. In the pale fluorescent glow of the overhead lights, the chunks in the bins radiated with a dull seafoam green, mixed with rusty reds.

"Now, why on earth would he have this here?" Bob wondered out loud.

Dak turned, searching the older man's face for an explanation. "What do you mean? What is it?"

Bob's shoulders rolled. "Looks like copper ore," he said. "I'm no geologist, but I've had a few friends who were miners. Showed me a few chunks now and then. Nothing special. Not like it was gold or anything."

"Copper? What is Baldwin doing with copper ore here in a quarry?"

"Your guess is as good as mine, son. But if I had to guess, it looks like my boss isn't only in the rock business."

Dak frowned at the lack of answers. He continued walking down the line of wheeled bins until he reached the end of the machine. He stopped at another row of steel drums and inspected the top, where a faded white label stuck to the lid. Dak read the black lettering, and the answers smacked him in the face like a wrecking ball.

"These are the chemicals he's using to process the ore," Dak said. He took out his phone and snapped several pictures, then walked quickly back down to the bins and took photos of the ore. He switched the mode to video and filmed sweeping views of the vast basement so anyone who saw it would have context. Then he stuffed the phone back into his pocket.

With his visual evidence collected, he reached into the nearest bin and pulled out a small chunk of ore, about the size of his fist, then unzipped his rucksack and placed it inside, carefully wedging it into the bottom.

"What are you going to do with that?" Bob asked, watching Dak with curiosity.

"Evidence," Dak said.

Bob looked back into the bin, picked out a smaller piece, and stuffed it in his pocket.

Dak asked the question first with his eyes, then said, "What are you doing?"

"Evidence," Bob replied. "Just in case."

Dak smiled at the man and gave a nod. "We best be getting out of here. Your guys are only going to hunt for me for so long."

Bob looked at the trespasser, searching his emerald eyes for motives, answers, and the future. "What will you do?"

"I think it's time I pay our friend Mr. Baldwin a little visit."

The security guard let out a pfft. "Good luck with that. He has a small army of guards at that mansion of his."

"Haven't you heard?" Dak asked with a mischievous smirk. "Half of his men are gone. Now it's time to take out the rest of the trash."

32

Dak knew his play would spark a desperate move from Baldwin. Which meant time wasn't on his side.

The second he left the quarry, he made his way to the outskirts of town. Rain pummeled the car with heavy drops. He continued driving until he found a pullout on the side of the road. He steered the car onto the gravel path between tall stands of green and golden grass and killed the lights.

Dak took out his phone and began sending the photo and video evidence to his friend Will. Then he sent it to the *Charlotte Times*, then to four other national media outlets with the subject of the email reading, The Contamination of a Town.

Will would make certain the mainstream media got hold of the story. While Dak didn't always trust the news, he knew they salivated over stuff like this, and that fire would only rage higher once social media threw fuel on it.

Once he was done sending out the evidence against Baldwin's illicit activities, he pulled back out onto the road and drove toward Hattie Markham's place.

The deluge continued as he guided the car down the road. Lightning flashed intermittently in the churning sky overhead. A spectacular bolt seared the air off to the west.

The thunder rolled in the distance, cracking and booming like sounds of nature's warfare. He'd always loved watching thunderstorms back in Tennessee, though in recent years there'd been more tornadoes than he remembered as a child. Those were the kinds of storms he didn't enjoy, the ones with so much uncertainty. Then again, unknown variables were built into weather. Much of his life was an unknown variable.

He continued driving until he reached the turnoff into Hattie's property. He slowed down and looked around, wary that Baldwin might have someone watching the place, even in this raging downpour. He was the kind of guy who viewed the people who worked for him as expendable, unimportant, pawns in his game.

Miserable working conditions for those serving him didn't matter to Baldwin. He wanted results, and in this case, he also wanted Hattie's land. Now Dak wondered if a huge rock deposit was the only thing driving his obsession with the Markham property. Based on what he'd seen at the quarry, he started to think that maybe there was more to that land than just a huge rock deposit.

He guided the car along the gravel driveway and then pulled off into a clearing where several tall bushes blocked his view of the main road. Dak turned the car around to face the driveway, then killed the engine and lights.

He'd passed no other cars on his way to Hattie's place, so no one had seen his vehicle or him. Not that anyone would remember the midsize, nondescript black sedan.

Dak leaned his head back against the headrest and allowed his eyes to close. He didn't want to sleep, but he needed it.

The fatigue of a long day melted his body into the seat. He felt himself being dragged into the dreamy underworld of slumber with every passing second. Adrenaline had kept him going for the last few hours, but the human body could only run like that for so long.

His reason for parking here on Hattie's property was simple. The brazen note Dak left in the bin back at Baldwin's facility would create a panic with the man. He would act swiftly, perhaps irrationally. He'd scour the area for Dak, as he had been for the last few days. But Dak figured the last place the tycoon would look was Hattie Markham's farm. On top of that, if someone decided to pay her a late-night visit, he would be there.

The minutes ticked by, and Dak found himself in a dream world, where monsters looked like men and women, each wreaking havoc on millions of people. The monsters stood like giants over the writhing throngs, as if ruling over them with the threat of pain and punishment.

Dak awoke and looked around, thinking he'd only been asleep for a few seconds. But as he cracked his eyes, he realized daylight pushed against the darkness in the sky overhead. He checked his watch and noted the time.

He'd been asleep for five hours.

With a deep breath, Dak reached out his hand and turned the key in the ignition. The engine revved to life, and he rubbed his eyes as the vehicle warmed up. Then he rolled down the window to let out the stuffy air and clear the fogged windows.

"Guess I was more tired than I thought," he muttered to himself. Usually a light sleeper, Dak didn't sleep deeply that often. It was, as he'd thought many times, a blessing and a curse.

He'd always been easily awakened in the night, by almost any sound or unusual light passing by. Adjusting to military life had been easy for him in that regard. Having to always be ready at a moment's notice was more of a natural thing than a learned habit. Dak wasn't sure why that was the case, but he'd always just dealt with it.

He climbed out of his car and walked over to the trunk, popped it open, and inspected the interior. Two black bags—one long, one shorter—sat neatly next to each other. He opened the longer one first and pulled out a sniper rifle. After running a quick once-over on the weapon, he put it back in the bag and opened the smaller case. Two black pistols lay inside, along with a few gadgets, spare magazines, and two leather pouches containing small amounts of explosives.

His favorite tool, a small drone, sat in the bag next to the pistols.

He'd become a fan of the miniature aircraft after making of use of one in Kentucky a few years before, and Dak realized he wanted to always have one on hand for reconnaissance. With a few minor tweaks, he'd been able to weaponize the drone, adding flash-bang discs and a single crossbow-style projectile system with a tiny tranquilizer dart attached. The dart was no longer than a golf tee, with a needle only a centimeter long. The mixture within the dart, however, was strong enough to knock out a Clydesdale.

After checking his gear, Dak closed the trunk and walked around to the driver's side front door. He looked up to the top of the hill, thinking of the strong woman who lived just on the other side of the ridge.

Hattie Markham was a survivor. She'd managed to stave off Baldwin and his goons for a few years all on her own. In a distant sort of way, Dak almost wished the tycoon would show up here again and try something. The thought of Hattie taking shots at a terrified Baldwin amused him, probably more than it should have.

He climbed back into the seat and closed the door, a single thought taking the place of his previous ones about Hattie. His battle senses took over, and Dak focused on the mission at hand.

Now, when Baldwin and his group were in disarray, was the time to strike.

33

Johnny nearly burst into Baldwin's study like a bull barging through the doors. He found his boss sitting at the oak desk, staring at his computer screen with a pair of reading glasses perched on his nose.

The billionaire was already dressed in an expensive black suit with a red tie tightly knotted below his neck. A white porcelain cup containing coffee sat next to the keyboard. Baldwin absently reached over and picked it up, took a sip, and set it down as Johnny strode across the room to the desk.

"Sir?" Johnny said, interrupting the man's drink.

"I know," Baldwin said.

A look of befuddlement splashed across Johnny's face. "I'm sorry?"

"I know," the boss repeated. When Johnny only responded by staring dumbfounded at him, he added, "You're going to tell me about the attack at the hotel. Right?"

"No, sir. I figured you already knew about that. Everyone knows. There are even reporters coming in from Charlotte and Knoxville to cover the story. They're calling it a domestic terror attack."

"Yes. The late Sheriff Meachum and his men will be called heroes. A minor setback in the grand scheme. Our friend the sheriff had been sloppy lately. I think he was getting complacent. There is an upside, though. Now every cop and fed within two hundred miles is going to be looking for the killer. Not to mention the nationwide manhunt. This Harper can only hide for so long now."

Baldwin's brow furrowed as he realized Johnny looked anxious. Then it struck him that his head of security had said the issue with the explosion wasn't why he was here. "What else happened?" Concern reddened his face.

"Someone broke into the facility, sir. Security reported a trespasser last night, but they weren't able to find the person. One of the surveillance cameras was destroyed. Looks like whoever snuck in shot it at fairly close range. We have a group sweeping the area."

"Not your men, I hope," Baldwin said. A thread of fear tainted his words.

"No, sir. What's left of the police, and a team that handles the quarry."

"Good. Are all of your men here now?"

"Yes, sir. What's left of them."

Baldwin caught the ire in Johnny's voice. There was no sadness there, more like a bitter resentment, and the boss couldn't tell if it was toward him or just in general. "What did they do, this trespasser? Did they get into the building?"

Johnny sighed, reluctant to share the last bit of information with his employer.

"Spit it out, son. Did they get in? Did they find anything?"

Johnny's head bobbed. "Yes, sir. They left a note in one of the ore bins." He produced the paper and set it on Baldwin's desk.

The note read, "I know what you did."

Baldwin stood and cracked his neck to both sides. Grim determination tightened across his face. He planted his fists on the desk as if he might shove it all the way to the earth's core.

His lips trembled as he spoke. "Where is he now?"

Johnny blinked as though a gentle breeze tickled his eyes, unafraid of the wrath he might face. "We don't know, sir. But I believe he may try to get to you."

"You think?" Baldwin roared. He swung his right arm and knocked the keyboard off the table. "Of course he's coming to get me, you nitwit!"

Johnny remained ever calm. "I recommend you evacuate the mansion, sir. I'll escort you to your boat on the lake. We'll put as many men on board as you want. You'll be safe there until we handle this situation. I have some contacts I can reach out to for reinforcements."

"Reinforcements?" Baldwin sounded like the word was comical. "You mean like the men this Harper has already killed? The men that you vetted and brought in?"

"We already have a plan, sir," Johnny continued, ignoring the barb. "All you have to do is get on the boat. We'll handle the rest."

"Maybe you're forgetting who's in charge here, Johnny. I'm not going to run from this nutjob serial killer." He breathed hard through flaring nostrils; his eyes locked on Johnny's.

"I wouldn't think of it, sir," Johnny said, with more than just a touch of vitriol. "What would you like us to do?"

Baldwin drew in a long breath as he straightened. He put his hands behind his lower back and walked over to the window the same way Johnny had seen him do many times before. The head of security suppressed his urge to draw his pistol and shoot Baldwin in the head for talking to him like a child. Baldwin had been good to him, especially from a financial viewpoint.

But that came with a price.

Johnny was always at Baldwin's beck and call. He served his boss more like the guy was his master, and he the lapdog. He tolerated being talked down to on occasion, but it never sat well with Johnny. Tonight's display only deepened the rift between the two, though Johnny doubted Baldwin even had the slightest inkling anything might be wrong.

Baldwin stopped at the window and looked outside. The sun's rays beamed onto the hillside to the west.

"Glorious, isn't it?" Baldwin asked. "I remember when my father bought this land, Johnny," his tone shifting from raging to nostalgic. "Back then, he didn't have much money. We were just getting the business going, but he knew he could do it. My father knew he could build something bigger, a business that would thrive and put us on the map as one of the power-player families on the Eastern Seaboard. People stood in his way, of course. My old man never let that get to him. He powered through every roadblock like a tank...and forged the Baldwin empire."

Johnny nodded. He'd heard the story before and wasn't sure why Baldwin was telling it to him again. He didn't care for meandering drives down memory lane. Especially when they weren't his memories. Unfortunately, he had to play along. For now.

"Sir," Johnny insisted, "we need to either get you to a safe location or prepare a plan to catch this guy. You can bet everything you own that he's coming here, if not next, then soon."

The boss shook his head defiantly. "I never had any children of my own," Baldwin said. "After my wife left me, I had no intentions of ever walking down that road again." He chuckled once. "Especially when you consider how much money she took off me in the divorce. But that was my chance to have children. I suppose it wasn't in the cards."

Baldwin turned his head to face the head of security. "That's why I'm going to leave everything to you, Johnny. When I die, you will inherit this empire my father built. You've been by my side through most of it. But there is one thing you must never do. Don't ever run from a fight. Someday, when you're in my shoes, I don't want you to tuck tail and run to a boat in the middle of the lake because you're afraid someone might get to you. You will have to be stronger than that, and frankly, I'm surprised to hear you sound worried."

Baldwin turned and faced the bodyguard. The look on Johnny's face wasn't the surprise Baldwin expected to see. He thought the younger man might at least show some form of appreciation. He'd just been told that he was going to inherit a billion-dollar company, and all the guard could muster was a blank stare, not that the boss should have been surprised. He always remained cool, emotionless, stoic.

"You're serious?" Johnny asked in a bland voice.

"Of course. You know me as well as anyone. I rarely joke around. You are going to be the next leader of the Baldwin Corporation. I know you're not a Baldwin, but there's nothing in the rules that says you have to be. I've already taken care of everything with my attorneys. It's official and finalized."

Johnny hid his shock behind vapid eyes. "I'm honored, sir," he said.

"Now, before we put together our plan to eliminate this murderer, we must have a toast."

Baldwin walked over to the bar in the corner and pried the lid off a $6,000 bottle of bourbon. He poured two glasses then returned to the front of the desk where Johnny stood. He handed one of the tumblers to the guard and raised his own in toast. "To the future of Baldwin," he said. "May you, and the company, always prosper."

"Thank you, sir," Johnny said, raising his glass. The tumblers clinked, and Baldwin eagerly drew the whiskey to his lips.

He dumped the bourbon into his mouth and swallowed, finishing with a satisfied "ah."

A loud click echoed through the room and dissipated into the walls. Baldwin teetered for a second and then toppled over. The glass in his hand smashed against the hard floor next to the rug, a fresh bullet hole in his right temple.

Johnny immediately lowered the pistol back to his side, removed the suppressor, and stuffed the pistol into the Baldwin's right hand.

"Thanks for the drink, Mitchell," he said as he raised the glass again. "And the job."

He continued staring at the body with dark amusement. "And the empire."

Johnny drank the whiskey in a single gulp. He blew air out of his mouth, looked at the glass, and shook his head. "I gotta be honest. I thought six-thousand-dollar bourbon would be a little smoother than that, Mitch. Although I'm more of a tequila guy myself."

He tossed the glass onto the floor, shattering it with the other one, then looked back toward the door. "If this Harper wants to play, I have a little game for him."

34

Dak arrived at the Baldwin mansion after a short ten-minute drive.

The sun had just peeked over the horizon to the east. Dak had no plan to sneak in through a chain-link fence or try some sneak attack. Maybe he should have, but sometimes he preferred the direct approach.

He turned off the road and onto Baldwin's driveway, stopping between two guardhouses. Behind the buildings, dense forest stretched in either direction. Dak saw Baldwin's mansion at the other end of the long, straight asphalt drive.

With the note Dak left him, Baldwin would be watching for him —if he hadn't tucked tail and run. Dak had considered that possibility, but if the man were still around, he'd be here, probably waiting somewhere in the house—whether it be his study or a panic room.

Dak felt that, if the man were smart, he'd have gone with the latter option.

Dak watched a huge beast of a man exit the guard shack. His shaved head and dark sunglasses made him look like a bouncer at a night club or perhaps a heavyweight prize fighter.

Rolling down the rental car's window, Dak grinned stupidly at the guard as the man approached. The second the guard recognized Dak, his eyes widened and he reached for the pistol on his hip. Dak already had his in hand, keeping it concealed on his lap. He raised the weapon and aimed it at the guard.

"I wouldn't do that if I were you," Dak cautioned.

The guard froze with his hand hovering over the butt of his weapon.

"Open the gate," Dak ordered.

"I can't do that. I have orders to kill you on sight." The guard's chilling response did nothing to deter Dak.

"Yes, I'm sure you do. Here's the thing: Baldwin has hurt a lot of people, killed some too. I'll never know how many. Maybe you did some of his dirty work for him. If you did, this is your chance at redemption. You let me in, I let you live. You can go on about your life, find another job somewhere, do the whole wife-and-kids-with-a-dog thing."

The guard blinked as he weighed his options. Dak could see in the man's dark brown eyes that he still appeared uncertain.

"Don't be stupid," Dak urged. "Open the gate."

The guard nodded slowly. "If I open the gate, you'll let me go?"

"Free as a bird."

"If Baldwin finds out, he'll kill me."

"He kills his own guards?" Dak asked. He already figured he knew the answer, but he wanted the man to confirm the doubts in his mind regarding his allegiance to Baldwin.

"Sometimes. When mistakes are made." The guard didn't sound regretful, but there was a pensiveness to his voice.

"You won't have to worry about that anymore. A big, strong guy like you can find work with any number of wealthy people. Maybe a celebrity."

The guard nodded. He lowered his hand and turned back toward the guardhouse. Dak watched him closely, never taking his pistol sight off the guy.

"Oh," Dak stopped him. "If you call for backup, instead of opening the gate, you die first. Okay?"

The man looked back over his shoulder, biting his lip. Dak visibly relaxed, allowing his pistol to drop slightly—a test to see what the guard would do.

As Dak suspected, the man failed. The second the guard saw Dak lower his weapon, the man spun around, grabbing for his own pistol. He drew the sidearm and twisted.

With a sigh, Dak raised the gun and fired three suppressed shots into the guard's chest. The man stumbled backward against the guard shack, stood there for a second with his back against the outer wall, and then slid to the ground as his bullet-riddled heart gave out.

Dak opened the car door and hurried over to the body. The man's eyes glazed over, staring blankly at the vehicle. Dak shook his head. "That was stupid."

He went around the corner, through the open door into the shack, and searched a small gray panel for the button that opened the gate. With only four buttons and a switch—all identified with stickers underneath—he located the one he needed and pressed it.

The black iron gate began slowly opening inward from both sides.

With the blockade out of the way, Dak trotted back to his car and accelerated through to the other side.

Straight ahead, Baldwin's palatial home gleamed in the early morning light, framed by the dense forest lining the driveway.

Going in through the front door was risky, but it was also the move Baldwin wouldn't expect. The billionaire would have taken every precaution, and probably had been expecting a sneak attack in the night.

Dak clenched his teeth at the thought of phase two of his plan. It was probably going to hurt a little, at least more than it would have when he was a younger man. Still, it was the best way to draw out the rest of the guards.

He slowed down as he neared the end of the forest line and squeezed the steering wheel. His eyes set on a huge fountain in front of the house. A sculpture of an angel stood in the center, pouring water out of a jug.

He put the car in park, calmly walked around to the trunk, and removed the two bags holding the rest of his arsenal. Then he set the bags down on a narrow strip of grass along the left side of the driveway and climbed back in the car.

Dak put the vehicle in reverse and backed up about one hundred feet.

"There's no way this works," he told himself. "Too many variables."

"Eh, screw it." He took a deep breath, lined the car up with the fountain, and stepped on the gas.

He accelerated to 25 miles per hour and maintained the line. He saw his gear on the side of the drive approaching quickly, switched on the cruise control, and at the last second opened the door and threw himself out. He tucked his arms into his torso a split second before he hit the ground. His shoulder struck the ground first, surprised at how soft it felt. It wasn't like jumping onto a mattress.

He rolled expertly to a stop and instantly bounced up to one knee to watch the car glide toward the fountain. Only content to watch for a second, Dak scrambled to his feet and sprinted the last several yards to where his gear waited in the grass.

He'd already unzipped both bags and went for the sniper rifle first.

Unfolding the bipod, he set up the weapon in seconds and got down on his belly with his eye on the scope, watching as the rental car barreled toward the fountain. If the alignment had been off, the vehicle would have careened off to one side, perhaps even into one of the mansion's corners.

Two seconds before the car reached its destination, Dak muttered, "Insurance company isn't going to like this."

The rental smashed into the circular fountain with a loud crash. Steam spilled out of the crumpled hood, sending out a smoke signal to any and all of Baldwin's men who would answer the emergency.

Just as Dak suspected, guards clad in black T-shirts and matching cargo pants began pouring out of the mansion with weapons drawn. He could have picked them off one at a time, but he needed as many of Baldwin's guards in view as he could get. Take out one, and the rest would hole up inside the building. But if he waited, he could get more for his money...or ammo, as it were.

Forcing himself to be patient wasn't an issue. Dak could wait all day if he needed to, but he knew that wouldn't be the case.

As expected, Baldwin threw everything at what he assumed was the attack. His guards circled the wreckage by the fountain, all with guns drawn. The seven armed men closed in around the mangled car, ready to take out the intruder.

Dak kept his finger tense on the trigger and lined up his first target—a guard with dark brown hair and a deep tan. The guard approached the driver's door with his pistol extended. When he was close enough to peer inside, Dak could see the man's confused expression in detail through the scope. He could even read the guard's lips as the man said, "It's empty."

Dak squeezed the trigger, and a pink mist blew out the back of the man's head. In an instant, Dak turned to the next target, fired, and moved to the third.

The suppressor on the end of the rifle kept the report to a dull pop, inaudible to the men around the wrecked car. The third of their ranks fell with another twitch of Dak's finger, and he turned to the fourth.

The remaining four guards in the welcoming party descended into panic. They spun around, desperate to find the sniper—all suddenly aware of how exposed they were out in the open in front of the mansion.

The fourth fell with a round to the ribcage as he tried to take cover behind the car. Dak targeted the other two on the far side of the vehicle, picking off one more before the last of those targets managed to slide behind the back right wheel.

He'd deal with that guy in a second.

One of the guards on the near side of the car tried to retreat to the house, running in a straight line toward the steps. Dak fired, drilling a hole through the man's spine, dropping him in midstride. The guard stumbled forward, smacking his face against the stone step at the bottom just before he died.

Dak returned his attention to the panicked man hiding behind the rental car. His body remained out of view, but Dak found a leg sticking out from behind the wheel. He adjusted his aim, lined up the crosshairs with the foot, and fired.

The guard's black boot exploded. The man leaned forward, then rolled over, grasping at the grotesque wound. The second his head came into view, Dak finished the job, sending a bullet through the back of his skull.

With the initial wave eliminated, Dak set the rifle back in its bag. He took out a pistol from the rucksack, then looped the bag over his shoulder. Carrying the rifle bag in his left hand and a handgun in his right, he charged toward the fountain.

Once in the clearing, Dak swept to his left and right, searching the fields on both sides and the lawns on either side of the steps. Satisfied the area was clear, he pushed ahead, up the steps to the massive oak doors.

He stopped and waited under the portico. A security camera overhead in the corner watched him. Dak didn't care about that. Whoever was left in the building knew he was there. The thought of Baldwin cowering in fear somewhere within the mansion gave Dak a warm, tingly feeling.

He took a breath to calm the adrenaline, then reached out and pulled the door open.

35

Dak stepped inside after checking the right side of the foyer, then the left, looking down the pistol's barrel. Two sets of marble stairs twisted up to the second floor on the right and left. Sculptures stood on the inner side of each railing at the base of the steps, each shaped in the same classical design as the great sculptors used in Ancient Greece. Dak wondered if they were from that era, and how Baldwin had acquired them.

He quickly dispelled the thought and surveyed the space. Dak had no idea where Baldwin might be, but the billionaire wasn't his only concern. Dak also needed to find Heather Markham. That meant he needed to check the basement first, if what he'd been told was true.

The stairs leading down to the lower floor started between the two staircases going up to the second floor. He trotted across the shiny marble floor, leaving the expensive rug, careful not to let his boots make too much noise.

He descended the stairs with caution but moved quickly. The clock in the back of his head continually warned Dak that time was running out, even though Heather had been missing for several days now.

Dak passed portraits on the wall that featured Mitchell Baldwin and what Dak assumed to be the man's father. The elder Baldwin sported a thick mustache and wore a suit that appeared to be from the 1960s.

At the landing between floors, Dak spun around the corner, pointing his weapon down to the bottom.

No sign of any guards.

Despite having eliminated most of what he believed to be Baldwin's security team, Dak took nothing for granted and knew the man could have easily brought in reinforcements.

Dak descended the last flight of stairs to the basement level and twisted from right to left, checking the corridor in both directions.

Two open doors to his right and one at the end of the hallway told him there was no one in that direction. So, he focused his attention on the door at the end of the corridor to his left. It was cracked open, almost as if inviting him to enter. Dak moved down the hall, passing two more open doors on either side. He stopped, peeked through the crack, and then nudged the white door open.

It swung easily and revealed a room that looked more like a fully furnished apartment than a basement. Dak didn't pay much attention to the bed, the couch, the fireplace, the kitchenette in the corner. His focus squared firmly on the bald-headed man with a pistol held to the temple of Heather Markham.

"Let her go," Dak ordered.

The thickly muscled guard shook his head. "Drop the gun."

"Then go ahead and kill her," Dak said, lining up his sights with the man's forehead. "You die next. I hope it's worth it."

"You're bluffing. And not very well." The man's deep, rumbling voice sounded like distant thunder.

"Am I? I don't know her from Adam. I'm here for the pistols. That's it." Dak put on his best stone face, hoping the man would buy it.

"You can't fool me, Harper."

Hearing his real last name shocked Dak, but only produced a few confused blinks.

"Oh, a stalker? You a fan?"

The bald man grinned, as if amused. "Nope. I just want to see you beg for mercy. Or dead. I don't care either way."

If the man using Dak's name didn't catch him off guard, the name of his former CO certainly did. A chill ran across Dak's skin, causing the hairs on his arms to stand up.

"So, you obviously have a twisted sense of entertainment. How much he paying you?" Dak tried to keep his cool, pretending that the name hadn't affected him. Meanwhile, he waited for the gunman to make a mistake. If this guy were a bounty hunter, though, he'd be careful, and Dak knew those types weren't given to making many mistakes. They were professional killers for a reason, and the ones that had been in the game for a while survived because they weren't stupid.

The gunman shrugged. "A few million."

He said it as if it were a pittance.

"A few million, huh? I have to admit, I'd probably do it too."

Heather tried to struggle amid the conversation, but the hulking man holding her against his chest wouldn't budge. On top of that, she was too afraid to do much out of concern for the gun going off, even by accident.

Dak saw the fear in her eyes. He didn't blame her. He'd be afraid too if he were in her shoes. "If this is between you and me," Dak said, "then let her go. You can take me to Baldwin if you want. Just let Heather go. She has nothing to do with this."

The man narrowed his eyelids. He glowered at Dak with suspicion, as if considering the request. "Tell me what you know about those pistols," the man said.

The shift in subjects surprised Dak, but he didn't miss a step. "Rare antiques, made by Samuel Colt himself. He gave them to Abraham Lincoln's secretary of something. They belong in a museum in Pennsylvania. I'm here to collect them."

"And these pistols are worth, what, you think?"

Dak relaxed slightly and allowed the gunman to see it. "I don't know. They're priceless artifacts. Last I heard, around a mil." He embellished the price, but it didn't matter. Dak had no intention of letting this guy have the pistols, or harm Heather Markham.

He watched as the gunman thought about it, weighing his options.

"No," the man said. "You're still worth more, but there's no reason I can't have both."

"That's true," Dak said, "but you won't make it out of here alive."

"I think you overestimate yourself."

The sound of a helicopter's rotors thumped in the distance. Dak used it to his advantage. "Right now, my guys are surrounding this place, including air support. You hear that? The cavalry is already here. There's no amount of money worth dying for. Let the girl go. And I let you walk out of here, no questions asked."

"I can't do that," the man said. A tremor of fear tickled his voice for the first time, and Dak knew he had him.

"Sure you can," Dak urged. "You have a choice. You can walk out of here, and never look back. No amount of money is worth dying for."

The helicopter drew closer, reemphasizing the looming threat outside.

The gunman flinched, twitching his head to the side for a fraction of a second. It was the window Dak had been waiting for.

He squeezed the trigger, and the bullet tore through the man's forehead and out the back of his skull.

Heather screamed and involuntarily jerked free of the man's now-limp hold on her. His finger twitched, and the gun fired as he fell to the ground. The round missed her by a foot, cracking through the air behind her head and drilling into the wall to her left.

Dak rushed over to the gunman and immediately kicked the gun away from his hand. Even though he'd just taken a bullet to the head, Dak wasn't going to take any chances.

Once the weapon was away from the body, he put his arm around Heather, who stood there shaking with her hands over her mouth.

"It's okay, Heather. Everything is going to be okay. He can't hurt you now."

She couldn't take her eyes off the dead man in the floor. She stood there staring at him, appalled, angry, terrified, and generally in shock.

"You...you just killed him," she stammered.

"I didn't have a choice."

"He...could have killed me."

"I wasn't going to let that happen." Dak wasn't about to tell her how risky his play had been, that the gunman could have easily killed her by accident the second Dak fired. "We need to get you out of here," Dak insisted. "I don't know how many more of them are here."

She nodded. Tears formed in her eyes, and Dak squeezed her harder.

"It's going to be okay, Heather. We need to get you somewhere safe. Come with me."

He pulled her toward the door and stopped when he reached the threshold. She waited as he checked out the hallway, making sure the coast was clear, then stepped out.

"Is there a garage or something here with Baldwin's cars?" he asked, hopeful.

"I don't know," she said, shaking her head. "I haven't seen the rest of the property. Only the basement. They brought me here after drugging me. I assumed it was Baldwin's mansion, but I had no way of knowing for certain."

"That's okay," Dak said. He looked at the doors along the corridor and surmised one of them must lead to a garage. "Follow me. Stay right behind me in case we encounter any other guards."

She bobbed her head once. Then she furrowed her brow. "What about your reinforcements? The helicopter?"

He smirked. "Oh, that? That was a lie. He was right. I was bluffing. I'm the only one here. So, I suggest we get moving."

Dak stalked down the corridor, checking the first two rooms on his right and left, but didn't find the garage. They continued beyond the stairs to the next two doors. A pair of double doors on the left led out into the pool area. One on the right housed an office, which turned out to be full of security camera monitors, computers, and other tech the guards used to protect Baldwin and his home.

The two kept moving until they reached the end of the hall, where it made a sharp left. Dak hadn't seen the turn when he arrived at the bottom of the stairs and followed the corridor around until they discovered another door. He took the handle and pulled it as quietly as he could, then opened the door. Thankfully, it didn't make a sound.

On the other side, an enormous garage housed six expensive vehicles. One SUV, four sedans, and one two-seater.

"At least Baldwin has good taste in cars," Dak said, noting the keys hanging over the garage door opener to his left.

He grabbed the key with a Maserati keychain attached. Then he pointed at the gray sedan at the end of the row closest to them. "Here," he said, pushing the button to open the garage. "Take the Mazer. Get out of here as fast as you can. There shouldn't be any police to slow you down, but if you do encounter any local cops, keep driving. Don't pull over even if they turn on their lights. Don't stop until you get out of Dawsonville. Understand?"

She shook her head in protest. "Wait. What are you talking about? I can't just leave."

"You have to," Dak said. "I have some unfinished business here, but you are safe. That's all that matters. And that's all your mother cares about."

"My mother? Did she send you?"

"No," Dak said. "I was coming here anyway. But I did talk to her, and she's fine. Still, it's not safe for you to be here. Get out while you can. Remember. Don't stop until you're somewhere safe, preferably with a lot of people around."

She swallowed and nodded her understanding.

He pressed the keys into her hand and closed her fingers around them. "Go," he said.

Heather wiped a tear from her right eye then turned and climbed into the sedan. Dak looked back behind him, down the corridor, to make sure no one was coming as the engine roared to life. He watched her back out of the garage and drive off, then returned his focus to the hallway.

It was time for Baldwin to get his.

Dak closed the door and hurried back down the hallway, then up the stairs to the main floor.

He scoured the place, checking every bedroom, the kitchen, living room, and every inch of the first floor. To his surprise, the place was completely devoid of life. Dak didn't allow himself for a second to believe he'd eliminated all of Baldwin's men, and then there was the boss to consider.

When he finished checking the main floor, Dak ascended the stairs to the second. With every passing second, the silence of the mansion overwhelmed him, tempting him to think he was the only person there.

He couldn't allow that. It would take him off his guard, and he needed to be alert. The second he lost that edge was the moment one of Baldwin's thugs popped out of a corner with a gun.

As with the downstairs, Dak investigated every room on the second floor, including Baldwin's lavish master bedroom, complete with a four-post bed, high vaulted ceilings, expensive artwork adorning the walls, and a view from a balcony that overlooked the pool and the massive rose garden beyond it.

He retreated the other direction and found a door open at the end of a wide hallway at the opposite end of the house.

Dak pushed open the door and jammed his pistol through, sweeping the area to the left then right.

He spied Baldwin's impressive library collection first, then the behemoth of a desk, the fireplace, and...a foot sticking out from behind one of the guest chairs near the boss's workplace.

Dak frowned. The light brown shoe was shined to perfection, and Dak immediately recognized the expensive leatherwork. He gave one last check in the room, and in the corridor behind him, then entered the study, closing the door behind him. He twisted the lock in case someone was trying to ambush him, then walked over to the desk where he found something he never suspected he'd discover.

"What the...?" His words fell off.

There, on the rug in front of the desk, lay the body of Mitchell Baldwin.

Dak let out a breath. It wasn't a sigh of relief, more of frustration. *Someone else killed Baldwin? But who?*

He searched the room again, finding no evidence of a struggle. The pistol in the man's hand was meant to lead any investigator to believe that the man had killed himself.

Dak wasn't buying it.

This was a guy who had enough money and power to get out of any sticky situation. He could buy a super yacht and disappear in international waters for years if he wanted, lying low until any heat back home cooled down. And all the while reaping the benefits of his corporation's profits.

The suicide thing didn't make sense, and that suspicion was confirmed when Dak turned to his right and noticed a piece of paper on the desk.

He inched closer and turned the sheet around so the words were right side up.

"I'm in control now. And it looks like Hattie Markham is ready to do a deal."

Dak's blood reached boiling point before he read the last word. He clenched his jaw then scanned the room. He saw a metal case behind the desk on a counter beneath a bookshelf.

He sighed. *All this trouble for a couple of antique guns.*

Dak stepped over to the case, picked it up, and left the room. No questions haunted his mind about where he was supposed to go.

Whoever left this note had Hattie Markham. He'd just freed one Markham...and thrown the other into the fire.

36

Dak's heart sank the second he saw the gray Maserati parked next to one of Baldwin's SUVs in front of the farmhouse. He'd told Heather to get out of town, to somewhere safe. He could have sworn he'd cautioned her against going to her mother's home, but now he wasn't sure.

He'd stopped at the top of the ridge overlooking the valley. The Markham farm spread out below him. Short corn stalks stood in a field to the east. In a few months, they would be shoulder high—if the weather cooperated.

A warm breeze blew across the ridge and through Dak's hair as he climbed out of the car and walked over to a tall pine tree. He leaned against the trunk and pressed a pair of binoculars to his face. No signs of life.

He watched for a full two minutes but saw nothing. Whoever left the note on Baldwin's desk wasn't being careless.

On the drive here, Dak had tried to piece together who could have killed Baldwin, but he never came up with the answer. Lots of people in town loathed the tycoon, but no one was willing to stand up to him. They cowered in fear, every day growing sicker, or their land dying from the toxins the billionaire dumped into the soil.

Dak knew that within the next twenty-four hours the Baldwin Corporation would be facedown in multiple investigations. The authorities would assume the tycoon killed himself in the wake of devastating news hitting his company. No one would question the death, not even the cops on Baldwin's payroll—the ones that were still alive.

None of that answered the question Dak had been trying to answer. Soon enough, he would find out.

Baldwin's killer was down there, somewhere. Maybe the man was in the barn, or perhaps in the house with Hattie. He hoped the old woman was still alive.

And then there was Heather to consider.

With both the Markham women in the house being held hostage, that was going to make things far more difficult. It would have been bad enough with one hostage. And he couldn't deny the frustration knocking on the door of his mind at having just freed one of them.

Dwelling on that didn't solve anything. Dak needed to get into the house. On top of that, he had to find where the killer was *before* going into the home.

If he had two hostages, and had left a note, Dak figured the last place he would be was inside with the captives.

No, I would use them as bait.

He returned to the Cadillac Escalade he'd *borrowed* from Baldwin's garage and took the sniper rifle from his bag. Then he moved downwind along the ridge until the living room window came into view.

Getting down on his belly, Dak propped the rifle on its bipod and peered through the high-powered scope.

He saw a figure tied to a chair and immediately recognized Hattie Markham. Her daughter sat in another chair a few feet away, also tied to the seat.

But there was no sign of their abductor.

Dak turned his scope to the barn and looked into the open window, but found no sign of the enemy. He scanned the rest of the property and saw nothing unusual. That meant the kidnapper was either hiding, waiting in the shadows, or he was in the house with the two women, waiting for Dak to arrive.

"Where are you?" Dak muttered.

He remembered the drone in his bag, and an idea began to form.

Dak rushed back to the SUV and retrieved the drone bag. Armed with his two pistols and the sniper rifle, he left the Cadillac out of sight just beyond the top of the ridge and picked his way down the slope between the trees, under the cover of the leafy canopy above.

He assumed that whoever was down there would be watching the driveway, but there was no way they could see through the treetops, not until he reached the clearing below.

Then, all bets were off. Which was why Dak brought the drone.

When he arrived at the bottom of the hill, Dak stopped several yards short of where the trees ended and the fields began. He set down his gear, took out the drone, then propped up the sniper rifle once more. With the drone ready, Dak launched the machine into the air. Usually, he preferred flying it via FPV goggles, which allowed him to basically control the drone with his eyes. In this instance, though, he needed to be able to go from flying the aircraft to shooting position in a matter of seconds.

For that reason, he remained crouched down by the rifle, watching as the aircraft took off and weaved between the last remaining trees before the clearing.

He sent the drone skyward. The motors whined loudly as it ascended. Dak watched the machine grow smaller as it zipped away from him. He leveled off and sent the machine forward toward the barn. Something told him the enemy was there. Dak knew that's where he would be if someone were coming for him. The red barn's big window allowed a view of most of the property.

Dak steered the drone over the space between the barn and the farmhouse, then got down on his knees beside the rifle and slipped the goggles onto his face. He kept the fit loose so he could toss them aside at a second's notice.

Now he had a drone's-eye view of the property. He turned the aircraft toward the barn and then pulled back on one of the radio controller sticks. If he'd been on board the drone, Dak's stomach would have soared into his throat. Even using the goggles with such a dramatic move threw his senses off, but he'd practiced with the drone for hours and had become an expert at flying it, even navigating through tight spots.

Dak slowed the machine's descent with a flick of his thumb. He stared through the opening of the barn and pushed the drone forward to get a closer look. Dak flipped up the safety cover for the tranquilizer dart on board the aircraft, ready to fire the aircraft's only weapon if necessary. *Who knows? Maybe I'll get lucky.*

He let the thought evaporate as the drone neared the opening. Then, suddenly, the screen flickered and went to static. A split second later, Dak heard the rifle report.

He was too far away to see the drone, or what was left of it, hit the ground. Losing the aircraft was regrettable, but he'd been given his answer.

The killer was in the barn, probably hiding in the shadows. The shot had come from inside the red building, and that meant the shooter had played things exactly as Dak would have.

Down on his belly, Dak peered through the scope once more, looking into the front corner. He saw no sign of the shooter, but this was the only angle he could get without being exposed and putting himself in a vulnerable position.

He grunted in frustration, clambered to his feet, and sprinted to the right. He left the radio controller behind on the ground. *No sense in carrying the extra weight now.*

Charging through the woods, Dak wondered what the shooter was doing. The man gave away his position with the single shot from his rifle, but would he stay there? Or would he alter his plan and adjust to the distraction Dak sent his way?

Dak could only play it one way.

He couldn't approach from the front, but on the side, there were no windows, no way of seeing out unless the enemy opened one of the horse stalls windows. But all of those were closed for now.

Either the shooter hadn't considered other options, or he believed his plan was still the best course of action.

Dak cut to his left and sprinted across the field, the tall blades of grass nipping at his knees and shins as he rushed toward the barn.

Out in the open, he felt almost helpless, with nothing but his mobility as a shield. He still had his weapons but preferred not to go on the offensive without some kind of cover in place.

He skidded to a stop just outside the barn and paused to catch his breath at a side door. Pressing his shoulder to the wall, he listened closely for any sign of movement from inside the barn. Hearing nothing, Dak set down the sniper rifle and drew one of his pistols. He shuffled over to the rusty handle on the door and pulled slowly. The sliding door moved silently, much to Dak's surprise. He expected the wheels on the rail to be just as rusty as the handle, and ten times as squeaky.

Then Dak heard something that sent him sprawling to his right. It was nothing more than a click, but he immediately recognized the danger and dove as hard as he could.

The booby trap exploded, destroying the barn door and sending a deadly hail of shrapnel out into the field. The concussion of the blast didn't injure Dak, but the sound of the explosion caused his ears to ring at a deafening level. He dropped his weapon out of sheer instinct, putting his hands over his ears as if that might help. It did nothing to silence the high-pitch ring.

He tried to focus his thoughts, but the smoke and dust swirling in the breeze disoriented him. A single thought streaked through his mind—*Where is the shooter?*

He got his answer sooner than he would have preferred. A shadow cast across the ground near Dak, and he instantly scrambled, clawing at the ground to find his discarded weapon.

A silhouette stepped over him, and he felt a hard boot step onto the back of his hand. A second later, another boot kicked him in the ribs.

A sharp pain shot through his torso and his hand. He let out a grunt, but nothing more.

"We meet at last," the blond man said.

Dak winced, ignoring the muted words as they blended with the ringing in his ears. It took a gargantuan effort to simply roll away, and the movement sent a fresh stabbing pain through his side. He fought through it enough to avoid another kick from the attacker and scrambled to his feet.

The world in his vision tilted and dipped at a sharp angle. He staggered sideways as the blond man laughed, his head rocking back in enjoyment.

"Dizzy?" The blond man stalked toward his prey even as Dak continued his attempt to retreat.

"I've felt worse," Dak spat through the haze. The ringing in his ears started to fade, though was still clearly dominating the rest of his senses. "Maybe you've never been to PCB during spring break."

The assailant snickered. "I have to hand it to you. Making jokes, even at the end. You got guts. I'll say that. Not that it's going to save you now."

Dak continued stepping backward, still fighting against the off-kilter gravity his equilibrium perceived. He needed to stall, at least until his senses corrected—if they could.

"I'm sorry," Dak groused. "But I don't know who you are."

The man shook his head. "It doesn't matter. You'll be dead soon. And I will be the head of the Baldwin Corporation." He made a sweeping show of looking around the landscape. "All this will be mine."

"Fine," Dak said. "I don't need to know your name to kick your teeth in."

A twisted smile creased the blond man's lips. "You can call me Johnny," he said. "You have a reputation, you know. Former Delta Force. I imagine you did a lot of dirty things for the military."

"I obeyed orders. That's it."

"Yes," Johnny drawled. "I'm sure by now you're wondering why I didn't just shoot you when I had the chance."

"Crossed my mind." Dak took another wary step backward

toward the forest. He still had one pistol strapped to his hip, but so did the enemy.

Johnny inclined his head, assessing his opponent with hawklike eyes. "You killed all of my men."

"Yeah," Dak confirmed. "One more to go."

"I selected them myself. And you eliminated all of them as if they were nothing more than a bunch of street thugs."

"You should talk to your HR department about their hiring practices. Should be a short conversation, I imagine."

Johnny shook his head. "I'm giving you one chance. You come work for me; I'll make sure you're well paid. We can clean up the pollution Baldwin's sloppy practices created. No more people will be sick. We'll make billions. And you'll be my right hand. As head of security, you can choose your own team."

"Nice offer," Dak sneered. "But I already have a job. And it doesn't involve hurting innocent people."

"It's true," Johnny agreed with a shrug. "You may have to keep a few people in line here and there, but we'll have the cops on our side. After we hire some more, obviously. And we'll need to groom a new sheriff since you killed the last one. Although Meachum was weak, and greedy. So, in a way, you did me a favor by taking him out."

"No need to thank me."

"Oh, I wasn't. You killed a few others, too, in that little hotel explosion. I figured you would appreciate the irony of my doing the same thing to you here. Obviously, you're not a man who would just run straight into the house and allow a sniper's bullet to take you out. You're too smart for that."

Dak felt his vision correcting, and for the first time in what seemed like hours, the world stopped pulling so hard at the side of his head. The conversation was going nowhere, and he wondered if the enemy was stalling as much as he was. From what Dak could tell, Johnny's offer was genuine. And if he were going to kill Dak, immediately following the explosion would have been the time to do it.

"You make a good offer," Dak said. "I got no problem doing what's best for the greater good, either. But I'm just not sure, Johnny. Something about this doesn't seem right."

Johnny took a long breath through his nose, then exhaled. "I'll start you off at half a million a year for your services."

Dak whistled at the sum. "That's a good start, but you're going to have to promise that no harm comes to the Markhams. Neither one of them are to be hurt, and Hattie gets to keep her land." Dak knew the man would never go for it, but with every passing second his right hand drifted a millimeter closer to his open holster.

"I know there is something far more valuable to you. Something that money couldn't buy. It's something you've been wanting for a while."

Dak's eyelids twitched, and he felt a sickening stream of fear slither through his veins. The image of Nikki's face appeared in his mind—beautiful, healthy, going about her life. He doused that fire before it even sparked. *This guy doesn't know who she is,* he thought. *But what else could it be...?*

Nicole was safe. Dak had to remind himself of that. It was why he couldn't be with her now, and while the last place he could go was Istanbul. At least there, she wasn't on anyone's radar.

"Colonel Tucker," Johnny said, tilting his head to the side.

Dak froze, his right hand hovering over the pistol. "What did you just say?" *Did I hear correctly? How would this Baldwin goon know who Tucker is, unless...?*

"I know about the bounty hunter network. How do you think I found most of my men? Although now that I think about it, that doesn't really say much about the network, now does it? Considering you killed them all."

"They weren't all bounty hunters," Dak argued. But all he could think about was getting back to the subject of Colonel Tucker.

"No," Johnny concurred. "They weren't, but the core of them were. The rest I pieced together. With poor judgment, I must admit. You, however, are a rare talent. And an asset I need."

"What do you know about Tucker?" Dak pressed. "Where is he?"

The pragmatic look on Johnny's face curled into a one-sided grin.

"You join me, and I'll tell you exactly where to find your colonel. I imagine you've been on the run, what's it been, a few years now?"

"Something like that. I haven't counted the days."

"Oh, but we both know that doesn't make them any shorter. Does it?" Johnny paused for a second to let Dak consider his offer. "I can help you end those long days. No more hiding. No more running. Settle down. Marry a woman. Have a family. I'll even let you quit after you've selected my security team."

Dak knew Johnny was leaving something out, and he wasn't going to get roped into this timeshare seminar. "What's the catch, Johnny?" He hadn't missed the way Johnny steered the conversation away from his primary demand.

"The catch is I take the Markham land. And I know this pains you, Dak, but the Markham girls are going to have to die."

Dak's face darkened. "Well, then I have to decline your offer, Johnny." The muscles in his right hand tightened, ready to dive and draw the pistol.

"Don't be a fool." Johnny cautioned. "And what are you going to do? An Old West-style shootout? We both know you're not fast enough to beat me." He shook his head, but Dak saw his hand slide toward his hip. "I imagine you're probably still feeling the effects from that mine. I wonder, are your ears ringing? Maybe you haven't heard me clearly this whole time."

"I can't let you kill them," Dak said. "Or take their land. If you know anything about me, you'd know that offer is a nonstarter."

"That is unfortunate. I thought maybe you were my kind of guy, an intelligent man who sees the bigger picture. Last week, you probably didn't know who the Markhams were. If they had died before you met them, you'd have never known the difference."

"But I know them now."

"Pfft," Johnny scoffed. "I'm sure you and those two got real close in the last seventy-two hours. Don't be an idiot. I'm offering you the chance to live your life, free and clear. Just help me set up my team—guys with your skills."

Dak stood there, letting his hollow stare do the talking for him.

He had no intention of letting the Markhams die. It didn't matter how much money, or revenge, this guy was offering. "Only a sick person would make that deal, Johnny. Someone without a conscience."

"So, your answer is no."

It wasn't a question. And Dak felt the ice in the words. "Thought that was pretty clear, Johnny. So, do you want to die today? Or do you want to go to prison?"

Johnny snickered at the notion. "For what, Harper? I've done nothing wrong. What crime have I committed? You, on the other hand, killed cops; not to mention one of them was a sheriff. How do you think that's going to go over in the media? Would be a shame if someone leaked a little information to the feds, or the press, right? Or both? A little eyewitness testimony?"

"Those cops worked for Baldwin. You, Baldwin, none of you would have risked dragging an innocent in on your witch hunt. I knew that would be the case. How many people did those dirty cops kill, your comrades? How many did they hurt?"

"Spare me. All of them are dirty in one way or another. And you act so high and mighty. You're the biggest hypocrite of them all. Last chance. You either come with me and we do this together, or I kill you...and the Markhams. Nothing's going to save those two women now. The only thing in the equation that can change is you living or dying. It's up to you."

"Doesn't sound like much of a choice," Dak hedged.

"I agree," Johnny said. "So, what's it going to be? You in?"

Dak sucked in a deep breath of fresh, warm air and shook his head. "No, I'm afraid not, Johnny. And I've already made sure the Markham girls are okay."

Johnny frowned, then he heard the sounds of sirens from just over the ridge.

"Right on time," Dak quipped.

Johnny twisted his head around and looked over his shoulder, fear streaking the color in his face with pale splotches.

"You think they're coming to help you? You killed their brethren. Your only option to get out of this valley alive is with me. I can explain to them that you were helping me to free the hostages, but we arrived too late."

"Sounds like a peach of an idea, Johnny. But I'll pass." Dak declined. "Besides. I already called the cops."

Johnny's face burned red now, dispelling the pale spots from a moment before. His breathing quickened, and Dak knew what was coming next.

In a rage-filled haze, Johnny reached for his pistol. Dak's right hand dropped to his own weapon, and he drew it a nanosecond before Johnny. A loud pop echoed through the valley when Dak pulled the trigger.

Johnny had been in the act of raising his weapon, but the bullet that went through the base of his neck stopped him cold. He choked, coughing as blood pulsed out of the wound. He barely had enough strength and focus to fire his pistol one time, sending the round uselessly into the dirt, before dropping the weapon to clutch at the wound.

His fingers did nothing as the sticky crimson liquid seeped through, draining his life by the second.

Dak watched with his pistol still trained on the man. He only lowered it when the body went limp, and the twitching stopped.

Sirens screamed at the top of the hill now, and Dak knew he had to go. He glanced over at the farmhouse. He would have preferred to go in and get the women out, but he needed to hit the road.

He had what he came for, the two pistols in the Escalade at the top of the hill. And the Markhams were safe once more.

Dak scooped up his weapons and sprinted back toward the woods. Just before the first police car came into sight, he disappeared into the shadows.

37

After Dak was safely out of the United States, the news reports quickly emerged about Mitchell Baldwin's seedy activities. The illegal copper refinery, the killings, the mysterious deaths, the illnesses...They all fell on his head. Dak would have preferred to see him suffer through losing everything, the way he'd made so many others suffer. But in the end, Baldwin got what he deserved, as did nearly everyone who worked for him.

The Department of Justice uncovered emails and text messages that further implicated Baldwin in illegal activities. Of course, they'd been given an anonymous tip. The federal investigators couldn't locate who sent them the information. All they could find was an ISP in Portugal.

Fortunately for the workers at Baldwin Corporation, the government didn't shut down the entire operation. Once they located the illegal copper refinery, they isolated that building and let the others continue with business as usual, although it was never clear who directly operated the copper side of things. If any of the employees were to be blamed, no one said a thing. Dak figured those workers were simply doing what they were told, probably under threat of harm to themselves or their families. So, he didn't blame them for keeping their involvement hush-hush.

Dak read the headlines with a smile, especially the one that featured the new sheriff in Dawsonville, Officer Mills, who'd received an anonymous phone call that Hattie and Heather Markham were being held hostage in their own home.

The police arrived on the scene mere minutes after Dak vanished. They'd been in such a hurry, they never noticed the Cadillac Escalade parked in the woods off the driveway, tucked away in a nook, blocked from view by the forest undergrowth.

Heather and Hattie Markham gave a complete description of the man who'd abducted them, the same man the investigators found dead from a gunshot wound to the throat. The body lay by the barn, where an apparent improvised explosive device had blown out the side door.

Thanks to the testimony of the two women, and the pile of evidence on their property—including the body of Arenson— the authorities had one of the easiest open-and-shut cases they'd ever seen. While the feds wanted to know who Arenson's killer was, Officer Mills had a feeling he already knew, and he made a conscious decision to hand out a little misinformation to keep the federal investigators off this mystery man's trail.

It didn't take much for Mills to put together that the man who saved Joe Notekabortsky's life in the hospital was probably the same guy who took out Johnny Arenson. Of course, the Markhams kept that secret locked up in a vault and claimed they had no idea what the man looked like who'd rescued them and killed Johnny.

Dak sat in the rental condo overlooking the water. The port city had changed over the decades, morphing from a beach town to a thriving business center for import and export. There were still, however, a few choice spots where the greenish-blue water lapped against the golden sand, and where Dak could reset and take some time off before his next mission.

He picked up a glistening bottle of cerveza from the table next to him and took a swig. Then he switched the tablet's page to the next bit of news.

His smile broadened as he read the headline: "Stolen Civil War Artifacts Returned! Mysterious donor remains anonymous."

Dak's employer, Boston, had received the Colt pistols and subsequently had them delivered to the National Civil War Museum in Harrisburg, Pennsylvania. It would have been quite a thing to see the curator's reaction when he opened the mysterious delivery box and discovered the priceless relics packed inside. Dak didn't want to know how much insurance for that package must have cost Boston. Then again, it wasn't his concern. If the kid wanted to donate his money to a cause like that, it was up to him. Dak admired that about the boy. The world needed more people like him.

The only unknown left on the slate were the Markhams. Dak wondered what happened to them, how they handled everything once the cops showed up, but he knew he'd likely never seen Hattie and Heather again. The thought saddened him now and then. That was the nature of his work, though. He looked into the future and considered how many more people he might meet that he'd never bump into again.

In truth, that didn't really matter. At least it shouldn't. He'd helped an entire town rid itself of a scourge.

Susan the diner waitress, Joe the mechanic, the family of Mike Hamilton, and so many others. Even the old security guard from the quarry came to mind. All of them would have a better future because of Dak.

He'd done many things in his life, some of them extremely dark. But he slept at night knowing those actions made a difference in the lives of those who couldn't help themselves, or didn't know how.

That was good enough for Dak.

As he sipped the cerveza, he stared out at the ocean and the setting sun as it glistened off the gentle waves of the Pacific. His thoughts drifted to where he might go next.

HATTIE AND HEATHER MARKHAM sat on the front porch of the family farmhouse. A pitcher of sweet, iced tea sat on the table between them, and each held a glass.

Heather took a sip and immediately shifted her gaze to her mother. "Did you put bourbon in this?" she asked with suspicion.

"Of course," Hattie said, shrugging. "I always do."

Heather chuckled and shook her head. "I have to admit, it's a good combination."

"Darn right it is."

The conversation fell silent for a minute, and the only sounds that tickled their ears came from crickets, frogs, and a few night fowl in the forest surrounding the farm. The crescent moon hung low in the sky to the east.

"I love that smell of honeysuckle," Heather said after the long silence. "And the feel of the cool evening air on my skin."

"Yeah," Hattie agreed. "Me too."

"I've been thinking. I'm going to come back here more often, Mom." Heather stared out into the darkness as she spoke. "But I can't move back yet."

"I know. You have a career you love. I don't want you to walk away from that."

Heather passed her mother a grateful smile. "I appreciate that. But my place is here, Mom. With you and with the people of Dawsonville. I spent so much time growing up thinking about how I just wanted to get out of here. Now, all I feel are the strings trying to pull me back."

"This place will do that to you, sweetheart. It's a little piece of paradise. I always thought if John Prine had been here, he might have written that song about this valley instead of that spot in Kentucky."

"Funny, since this place could have faced the same fate if it weren't for Dak."

Hattie nodded in rhythm with the rocking chair. "That's very true."

Silence settled over them again, and neither said anything for two minutes.

"I wonder," Heather said, "where he is now."

"Can't say I know, dear. But I have a feeling he wants it that way."

"Yeah, I was afraid of that," Heather confessed. "I'd at least like to tell him thank you."

Hattie turned her focus to her daughter. The hard expression on her face that had been earned through years of hard work and struggle softened. "I would too. But I don't think we'll ever see him again. Then again," she added upon seeing the disappointment on Heather's face, "you never know."

THANK YOU

I just wanted to say thank you for reading this story. You chose to spend your time and money on something I created, and that means more to me than you may know. But I appreciate it, and am truly honored.

I hope you enjoyed it, and will stick with this series as it continues through the years. Know that I'll be working hard to keep bringing you exciting new stories to help you escape from the real world.

Your friendly neighborhood author,

Ernest

OTHER BOOKS BY ERNEST DEMPSEY

The Relic Runner - A Dak Harper Series

The Relic Runner Origin Story

Two Nights In Mumbai

Country Roads

Sean Wyatt Adventures:

The Secret of the Stones

The Cleric's Vault

The Last Chamber

The Grecian Manifesto

The Norse Directive

Game of Shadows

The Jerusalem Creed

The Samurai Cipher

The Cairo Vendetta

The Uluru Code

The Excalibur Key

The Denali Deception

The Sahara Legacy

The Fourth Prophecy

The Templar Curse

The Forbidden Temple

The Omega Project

The Napoleon Affair

The Second Sign

The Milestone Protocol

Adriana Villa Adventures:

War of Thieves Box Set

When Shadows Call

Shadows Rising

Shadow Hour

The Adventure Guild:

The Caesar Secret: Books 1-3

The Carolina Caper

Beta Force:

Operation Zulu

London Calling

Paranormal Archaeology Division:

Hell's Gate

ACKNOWLEDGMENTS

As always, I would like to thank my terrific editors, Anne and Jason, for their hard work. What they do makes my stories so much better for readers all over the world. Anne Storer and Jason Whited are the best editorial team a writer could hope for and I appreciate everything they do.

I also want to thank Elena at Lɪ Graphics for her tremendous work on my book covers and for always overdelivering. Elena definitely rocks.

This one also needs to go out to my good friend Dr. Jack McClarty for his medical consultations throughout the research and writing of this book. His expertise was critical in making sure I got certain elements of this story correct.

Last but not least, I need to thank all my wonderful fans and especially the advance reader team. Their feedback and reviews are always so helpful and I can't say enough good things about all of them.

Made in the USA
Middletown, DE
26 August 2021